Visions Through a Glass, Darkly

Visions Through a Glass, Darkly

David I. Aboulafia

Winchester, UK
Washington, USA

First published by Cosmic Egg Books, 2016
Cosmic Egg Books is an imprint of John Hunt Publishing Ltd., Laurel House, Station Approach,
Alresford, Hants, SO24 9JH, UK
office1@jhpbooks.net
www.johnhuntpublishing.com

For distributor details and how to order please visit the 'Ordering' section on our website.

ISBN: 978 1 78535 022 1
Library of Congress Control Number: 2015934117

A CIP catalogue record for this book is available from the British Library.

Design: Stuart Davies

Printed and bound by CPI Group (UK) Ltd, Croydon, CR0 4YY, UK

for my father

But whether there be prophecies, they shall fail;
whether there be knowledge, it shall vanish away.
For we know in part, and we prophesy in part.
But when that which is perfect is come,
then that which is in part shall be done away.
For now we see through a glass, darkly...

Corinthians 13

Yesterday monsters, tonight perfection.
From the grotesque to the sublime.
Visions through a glass darkly.

James Herbert

Prologue

I am driving north on the Taconic Parkway in New York, approximately forty miles from the City. Fall is coming here, arguably the most beautiful time of the year anywhere in the world.

I am passing the Pleasantville exit five miles south of the Croton Bridge, a pretty little span crossing the New Croton Reservoir. It has always been one of my favorite places.

The trees are passing by so quickly now; too quickly to be able to reflect upon any one by itself. Every now and then, though, one appears so large, so magnificent, that it stands out from the rest, causing one to crane in such a way that neck and vehicle move in different directions.

It is an attempt, I suppose, to keep a special moment of one's life still and fresh for a second longer in the mind's eye.

What am I doing here? How did I get here?

I adjust the rear view mirror to look at my face. It is a familiar face, except for the large bruise on my left cheek bone and the multiple lacerations I see elsewhere. There is a starburst hemorrhage in my right eye.

That explains the tears, I guess.

I readjust the mirror and survey my immediate surroundings. They are decidedly unfamiliar. I do not own the vehicle I am driving.

It is an old Ford, equipped for a physically disabled driver. Two levers on the left side of the steering wheel – similar to those found on a bicycle – control the brake and the gas. An over-sized electric clock sits in the center of the dashboard. I watch as a minute passes with a tick of the mechanism.

An old children's bedtime story forces itself into my mind. For some reason, I smile.

Strange.

My hands feel peculiar. I attempt to lift them from the

steering wheel and find there is an odd adhesion; they yield with an audible smack. I take my eyes off the road for a moment.

The sun, that most ancient of timekeepers, is rising now over the reservoir. The moon, its distant cousin, is still visible above the horizon.

I look down.

Blood. My hands are covered in blood.

The clock ticks again. It is 5:54 a.m.
Oh yes; I remember now…
In four minutes, I will be dead.

Visions Through a Glass, Darkly

Time is not real.
And if time is not real,
then the dividing line that seems to lie
between this world and eternity
is also an illusion.

Herman Hesse

I

It is always dark in some part of the world.

I find the light a transient thing. It is the darkness that pervades. We are born from it; we die into it. At some time, in every evening anywhere, someone closes their eyes and immerses themselves in the black.

We depend on the darkness; we require it like food, like water and like oxygen. Deprived for any significant time of the murky emptiness that sleep provides we find ourselves mad. Our time in the sun is made possible only by the moments spent in the shadows.

The universe itself is dominated by darkness. The stars are not the entranceways to the heavenly realm that the ancient mariners believed they were. They are mere pinpoints; anomalies, abstractions and distractions, filling the void in only the most infinitesimal way, offering only the vaguest, most tenuous respite from the surrounding beyond. Perhaps they struggle each moment to avoid being swallowed whole by the very giganticness of it.

Yet it is the light that we walk in, and to which we ascribe all manner of attributes. That it is good and omnipresent and that the physical energy of it washes away the gloom. That the light of God, or the light of truth or the light of justice shall shine forever through the darkness of evil or cruelty or hatred, or that of Hell itself, making all these terrible things disappear, or dissipate, or be rendered moot.

You poor fools. The light is never there for more than a few moments. Only for as long as it takes the sun to go down on your side of the world. Only for as long as it takes you to flip the switch of the lamp beside your bed.

Or for as long as it takes for you to close your eyes.

Of course, for some, there is more time in the dark than for others.

Time. For most of us unconcerned with Einsteinium theory, metaphysics or astrophysics, time is merely a straight line that we walk upon; a path with a discernible beginning and a definite end.

But most hope that there is more. Many *believe* that there is.

And to me, *that's* what's *really* funny. Because *I* know there *is* more. Ohh, *so much more.* But that "more" bears little resemblance to fiery pits of molten flame, or depths of ice where Judas hangs halfway out of the mouth of the devil; it shares little similarity with any artist's vision of a celestial Promised Land, where white people with blond hair and halos take flight among the clouds and smile all the time at everything and nothing at all.

Can we talk? You don't mind if we talk, do you?

You see, I know nothing of bearded men with stone tablets on mountain tops. I don't know if flocks of virgins wait patiently in some distant reality for the holy of heart. I can't tell you whether we all repeatedly reincarnate from one existence to the other or, if we do, whether we are reborn as cows or as millipedes. I do not know if an ancient wise man sits judging us all upon a throne in another dimension, or whether that wise man is in fact a youngish looking black woman, an Asian youth with a tricolored Mohawk haircut, or someone else.

I cannot say whether there are two immortal beings engaged in an eternal struggle for the souls of mankind, or whether there are two immortal beings who simply don't give a crap, who activate the Earth like we turn on television sets, and who sit and merely watch – for time immemorial, like some kind of eternal couch potatoes – real life sitcoms, horror stories, dramas, mysteries, crime series, divorce courts, animal planets, music videos, and the like.

I know only what I see, what I experience, what to me alone is true, eternal, and proven beyond any reasonable doubt or calculation. And what I see are things that no one else can see; what I experience, things that I alone of all the people in the world am capable of experiencing.

In many ways, I suppose, all of us are unique. But this trite assertion has little meaning to me. For I, among all of you, am inimitable, one of a kind. And because of this, regardless of any human association I may attempt to construct, I am utterly, and completely, alone.

My name is Richard Goodman.

II

My parents were products of the Depression, my father, working from the age of nine, was desperately poor throughout a childhood that was not much of a childhood at all. He never owned a bicycle or a baseball glove, never went to a ball game, never had a radio, never had ice skates or a football. As a boy he made his toys from scraps of wood and discarded rubber bands and shined shoes for a penny on cold street corners; a penny that might buy a sweet potato for dinner that evening. He loved animals and would frequently rescue stray dogs from the street. If they were small enough, he would keep them at home and hide them from his parents. If he couldn't, he would escort them to makeshift sheds he built on a nearby vacant lot. He would care for them there, saving small scraps from the dinner table, even when he barely had enough to eat himself. Sometimes, he would have to beg for food for them from local merchants, reliably softened by the lad's obvious concern and conviction. He nursed most back to health and saved a few lives along the way.

Some would eventually just disappear, never to return. Others lived to a ripe age in their homes made from wooden milk cartons and cardboard boxes, complete with a backyard and regularly served meals.

He loved his animals. He dreamed of being a veterinarian when he grew up.

However, by the time he was seventeen, the United States was at war, and he was in the Air Force, a tail gunner on a B-29 Liberator Bomber. By the age of eighteen, he had saved a man's life, cost twenty-four Japanese their own, and had been shot out of the sky, parachuting on that occasion into the jungles of the Philippines.

All members of the crew were able to parachute out of the plane before it crashed. My father landed, somewhat miraculously, into a small clearing through thick stands of trees and otherwise impenetrable undergrowth. As the story goes, he was covered by his parachute upon landing, and, after a few frantic moments, freed himself from its constraints. In his possession were a .45 caliber semi-automatic and ammunition, a pocket knife, a mirror, two packages of topical disinfectant, a gauze bandage, and a small packet of safety matches. He drew his gun immediately. He was, after all, on a Japanese controlled island. Enemy combatants, he knew, were beheaded on the spot.

He looked around him and saw nothing but jungle. Relative quiet abounded, and he wondered what had befallen his comrades, most of whom had jumped before him. He looked up.

Small green lizards observed him from their precarious holds on tree trunks. The occasional parrot squawked in the distance. Sunlight barely filtered to the jungle floor through huge stands of bamboo – some 100 feet tall – and ancient ficus with leaves three feet wide and five feet long. When a glint of sunlight did meet his eye, it was like a miniature heat lamp, burning through his cornea and into his brain, blinding him momentarily. He realized he was sweating profusely; it was May and 102 degrees.

He saw their shadows first, backlit spirits seemingly suspended in mid-air. And they were spirits indeed; the remains of a flight crew primarily composed of eighteen and nineteen-year-old boys; not merely suspended, but impaled upon the branches of the trees they had landed into.

The scene was reminiscent of the roadways leading to ancient Rome, lined on both sides with the bodies of men, women and children nailed to crosses of wood.

Despite his fear of capture he screamed, and screamed again. He ran blindly through the jungle, following a sickening trail of hanging corpses, mangled and contorted into impossible positions, unambiguously relating the tale of a rapid plunge from fifteen thousand feet through the equivalent of barbed wire and spears that ripped limbs from torsos, pierced lungs, tore kidneys, and popped eyes from their sockets.

He was counting them as he ran, screaming, through the jungle, or at least he thought he was; he finally stopped running when his former friends appeared to be accounted for, and when the ghastly trail ended of its own accord. The jungle continued to enjoy its relative peace and quiet. This was not unusual. In this place, death often came silently; sometimes by biological design; sometimes through the cruel and inexplicable workings of an arcane and unknowable fate.

For three days, he wandered without either food or water. On the fourth day, half mad with dehydration, fatigue, and fear, he was surprised by a troop of soldiers, whose presence was announced by the crack of branches and then by the crack of gunfire. Later, he would not be able to recall who had been the first to fire, but by the end he had emptied his weapon twice, wounding six and killing one of the twelve Australian soldiers who had come to his rescue.

Madness.

Anyway, with little regard for an unfortunate misunderstanding that had occurred on an island in the Philippines, my father was ultimately discharged honorably as a much-decorated staff sergeant. He, like so many thousands of his peers, had entered the conflict a boy, and been lucky enough to leave it intact as a man.

In a manner of speaking.

The war had changed the world, and the world was about to change significantly more.

The prime of America's youth were returning to the Homeland, a different kind of youth that had risked their lives and fought the good fight against unspeakable enemies and had prevailed. They brought with them their energy and optimism, their talents and ideas, their confidence and limitless potential. They offered loyalty and hard work and, in turn, they were welcomed with open arms as conquering heroes.

The returning GI's settled down, married, had children, and began the quest for the American Dream at a time when dreams could come true, and often did; when opportunities were real, when hard work and honesty and service to your country meant something; when talent was appreciated and often rewarded. It was a time when a poor immigrant's son might realistically expect to succeed in his life.

The vacant lot of my father's youth was now a six-story tenement under construction. Soon after his return to The Bronx, New York, he stood before that emerging structure, feeling somewhat numb, in his Air Force greens with three stripes on each shoulder and three rows of medals on his chest, looking upon that once-vacant space as if it were some kind of vanishing species. His childhood, such that it had been, officially ended that day when he looked at the playground of his youth and saw the ghost of a hungry child and his furry friends.

Three years ago. A lifetime ago.

Gone today but not forgotten.

His world had changed; the war had left him changed. And he was to change still more, undergoing a transformation that had started long ago, one evening as he rushed fourteen blocks through the rain on a September night…

…It's after 9:30, a half hour past my bedtime. I'm home, getting ready to go to bed; today's Tuesday and tomorrow's Wednesday, a school night. Mom is sick again and has been asleep for an hour already. She goes to sleep earlier and earlier these days.

Someone knocks loudly at the door.

Stevie, my eldest brother, is out somewhere. He seems to be out of the house more and more lately. Marcus, the middle child, is working, and Dad is working, too, running the coat check at the Club. Mom doesn't stir at the big bang.

I ask who it is. Dad says to always ask who it is before you open the door. Ricardo Espinoza answers back. I recognize his voice because he's Spanish, and he works with Dad as busboy. They call him Ricky-Boy. I open the door and let him in. He's holding a wet, black cap in both hands, the kind the cab drivers wear, and he keeps turning it around and around in his hands. Ricky-Boy keeps looking down at the ground, and he's trying to say something, but for some reason I'm not paying attention, not yet. I'm just looking at him turn his wet cap around and around. It's as if he's nervous, as if he wants to hold back what he has to say for a few more seconds.

I'm old enough to know that words can hurt, like when Stevie calls me a shrimp, and I think Ricardo has words that might hurt, words that might change things: that might change everything.

Now the words come. He says Dad fainted and that he's very sick and that he's in the hospital. A lump gets into my throat and I can't swallow. I look back at Mom through her open bedroom door. She'll be difficult to wake. Even if she were awake, she couldn't do anything or go anywhere; her legs don't work very well anymore.

Ricky-Boy is just standing there, head down, looking at the floor. So I take off my pajamas, put on my clothes, grab my only jacket and run right past him; through the open door, down the stairs, out of the house and into the street.

It's only September but it's cold outside, and it's raining hard. It didn't seem to be raining a little while ago. I don't have an umbrella or hat. My left shoe has a piece of cardboard inside covering the one-inch hole in the sole. I feel the bottom of my foot getting wet as I begin to run.

Running, running, running.

I know where the hospital is. It's a long way off, but my feet will take me there. I'm small, but not weak and I'm fast, very fast; everyone in the schoolyard tells me so…

By the fourth block, the downpour has become a freezing rain. The wind is blowing harder. I round a corner, and I am nearly knocked off my feet by a cold, wet blast. I fall, and crash into a stand of silver metal garbage cans put out for the morning's collection. I slowly get to my feet. I look at my pants. There is a long rip at the left knee. I only have two pairs of pants. There is an ache where the rip is and I think I'm bleeding. My shoulder hurts. I start to cry. And, then I start to run again.

By the seventh block, I am soaked to the bone. My knee is stiff and it hurts every time it moves. Two blocks later, I can feel my heart pounding in my chest, and I can't catch my breath, so I start to walk.

By the eleventh block I am running again, but my whole body is numb. I am shaking and shuddering and I can't do anything about it.

I never thought I could do anything to make my body stop working, but it feels like it's going to stop working now. But I'm not gonna stop unless it does.

I'm not gonna stop. I'm not gonna stop no matter what.

In 1945, Dad returned to The Bronx, met a beautiful girl and got married. It wasn't an unusual story, considering the times, but it was a nice one. He was quiet, shy and physically small, and not much to look at. But he was funny once you got him to talk: also honest, kind, hard-working and sincere. He possessed a unique drive to better himself, along with a powerful need to succeed. I guess he possessed enough redeeming qualities for Mom to love.

Early on, he got a job as a low-level bookkeeper for a small construction company on Long Island. He went to night school to earn his degree while helping to raise his infant son, the first of three. His young family lived in an apartment in a four-story walk-up tenement. Living there with them were water bugs the size of mice. The flat had a dumb waiter, and dark cubbyholes built into the kitchen walls, with funny knobs on the doors.

Dad owned a four-door, brown Pontiac Bonneville. It had no heat, minimal braking power, a broken AM radio, and took a half hour to start if the temperature dipped below freezing. But he had cut a great deal on the car, promising to complete and file the owner's tax returns for five years in exchange for the vehicle.

He wasn't quite sure whether he could make good on his promise without subjecting the man to significant IRS penalties, but he did know that he had a talent for manipulating figures. This aptitude extended to anything that had anything to do with numbers. By the time he graduated college – magna cum laude, with a bachelor's degree in accounting – his superiors had realized that his cost-cutting measures, tax strategies, and acquisition tactics had significantly increased their bottom line. He was promoted, and then again. With each expansion of his authority, the company grew and prospered. As the company prospered, so did my father.

So did we all.

By the end of his life, my father had acquired four homes; one for each season he used to say. He had a Swiss chalet in Lake Placid; a condominium in Manhattan overlooking the East River; the vast contemporary in Northern Westchester County and an oceanfront ranch in Key West. His assets included stock holdings worth over fourteen million dollars, a pension fund with five and three-quarter million, cash in excess of $750,000, and collections of Whistler originals, rare firearms, and Remington bronzes.

Strangely, my father never seemed to take much pleasure from his prosperity; the fulfillment of his personal American dream. He professed to enjoy what he did for a living, but his meteoric rise from abject poverty to significant wealth had not made him happy. He took pride in his accomplishments but appeared unable to extract any *joy* out of them.

It wasn't that he didn't laugh or joke around, or that he didn't appreciate that he had achieved financial security or, for that matter, that his family adored him. It wasn't that he didn't enjoy himself at work, or that he wasn't appreciated, respected, or even loved by his co-workers.

Ultimately, acting as chief financial officer, he conceived and created what became a major international development firm. The company built royal palaces for princes in Kuwait, prisons for the state of Montana and museums for the city of Los Angeles. The gross revenue of the firm eventually reached over $2.5 billion a year. The small group of partners – the four daughters of the original owner – were taking home annual after-tax profits of $37 million per.

My father was not among this elite group. He was still just an employee, just "a bird in a gilded cage," as he used to say. He had milked the cows but he didn't own the herd. He was just a well-paid farmhand.

I could understand how this might have troubled him. This and the fact that he never became a veterinarian.

But there was something more. There was a pallor, a dark cloud that hung over him; some deep, insidious sadness buried away, which he seemed to labor under every day. It was barely visible at times; its existence evidenced only by mysterious glances or expressions, a lowered voice, a furrowed brow. As he got older, this black hole expanded and blossomed with the sickening propensity of mold. It produced in him a pain that could only be described as exquisite, a temper that was volcanic, and a personality that was wholly unstable. His inner anguish slowly drove him to the brink of insanity. Then, beyond the brink.

As to the root cause of it all, I could never be sure, assuming there was just one. Whether his unique view of the world resulted from genetics, his experiences, or random forces mattered little in the end. At some point, his mind took a sharp turn down a dark and terrifying alleyway leading to a dead end from which there was no reprieve, no escape, and no exit.

If I have concluded anything at all I have concluded this: At some point Dad came to some terrible realization, some horrifying epiphany, sparked by an event in his life that marked and changed him forever.

Madness, apparently, was the natural result.

I get to the hospital. I put one hand on the entrance door which I also use to prevent me from falling. As I enter, I pass a tired looking security guard sitting at a small desk that looks like the desk I have at school. To my left is a long white counter. A woman about Mom's age is sitting behind it. On the wall directly above her is a large round clock with black hands and a plain white face, also like those at school. I smell disinfectant; it smells like the hallways at school.

The woman has a white dress on, but she doesn't look like a nurse. She uses reading glasses, and she has them on, attached to the back of her neck by a chain that looks like it's covered with diamonds. After a minute I realize they can't be real diamonds.

I walk to the counter, slowly, hesitantly, not sure if my legs are working. I approach and wait for her eyes to lift from her charts and meet mine. When they do, I don't wait for her to speak. I don't know whether she is going to be amused or angry or something else.

"Goodman…" is all I say. She just stares.

"Goodman..." I say again, as if it's the only thing I can say, as if it is my last word, the only word left in the world, the only word that matters, the only word that means anything.

She stares a moment longer, eyeing me through the thick glasses perched on her broad nose, saying nothing.

She begins to rustle papers, but I can't see what she's doing because I'm not tall enough to see over the counter. She stops rustling for a moment and becomes still. She's reading. I wait, and I realize I am holding my breath.

"A Richard Goodman was admitted at 9:20 p.m. He collapsed at work and hit his head when he fell. He's in Emergency right now, kid, still being worked on; no visitors."

I shift my weight uncomfortably from one leg to the other. I am embarrassed by the loud squirting sounds that come from my shoes. I am shivering, my knee is bloody and throbbing, and if I try to take a deep breath it hurts. I can't seem to get enough air.

I do not repeat my last name. I can't think of anything else to say.

"You can wait over there," the woman says, not unkindly. She motions to a long wooden bench. "I'll tell the doctors you're here."

I guess she knows who I am. I'm glad I don't have to explain.

I hesitate for a minute longer, and then drag myself to the bench. Exhausted, I fall asleep almost at once.

This madness eventually flowed from the father to the son as naturally as a creek feeds into the ocean. What else came along for the ride, I sometimes wonder.

Because of my father I have enjoyed a mostly privileged life. I have benefitted from advantages far exceeding mere food and shelter. I have received considerable financial support, a fully paid for college education, summer jobs, and business contacts. I have been freed from the debilitating constraints of insecurity or poverty and permitted to *evolve,* as humans are designed to do.

But this freedom has done little to release me from anything. My mind has not been unchained, nor has my imprisoned spirit been liberated. Whatever balm may remain available to soothe the tattered edges of my psychology has gone undiscovered. If some shining beacon of truth still awaits me *out there,* its light is still too dim to warm me, or guide me through the darkness of my path.

Madness.

The drugs help. Clonopan, Valium, alcohol and marijuana, each used most every day, in relatively moderate doses, are normally sufficient to hold off the demons that might otherwise come to me.

Demons.

They are strongest in the hours just before dawn. They ferment, like invisible bacteria, drawing their strength from our experiences, sucking the evil out of our actions and distilling them into a sustenance, feeding on our sundry acts and omissions as if they were a kind of perverse energy. They store this fuel and when we humans enjoy our deepest sleep, they come out and burn it in our subconscious, attacking our beliefs, shifting our mental universes, altering the very memories of our lives, exaggerating some, weakening or negating others, affecting the very foundations of our personalities, our belief systems, and our *Chi;* our spirits and our souls.

Do you think I am describing some metaphysical concept? Do you think I am espousing some pseudo-philosophical theory? *Do you?*

I cannot form a mental picture of them in my mind. I wouldn't recognize them if they appeared in a police lineup, or a daytime television talk show, if they masqueraded as drunks or addicts lying prostrate on a deserted street, or if they approached me on a subway station and whispered the maiden name of my dead aunt.

They don't have shape or mass. They require a form to inhabit, or the design of one. They require fodder with which to work, a fuel to burn, energy upon which to feed.

So, in the wee hours of the morning, usually sometime between three-thirty and five, they work the height of their insidious magic, bending and kneading my personality, concentrating my attention on the evils of this life, nourishing my weaknesses and negative experiences until they bloom like black flowers smelling of excrement and death, creating a psychic jungle of confusion and panic, subduing my logic, defeating my hard-won discipline, playing in my mental backyard and making it their playground.

I have never "seen" them in the way physiological perception is often defined, I have only felt them. They ride their own Wave, one unique to themselves, violently churning within the unknowable boundaries of an indecipherable sea.

Their power can appear absolute, unlimited, or as subtle as the faintest breeze, as inconspicuous as a momentary spark somewhere in the infinite cosmos, like the unrecognizable portent of a storm a thousand miles away.

They come and go as they please, and it matters little if by force of will or strength of spirit I am able to hold them off for a moment, a month, or a year. If they cannot come *through me*, they will eventually come *at* me through others. Meeting resistance from others, they will manifest themselves in random ways.

In sum, they will simply come; by directing their power like a laser, or by dispersing it in the widest possible pattern like a shotgun. They are not bound by the physics of this world. There is a simple explanation for this. They are not of this world.

So I awake each day in the grip of a gut-wrenching, paralyzing fear that I cannot articulate. Each morning my mental soil is just a bit more fertile than the day before, a more perfect medium for insidious plantings that yield only rotted fruit and sickly-smelling blooms.

I suppose I could explain all this using the words of Erickson, Freud, or Jung. There is always a perfectly lucid explanation for madness; a lack of faith, too, can always be rationalized.

But explanations are of little use. My condition progresses, and with every dawn I greet my madness. Which started around the age of nine.

I open my eyes and for a moment I don't know where I am. I sit up with difficulty. Bright light is shining in my face. The sun is glaring at me through a dirty window with a tattered shade. There is a large patch of dried, caked blood surrounding the slash in my left pants leg. I ache all over.

I remember now. I look around, expecting someone to be here, but no one is. No one seems to know I'm here. So I sit and wait.

The almost-nurse from before is not at the counter. There's another woman there who looks very old. She also is dressed in white.

She's playing with paper. She looks up at me with a blank stare, then continues playing.

I look down and stare at my shoes. The left one used to have a piece of cardboard in it covering a hole in the sole. Now I can feel a raw piece of my big toe touching the icy cold of the hospital floor. After what seems a long time, I see someone else's shoes facing mine. I follow one shoe to a knee; then to the tip of a long white coat that looks almost like a bathrobe.

I look up and see a man about my dad's age. He has no hair on his head except on the sides. He has big black glasses that I can't help but stare at. I look at his glasses but not at his eyes, although I know he's looking at me.

Now he's saying something; I know that he is, but I can't make out any of the words. Then I hear him say 'Mr. Goodman' and I finally realize he's asking me if that's my daddy and I nod my head. He continues to talk, but the words go away again. Somehow, though, I don't have to hear any to know what he's saying.

He says my daddy was in an accident and went to sleep and didn't wake up, and he asks me where my mother is. I don't say anything. I'm just thinking. I'm just thinking that someone is always there for me; someone always comes to me when I'm sad or hurt. Then I remember my dad saying that when you're poor, like we are, that you really have to rely on each other 'cause sometimes that's the only thing you have, and that we always have to hang on to that, and hang on to each other.

But no one's here to hang on to.

And, all of a sudden, I realize I don't have a dad anymore. I won't see him walk through the front door after work; there won't be any more stories about when he was a kid; he'll never kiss me good night again. I'll never feel his hand brush across my forehead, and I'll never have that feeling of being so safe, so secure, so loved by someone I look up to, depend on, and love. I realize the best and biggest part of my life is gone, and that nothing will ever be the same again. I'm alone; I will always be alone, and I'm afraid. I feel a great weight pushing all around me. My throat is clogged, and it's hard to breathe.

I look at the man, and I want to ask him how this could be. I want to explain to him that my dad isn't old and he isn't sick and that people who aren't old or sick can't die and I don't' understand where he is and I want to see him I want to see him and why can't I have my daddy anymore?

I am crying now. There are gulping sobs shaking my whole body. The man puts his hand on my shoulder, but he doesn't hug me. And, when he doesn't, I realize something else.

Today is my birthday. Today, I am nine years old.

I was playing in the snow with my father. It was a bright, crisp winter day. We were a block from our apartment, just down the street in Poe Park. It was called Poe Park because the famous author, Edgar Allan Poe, maintained a residence on the grounds for a brief time, and the house was still there.

It was a cramped, two-room cottage with low slanted ceilings, and to step into it gave one the feeling of being in a large doll house. Despite its notoriety, the house was poorly maintained and virtually unsecured for years, treated by the neighborhood youth more as park equipment – like monkey bars or swings – than as a local monument. Yet, it still had a few pieces of Poe's original furniture in it, scarred and battered but there, nevertheless. In the late 1960s, there were still some things that were for everyone; still some things that wouldn't be stolen.

Two feet of snow lay on the ground that day, the kind of snow you saw after a blizzard of it had passed through. We were throwing snowballs at each other in the park. I laughed and turned to run from him in mock fear but I tripped and fell, falling face down into a deep mound of fluff. I rose, my face stinging and my eyes tearing, and through a blur I saw my father holding a huge snow-boulder over his head, pretending he was going to crush me with it.

Only I didn't think he was pretending.

I had never considered the possibility that my father would ever hurt me; not counting the occasional *whack* I received every once and again, when I deserved it. But at that moment, I somehow understood what he *could* do, what he *might* do, what a part of him *wanted* to do. All he had to do was to twist the screw a half-turn to the left and take one more stride off the plank; one more half step bridging the gap between the improbable and the likely, gulfing the chasm between the unthinkable and the doable.

Like a *wave* coming over me, like an irresistible tower of water surrounding and engulfing me, at that one moment I became aware of all that he was, all that he felt, everything that he was consumed by

(demons).

I felt a rage within him, buried beneath the surface but hardly invisible, not to me. I felt his fear, as well; permeating every part of him, making his heart beat wildly and the sweat pour down his forehead; causing his legs to quiver and shake, barely able to support his weight.

I saw a look of confusion upon his face. But my *mind's* eye saw a little boy locked in a closet and unable to escape; screaming, grabbing wildly, futilely, at a doorknob, pulling at his hair, tearing clumps of it out, banging his head again and again against the walls of his enclosure in panic and frustration, clawing at the boundaries of his prison with nails that cracked and shredded and ripped from his fingers, leaving pieces of flesh and thin trails of blood behind.

There was no one to hear him, no one to come to his aid, no one to unlock the door, no one to release him from the prison inside his mind. There was no relief for him, no end, no escape, no exit, and there never would be. He was alone. Forever and for always.

At one point, I cried. Bewildered, he laughed uneasily and dropped the snow-boulder to the ground.

His madness was still *becoming* then; building to its own slow, inexorable climax. He didn't know what was happening to him. He couldn't know what was happening to me.

It didn't occur to me to question the surge of that wave that had descended upon me. The power and depth of what I had experienced – the momentary capture of the spiritual essence of a person in a moment of time – was overwhelming and absolute. Its validity was unimpeachable; its accuracy unassailable.

It didn't end there, of course. The Wave, as I began to refer to it, increased in frequency and intensity. As I began to rely more upon what I felt, rather than upon the information coming to me from the same five senses that you possess, I began to perceive a version of reality that no one else did.

However the world and its tenants may appear to the

ordinary man, they appear quite different to me. My ability is to pierce the veil of skin and flesh, to peer just underneath, to the decayed underbelly of humankind; to see the dark clouds of perversion and chaos hiding behind the strained disguises of trusting faces, reassuring gestures, kind demeanors, and soothing voices.

But there is more… so much more.

Listen…

Things come to me during the day. That they come is as much out of my control as is the coming of those nameless, faceless fiends that appear in my nightmares.

A dimensional veil parts. The thin film separating one reality from the next is stripped away. The unseen becomes visible.

What becomes visible to me are the dead.

III

I work as an administrator for a trade school in the Borough of Queens in the City of New York. The Waterman School of Watchmaking has been around for over fifty years. It is the finest of its kind in the nation, I am told. My position is necessary, but of no cosmic import. My co-workers are mostly kind people with good intentions.

By design, the school is filled with students possessing a variety of physical disabilities. Some came to their fate through that wheel of chance called genetics, crushed by the irreversible weight of their aberrant DNA. Others are simply casualties of their fatal choices; mangled and torn asunder by car accidents or gunshot wounds.

Or, if you prefer, perhaps they are all casualties of a disinterested god, who on one fine morning elected to umpire a cosmic game of softball, and simply took his eye off the ball for a time.

Many students are recent discharges from rehabilitation hospitals across the country, where some spend up to eighteen months recovering from their varied and sundry traumas. Follow-up surgeries are common. They experience recurring pain, perpetual assaults upon their self-worth and esteem, and engage in a daily struggle to maintain what little integrity is left in their physical bodies, or their belief systems, or their faith.

Or their minds.

In all of these souls there is an inability to escape the narrow circumscriptions of their lives. They always exist with an inherent powerlessness. Yet, in the words of Cyrano, they fight on.

My office is located on a second floor mezzanine overlooking a main classroom. It connects to a balcony running along the perimeter of the large hall and is lined with trophy cases filled with awards won by the school's athletic teams. These are prizes of a unique nature, as they were won by generations of wheelchair sports teams, going back to the very beginning of such sports in America. Here are plaques, medals and other memorabilia from innumerable regional, national, and international events, where athletes competed in sports such as table tennis, shot put, archery, javelin, swimming and weightlifting, destroying by example the common conceptions of what disabled people can and cannot do.

From my bird's nest, I look down on students – most in wheelchairs – as they study watchmaking and jewelry design, trades requiring patience, discipline, and tedious months of study.

The school was founded for disabled veterans returning from World War II. It greeted those shattered individuals with an offering of a new life and an opportunity to acquire skills much in demand. Many lives were rebuilt, along with the watches those fine young men worked upon. The school provided not just skill-building, but medical care and socialization, much like a modern rehabilitation facility today, but hard to find in 1945. Today, the institution is equipped with an indoor swimming pool and sauna, full dining room facilities, nursing care, a recreation room and a basketball court.

These days, the school is rarely populated by casualties of war, but of life; paraplegic students, deaf students, and amputees. Among the institution's apprentices, one will find those with checkered histories and violent pasts, trying to undo in small measure their largely self-inflicted injuries, often reaped by evil ways.

Even students with terminal illnesses sometimes decide to spend their final days in this place, learning and growing, searching for meaning in lives unfairly shortened. Here they often find what they are seeking.

I live in a house next door, a two-story job, adjacent to a small dormitory which is joined to the school. I live there *gratis* as partial consideration for my duties as the 24-hour supervisor. I pay for phone, electric, gas and that is all, and you can't beat that.

My duties are varied and often interesting. I promote the school's sports teams and recruit disabled students from all over the world. I handle press relations – the easiest part of my job – and often encounter kind-hearted or otherwise sympathetic journalists.

I try to find full-time jobs for the graduates, in jewelry and watch repair shops nationwide. In order to hire our students, owners may be required to change the physical structures that house their businesses. Some construct ramps, widen entrances or re-design bathrooms to accommodate wheelchairs.

More often, however, people are required to change themselves. Some must overcome a certain discomfort they have just being *around* people in wheelchairs, an involuntary repulsion of 'cripples' that is eventually broken down by exposure and familiarity. Others study sign language and learn to communicate with employees who live in worlds filled with silence instead of sounds.

It is often not an easy sell. Of course, it helps to be able to sense a person's hidden fears, their secret longings and desires, their regrets. But even this is not always sufficient. Sometimes – particularly with graduates able to acquire only a mediocre level of skill – my abilities are not enough. These students leave the school with little more opportunity than they had when they entered. When this occurs, it is as much my failure as it is theirs. I become frustrated, or manic, or depressed.

Today was one of those days. Today, after a full day's work canvassing over fifty businesses in four states, I came up empty handed. Fifteen students were pending graduation. While I had a small number of openings, some in obscure or far-away places, I didn't have nearly enough to fill the near future needs of the student body. I buried my head in my hands and slumped in my chair.

Suddenly, I heard a gentle thump, followed by a rustling, then a thump again. The thumping-rustling repeated itself; it originated from the stairs leading to my office. It occurred to me – not for the first time – that my office was not accessible to people in wheelchairs.

Marty Rodriguez was sitting on a tread in the middle of the staircase. His beaming countenance appeared just above the crest of the stairs, making it appear as if his severed head was lying on the floor.

Marty is Spanish, bearded, almost always cheerful, and has an incredible deadpan humor. He has a quick mind and a quicker wit, which he often displays with great effect. One cannot help but like him. Beneath this facade, however, lies a profound depression, along with feelings of inadequacy as deep as the ocean. Only I am aware of this, and he will never know that I am.

Marty also has spina bifida, a disease that arrests the development of an infant's brain or spinal cord while still in the womb. It causes a variety of symptoms, including bowel and bladder difficulties, paralysis, water on the brain, and learning disabilities. The effect is always permanent.

There is no cure.

A man with spina bifida will often find his lifespan shortened, and the prognosis is particularly poor for those who find themselves paralyzed by the ailment, like Marty. Yet, he seems completely at home with his disability and maintains an outward appearance of cheerfulness.

He had left his wheelchair at the bottom of the stairs. Like many people compelled into a chair, he has remarkable upper body strength, certainly greater than all but the most dedicated body builder. Riser by riser, he has hoisted himself up the staircase to the mezzanine level that is my office; a small display of courage and character that no similarly disabled student has ever exhibited. Once at the top, he "walked" toward me using his hands, which dragged his useless lower half along. Reaching the corner of my desk, he lifted himself onto an adjoining chair. He maneuvered his face until it was no more than a foot from mine and leaned on my desk with his elbow, placing a fist underneath his chin. He looked at me in a most serious and scholarly way.

"So, uh, Ricky, how's it going?"

"Fine, Marty."

"Everything OK today?"

"Just fine."

"I see you're working."

"I try to do a small amount of work almost every day."

"I'm not disturbing you, am I?"

"Never."

"Are you sure?"

"Quite sure."

"Because I know disabled people can be very disturbing."

"Not at all."

"Because if I am disturbing you, I'll be happy to leave you alone on your mountaintop…"

"That's OK, Marty."

"…looking at all the peasants beneath you."

"Well, that's true, they are peasants."

He cackles heartily. His laugh is genuine and infectious. "No, but I have to be serious for a second." He regains his form along with his mock-serious look. "If you have a moment."

"I have more than a moment."

"You know, I'll be graduating soon."

"I do."

"And, you know I want a job, right?"

"I'm sure you want a job."

"More than minimum wage. Not at McDonald's."

"I would never offer you a job at McDonald's. I wouldn't have you settle for anything less than Burger King."

He laughed again, somewhat uneasily. I really shouldn't joke about things like that.

"You know you really shouldn't joke about things like that. You know I'm very insecure, and I bruise easily." He was telling me the truth, now.

I'm sorry, Marty. You know I'll do everything I can to find you the right spot, and we'll be talking about that real soon."

"Of course we will." He brightened considerably. "You're a friend to legless people everywhere."

I laughed.

"I'll let you get back to your work, now."

"Thank you."

"Even though we both know you're not doing anything. You sleep all day long."

I faked a yawn. "I think it's time for a little nap right now."

"I'd never disturb your beauty sleep. You're an ugly slag, and you need it. But, I'll be back real soon. For my job."

"I bet you will."

"You don't have to see me to the door. Because you don't have a door."

"Just don't fall down the stairs."

"That's good advice. I might break my legs. Then, I wouldn't be able to walk. Then, you wouldn't have to find me a job."

"Don't try to cheer me up," I replied.

He laughed once more and turned to depart the same way he had come. He looked over his shoulder to issue a last volley of retorts.

"Hey, Ricky-Boy; we're tight, right?"

"Yeah, Marty, we're tight."

"You're my buddy, right?"

"I'm your buddy."

"I mean, even though I'm Hispanic, and you're a racist?"

"Despite those two facts, yes."

Unfortunately, Marty's skills are less impressive than his sparkling personality. He is in the lower twenty percent of his class. Normally, it would be difficult to find him a job. At this particular time, it is next to impossible.

What will he do? Where will he go? If he's lucky, he'll find himself in subsidized, government housing; "Section 8" it's called. There's a long wait for such lodging and it's often substandard, and in neighborhoods that are less than desirable.

He will subsist on social security disability or some other entitlement program. He will sit in his apartment most of the time, mostly alone. Television will be his usual companion; beer and illegal drugs, if he can afford them, as well, if he can physically get to where they are sold. Depression and physical pain will never leave his side for long. He will probably die young.

Were these predictions emanating from my expanded senses, common sense conclusions derived from facts, or simply false visions observed through a cracked and clouded lens? I couldn't tell, and it didn't seem to make a difference one way or the other. The future didn't seem bright for Marty and there was little I could do about it.

I buried my head in my hands again and closed my eyes. I was tired, so very tired. I tried not to think. But as I started to doze, I did…

I've just started the fourth grade and so has he.

His name is Timmy and he lives across the street. He is a head taller than me. He has a pale complexion and a lot of freckles on his face. In another place, at another time, this might make him look funny, – like that famous cartoon man they have a billboard of at Coney Island – but he's not funny at all, even though he's always smiling, particularly when he sees me. I never want to see Timmy because I will be hurt and scared every time I see him.

But I do see him, more often than not, no matter how hard I try to avoid him, even though I am always looking out for him, even when I know he couldn't possibly be there, like when I wake up in the morning to go to school, or when I'm leaving with my parents to visit my grandmother every Sunday afternoon.

He often tells me he's Irish-Catholic, as though this should mean something to me, even though this means nothing to me, and I don't know why he tells me this all the time. I know another kid who is Irish-Catholic, but he never wants to beat me up.

I don't understand.

Sometimes, I think I can just talk to Timmy as if he was just a normal kid, and sometimes I try; sometimes I even think he listens. Sometimes, I think I can talk to him without getting him angry enough to beat me up, although he doesn't really seem to be angry when he does. He seems happy. As if it is the best part of his day; the part of the day he really looks forward to.

He likes it when I'm scared. He wants the fear to build in me slowly. He wants me to roll it around in my mouth and taste it like one of those big lollipops Dad gets me when we go to Coney Island, or like one of those Tootsie Pops with the white sticks and chewy centers, or like one of those red candy balls that burn your tongue and make it red and that is hot and sweet all at the same time. I think he wants me to enjoy my fear as much as he does.

I'm here right now on Valentine Avenue, and Timmy's right here too. I have my back up against a parked car which is across the street from 2701. We live on the third floor in apartment 301. Our living room window faces the street, and mother always keeps the window open so she can hear me yell if I need her. I need her a lot, mainly because Timmy lives across the street. He won't hit me if he sees her, and she seems to spend the day waiting for me to call.

His chest is pressing against my chest. He's just talking with that terrible smile of his, with those freckles that look like they should be funny but aren't funny. He knows what's about to happen and so do I. His breath smells like the bubble gum that comes with baseball card packs. This would normally be a good smell, but when it comes from Timmy it's different. It smells stale. It smells like I think death would smell, even though I don't exactly know what death smells like.

I guess it smells like something you can't run away from.

He starts to push me, first. That's how it starts. He starts to push me, not because it hurts my body, but because it hurts something else, something deep inside me.

He pushes me again, a little harder now. I fall back against a car and the handle on the car door jams into my back. He slaps me on the face hard, and that hurts, that stings, and he takes a little step back as if to admire what's he's done. He licks his lips as if he tastes my fear. He's starting to have a good time. He punches me in my stomach, and that hurts, too, and he knows it, so he does it again.

He's not rushing. There's plenty of time. There's always plenty of time. There's no one around to see. There's never anyone around to see when he starts hitting me, although a lot of people probably know what he's doing because it's summer and everyone has their windows open.

I start crying and beg for him to stop. I ask him what he's doing and why he's doing it. I tell him I am only nine years old, but that's stupid because I always ask him this and tell him this and he always gives the same answers; because he wants to, because he feels like it, because I'm a punk, because I'm a shrimp, because he can, because there's nothing I can do about it.

"Call for your mommy, punk," he says. "Cry for Mama like the baby you are."

He really starts to punch me now, over and over again, and he's not going to stop. He's not going to stop until someone stops him, but no one is here to stop him.

So, at that moment I make a decision, the only decision I can make because he's not going to stop if I don't do something. I punch him back, and I don't know how hard I hit him, but I see his smile disappear. He starts to hit me faster and harder.

Then, I make another decision: I turn my back to him, I grab the roof of the car with both hands and I start to scream. I scream for my mommy just like a baby, like the punk he says I am, but I don't care at all, now.

My mother's head appears in the window like she was there all the time just waiting for me to scream. He hits me up until the very moment she appears. I can't hear what she's saying, but she's saying something and all of a sudden the beating stops and I turn to face him again. He's taken a half step back but he's still right in front of me. He's got that smile on his face, again, that terrible smile that tells me that's he's full for now, and that's he's happy, so very happy for what he's done. He looks at me and doesn't say anything but he's telling me something anyway. He's telling me 'I'll see you again, punk – maybe tomorrow, maybe the next day, maybe the day after that – but I'll see you and, when I do, it'll start all over again.'

I don't know it yet, but I will see Timmy's face for a long time. I'll see it at other times, in other places, in the faces of other people. I won't be the one taking the beating, someone else will; but I'll feel the same way then that I do now.

Mommy won't be around. There'll be no one to stop Timmy. Nobody at all.

Nobody, that is, but me.

I opened my eyes. At first, I wasn't sure whether I was asleep or awake. When my thoughts cleared a bit, I felt as if I had been violated. I looked to my left.

A red and green plaid couch is situated under a window. A planter sits upon the sill of the window. It contains just one scraggly plant, which I have owned for fifteen years. It ekes out a bare living on the meager supply of light, water, and fertilizer that I provide, and it refuses to die. I have left it much to its own initiative, and it fights on.

But, someone's blocked my view of the planter. As I turned, my eyes met a man's waist.

I didn't want to look up right away, because I knew what I would see. A part of me is always shocked; still another part can never be.

Timmy is here with me. He is wearing blue jeans and a white denim shirt with the sleeves rolled up. His shirt is open two buttons down at the neck, and he is wearing a white, sleeveless T-shirt underneath.

He is covered in blood. It does not appear to be his.

He smiled that wicked smile, a smile that I remembered, a smile that said 'I know what's going to happen and so do you.' An incisor was prominently missing from the center of his upper jaw.

"How ya doin', punk?" he asked.

Timmy was not alone. He was holding hands with Estrada.

Estrada was a Latin kid who lived in the neighborhood when I was around eleven. He was not much taller than me, and everyone knew him only by his last name. To encounter him was to risk injury. He was mean and crazy, and always armed with a knife or a bat. As life – yours or his – meant precious little to him, only your money would keep him from using one or both on you. It was usually good practice to pay him whatever cash you had, and suffer the parting blow or the spit in your face.

We rarely saw Estrada in school, yet we all knew he received a thorough education from his alcoholic father, who was frequently ill-tempered and occasionally violent. His mother was a meek, sweet woman who rarely spoke at all, much less raise a voice to challenge her husband, who used his son as a punching bag on the bad days, and as a target for his verbal abuse and denigration on the good days.

To survive, Estrada learned to filter this terrible physical and psychological cruelty, channel it, and then use it. The result was an unremitting rage fuelled by an uncontrollable hatred for everyone and everything. Including him, I think.

He, too, was covered in blood, but in his case, there was no doubt where it was coming from: a large, gaping hole on the right side of his head.

One day, Estrada chose to go swimming in a large sinkhole we called Bronx Lake. It was barely three feet deep during the dog days of August. He dove in recklessly and his head struck a rock lying at the bottom. He came out into a body bag.

He was fourteen years old.

They stood now, hand-in-hand and side-by-side, like demons on their first date, glaring and smiling.

Back from the dead. My own personal horror show. Fright Night, for real.

"He's a little punk, isn't he?" Timmy asked.

"Yeah, yeah," Estrada replied. His gaze held a ravenous, needful look.

I squeezed my eyes shut and held them shut for a moment. When I opened them, they were still there.

"He's afraid to do anything," Timmy said.

"We're going to kill you," said Estrada, always more succinct and to the point. "There's nothing you can do; there's no way you can stop us. We do what we want, when we want."

They both laughed. And took a step closer.

I believe that when the dead come, they come for a reason. They come at times when I am confused or fearful; when I need a compass or an answer. Whatever it was that they were here to say, it was in response to a question I had posed.

Their grip on each other's hands seemed to tighten. Blood squirted out from their palms. A thick green liquid oozed from the chasm that was the remains of Estrada's brain.

"All be over soon, punk boy," Timmy said. "Just close your eyes and let us end it."

"...all be over soon," Estrada chimed in.

"Just give up," Timmy breathed.

"Just give up," whispered Estrada.

They moved another step closer.

Estrada's face had become unrecognizable. The pit of his cranium was putrid and gray, and I was aware of the horrendous odor of rotting flesh.

There was a growing puddle of red, viscous liquid under Timmy's feet. The veins in his forearms were purple and defined, like a road map to Hell. I speculated they were from lethal injections; self-administered, or otherwise.

"Give up," they said in unison.

They stepped forward again.

Then, they were simply gone.

I realized I had risen to my feet. My arms shuddered as I tried to steady myself using my desk. I looked over the side of my balcony and saw the students busy toiling below. Each busied himself with the task at hand. No one looked up; not one of them was remotely aware anything had occurred.

Because, I suppose, nothing had.

I collapsed into my chair, stunned and drained, my typical state after such supernatural excursions. I realized then that in many ways I was just like Marty Rodriguez. I, too, was forever to be alone, with only dangerous visions I was weary of trying to understand.

But you tend to listen closely when the dead speak to you. There is insight to be gained from these dark tutors, though dreamed into existence from my repulsive memories, and taking the form of day-walking visions of horror. Perhaps this is their lesson:

That one day, each of us will come face to face with the unavoidable end of our lives. It is the nightmare that silently trails us, the horror that ultimately consumes us, and the great terror that we are so loath to face.

But what if we were to face it? What if we confronted the demons we have spent a lifetime pushing into the deepest recess of our brains? What if we choose to live out our lives without fear, without our demons, as if the worst had already occurred?

As if we were already dead?

Perhaps that's the only way we can get through any of this at all.

I don't know how long I can go on like this. One day I may give up altogether.

But not today.

I walked down the one flight of stairs that led to the main level, and then another flight that led me to the dining room. Smack dab in the middle of the dining room was a regulation size pool table. No one ever seemed to question its location there.

To the left was a conference room, and within that room a nurse's office. Emily Parson was the school's nurse. She had a true affection for every student whose health and well-being she was charged with. She was kind and empathetic. There was no request she had ever turned down, and no task asked of her that she had ever refused.

Everyone loved her, but no one wished to be treated by her. She was always drunk and had been for the last seven years. No one ever had the guts to fire her, and everyone hoped that no serious medical situation would arise to test her abilities. Amazingly, considering that the school was attached to a dormitory filled with disabled youths, none ever had.

In the rear of the dining room was a counter that demarcated the kitchen, always manned by Domingo. Nobody knew Domingo's last name and, for all we knew, he didn't have one. Domingo was a great guy, and did his best to provide for all the kids who sought a meal from him at most any hour.

He was a terrible cook, but a terrific pool player. He liked to refer to himself as "The Master," but in his deep Spanish accent it came across more as "De Mahstair". He has had his job for over twelve years, and his culinary abilities have deteriorated each and every year without exception.

No one has been inclined to remove him from his position either.

Marty Rodriguez was at a table drinking a Coke and stared with some disbelief at a shriveled piece of meat, a watery pile of mashed potatoes, and a serving of barely defrosted string beans. He was humorless for the moment.

"Yo, Rick, you gotta do something about this, Rick; this is jail food, my brother." He shook his head back and forth, and made circles on his plate with his fork, baffled as to which pile to navigate first.

"Reechard Goood-men, how are jou, Reechard Goood-men?"

Domingo was always happy. You had to love this guy.

"Fine, Domingo, fine... Is there anything edible tonight?"

"*Everyting* is ehdible, Reechard Goood-men. I make somting especial por jou?"

"No thanks, Domingo, just a Coke; I'm going to eat later on."

With obvious pride and an unmistakable flourish, Domingo joyfully dispensed a watery, flat Coke.

"Por my frend, Meester Goood-men."

"Thanks, Domingo."

You had to love this guy.

"Perhaps later jou want to play a game with De Mahstair?

"If you play left-handed, maybe, Domingo."

Domingo laughed heartily. "I play lehft-handed if it give jou *hoop*, Meester Goood-men, but you can never defeet De Mahstair!"

He was right, of course. No one had ever beaten Domingo at a game of pool.

I sat down with Marty.

"Yo, Rick, you gotta do something about this, Rick, this is convict food, man."

"At least it's free, Marty.

"Yeah, death is free, too, but I wouldn't want any part of it." He laughed at his own joke, and was at once himself again.

From the long hallway to the right of the kitchen which connected the dining room to the dormitory, appeared Dayne Dorio. Dayne was the only able-bodied student in the school, the son of a watchmaker who wanted his boy to learn the trade. He came from somewhere in the Midwest; for some reason nobody ever asked exactly where or seemed to care. The "Midwest" was far enough from Queens, I suppose. Everyone liked Dayne, and there was very little not to like.

He was a tall, good-looking kid without a blemish or mark on his angelic countenance. He was humble and unassuming, with a perpetual smile plastered upon his face.

Marty connected with him immediately, mainly because of his last name. To Marty, "Dorio" was like Oreo, as in the Oreo cookie. In the evolving lingo of Marty Rodriguez, Dayne's nickname became Oreo, then Cookie, and then simply just Cook, and that was where it usually stayed, give or take a daily permutation.

Dayne took his obligatory plate from Domingo, and joined us at the table, where he immediately became the target of Marty's good-natured ribbing.

"So, Cook, what's up?" Marty's demeanor was serious, which meant he was about to be anything but.

"Have you seen the dog?"

"What dog, Marty?"

"The Devil Dog, have you seen it?"

I couldn't help but chuckle. Rodriguez was always hysterical, and Dayne was always such a good sport. Dayne smiled.

"Very funny, Marty. No, I have not seen the Devil Dog."

"How about chips?"

"Chips?"

"Chips Ahoy, have you seen him?"

"Marty, I think that wheelchair is affecting your brain."

"Oh, now you're making with the disability jokes, making fun of the cripple. Hah hah hah on the man with no legs. Very good, Cookie Man." Dayne stopped eating and seemed to genuinely believe he had hurt Marty's feelings.

"I'm sorry, Marty."

Rodriguez laughed. "Ahh, that's OK, Cook, we love you man, even if you do have legs."

He turned to me and whispered for all to hear. "Rick, do *not* get this man a job." He turned to Dayne again. "Nah, we love you man; eat your gourmet meal, it'll give you leukemia, eat up, Cook!"

Cook dug in heartily. He was Domingo's best customer, and Domingo knew it.

"Secund helpings waiten por jou, Mr. Cookie Man."

"Thanks, Domingo," Cook replied, without lifting his eyes from his plate.

"Second helpings," Marty repeated mockingly. "You're like a frigging oncologist, Domingo; you're a Spanish Jim Jones, you know that?"

Domingo was a short order cook who knew very little of oncology or Jim Jones. Oncology is a field of medicine specializing in the treatment of cancer victims. Its practitioners gently supervise the death of more patients than can ever be cured. Jim Jones, of course, was the infamous cult leader of the People's Temple in Indianapolis. One fine day he served up his own short order to his starry-eyed congregation in the form of cyanide-laced "Flavor-Aid". Nine hundred fourteen members of his community were killed, including 276 children.

Domingo laughed. "Jou jus jealous," he replied to Marty. "Jealous of De Mahstair."

Then, from the long hallway to the right of the kitchen, came Derrick Vander.

Domingo began to whistle. He quickly prepared a plate and placed it on the counter and just as quickly retreated to the rear of the kitchen to wash dishes that may or may not have been there. Everyone else in the dining area looked at their plates. If they didn't have a plate, they looked at where one might have been. Except me.

"Hi, Derrick."

No one was happy I had said that.

Derrick picked up his plate without looking at it or acknowledging Domingo, and he sat down by himself at a table adjacent to ours.

* * *

Derrick was a 26-year-old African-American. He was six-foot-two-inches tall, weighed over 200 pounds, and was packed with muscle from head to toe. Both of his arms were covered with tattoos from his wrists to his neck. He walked with a distinct limp that made his entire right side rise noticeably with each step he took.

Every time he walked he looked funny. But no one had ever laughed.

Derrick was a student of the school's jewelry design program, which in itself was somewhat funny. Derrick had become disabled robbing a jewelry store at gunpoint. He made it out of the store successfully, but the store owner, similarly armed, followed him out as he retreated and shot him in the back. Thus, the limp. One year at a rehabilitation hospital and five years at the Riker's Island Penitentiary had been the prerequisite training for the course in which he was now enrolled. Like everyone else at the school, Derrick had a story behind him.

The story started with Derrick's father or, more accurately the fact that he didn't have one. No one else he knew did either. Most little boys in his neighborhood grew up with the idea that Dad had lived down the street once, or went to jail, or died a long time ago, or disappeared. They saw him once in a while, or they heard Mommy talk about him, or Mommy never wanted to talk about him; stuff like that.

You can't miss what you never had. Maybe it was better to have only one parent to tell you what to do, or stop you from doing what you wanted to. Of course, Derrick never resented his mama for doing these things, and he would never utter a bad word about her.

Neither would anyone else. One thing you never did was say anything about anyone's mother. You could (you would) get killed for something like that. It was best if you left "mother" out of your vocabulary entirely so that the word never slipped out of your mouth by mistake.

Hell, even your best friend would try to kill you for talking about his mother. Derrick had a best friend, once.

Reginald Slaughter – great name – bad dude, big balls, never had an argument with him, ever. We hung out together, got drunk, got laid, did crime, did everything together. My brother, Reg. It was that party, man, that fuckin' party. Me and Reg hanging out, smoking, laughing; we were pretty juiced. He was telling this joke when this fat bitch came walking by us, this wasted bitch who could barely walk, and she was wearing this pink dress – this tent of a dress with these animals printed all over it – lions, pandas, giraffes – animals everywhere all over this bitch.

For some reason, the first thing I thought of was the circus, so I said "Shit, Reg, the circus is in town," and Reg must have been thinking what I was thinking because he cracked and spit his beer all over me and I really didn't give a crap because we were juiced, ya' see?

Anyway, for some reason – for some other fuckin' random reason I never understood – the very next thing I thought of was that Reggie's mom had the same dress; she wasn't as wide as this girl, but she had the same fuckin' dress, and before I could stop myself I said

"Shit, Reg, isn't that your mom's dress?"

It was the way that Reggie looked at him then that Derrick would always remember. He looked confused; like a German shepherd that didn't quite understand the commands of its master. He never recalled seeing Reggie's eyes look like that before.

He clearly recalled having seen Reggie's '45 before, although never pointed at his face, like it was the very next moment.

Without a word, Reggie pulled the trigger.

The gun misfired.

Without a word, Derrick grabbed his best friend's head with both of his powerful hands and snapped his neck with a single crack.

There were twelve witnesses.

No one saw anything.

Derrick kept his hair closely cropped. The shadow of hair on his head accentuated a bony, well defined and pockmarked face. It wasn't a particularly ugly or handsome face, but it was a scary face.

That was fine with him. In his line of work, on his side of town, "scary" was an attribute, not a liability. It kept you alive, and it kept you employed. It had always been Derrick Vander's intention to keep both alive and employed, even if staying alive was sometimes a relatively short term goal.

His eyes were his most exceptional feature; the large, brown, puppy-dog variety that always made him look a bit innocent, or even cheerful; crazy, to some. But, whether one believed that they were innocent eyes, or cheerful eyes or crazy eyes, all concurred they were dead eyes, not windows to a soul, but portholes that overlooked a dark alley that led to a brick wall. Whatever hint they gave of the personality of the man to whom they belonged, they introduced an individual without much capacity for emotion; devoid of regret, or empathy, or fear.

Fear was what his personage inspired in others, and a lack of fear was the hallmark of his personality.

However, this Man with No Fear did fear something. He lived with a terror he was unable to articulate. It originated in a moment of time that had yet to occur, but would. It was a prophecy that bided its time in a dark corner of his mind and that came out to inhabit his nightmares. It took the form of a cold, steel instrument he would never see, tenderly placed against the nape of his neck by a familiar hand. After that, there would be only one final sensation: a curious awareness of a smoldering heat pressing against his ear.

Demons.

Derrick tried not to dwell on such things. He was fond of saying that demons would eventually kill him, and that it was demons lapping at his ankles that always seduced him back to the streets, and away from such pedestrian undertakings as the acquisition of usable skills or working nine to five. Demons filled his world when he closed his eyes, and just as completely when he opened them, taking the form of hundred dollar bills, bags of cocaine, or two legged hoodlums who had as little regard for life as he did.

Derrick had tried several times to advance from the streets, but the demons always lured him back. They were his constant companions, the parrots on his shoulder, his shadows, and his alter egos.

One day, he feared, they would kill him; but not today.

He knew he wasn't like everyone else, and that he would never be like 'everyone' else. He knew that people looked away when he entered a room. A simple stroll down the street was often enough to cause people to cross and walk to the other side, or lock the doors of their cars as he passed.

All things considered, however, he was perfectly content with the way that he was. After all, no one was perfect.

And, as the great Clint Eastwood once said, a man's got to know his limitations.

The ghetto was certainly the place to realize those limitations. To dream for something better out of life was like taking your eye off the road while you were driving. Dreaming was every bit as dangerous as cursing out someone's mother or robbing a jewelry store.

* * *

Derrick looked up and caught Rick's smile. Involuntarily, Derrick returned it.

"Hey, Rick," he said.

Everyone looked away quickly.

"Well, that's it for me, boys," I said.

"Where you going, *Walker*?" Marty asked.

I grimaced as I looked down at Marty. Everything he felt at that moment was known to me in an instant, as the Wave passed over me without apology or warning, reminding me of what I was. Marty was afraid that I was the only thing keeping Derrick in check, and he didn't want me to leave. I breathed a sigh of relief; that was simple enough.

"Don't be afraid, Marty." I put one hand on his shoulder and looked deeply into his eyes. "You've got the Cookie Monster to protect you." Rodriguez looked at me strangely.

"I'll take good care of him, Rick," said Dayne, good-naturedly.

"The friggin' Cookie Monster," repeated Marty, looking down at his string beans.

"Cook, you couldn't protect a condom from getting herpes."

Domingo thought this remark was a riot and collapsed in hysterics in his kitchen. Dayne passed his Coke through his nose, and Marty sat back with arms folded, obviously pleased with himself.

Derrick sat smiling at his table

IV

I walked down the long, gently curving corridor that led to the dormitory. Each step produced a short-lived echo. There were no side passageways or exits of any kind before you hit the dorm, with the exception of the twin doors leading to the indoor pool, located midway between the kitchen and the residence hall.

The pool building was equipped with saunas, as well as a specially designed hydraulic lift used to raise and lower disabled people in and out. One of the activities the school organized was the Ten Mile Swim, an event where local businesses would sponsor a disabled athlete to swim a total of ten miles over a period of time, with the proceeds donated to local charities. It was an innovative way to involve the business community in disabled "affairs," support the good works of similarly minded organizations, break down stereotypes and help build a more inclusive atmosphere for a disabled population. It also raised the esteem and built the bodies of the participants.

Those individuals who completed the required ten miles would be awarded a T-shirt aptly entitled "Ten Mile Swim". I commandeered one of these shirts for my personal use, though I could hardly swim a lick.

One day, I found myself wearing it on the beach. A beautiful, young woman approached me seductively, looked at my shirt, and declared, "Ten miles…that's a long way."

"Yes, it is," I proudly replied.

After about 100 feet the hall ended in an inverted "L". There were eleven rooms down a short corridor to the left and an exit straight ahead. The rooms were configured to accommodate disabled people, boasting accessible restrooms, lowered sinks, and cork floors, which offered maximum stability and traction for wheelchairs, canes, and artificial legs.

All appeared quiet.

I walked out the exit, going straight outside, negotiated nine concrete steps and turned left. In another twenty feet, I came to a steep stairway that led to the entrance of my house.

I vaulted up the steps, turned the key and crossed the threshold. The first thing I had to pass on the way to my apartment, down the hall, was the basement door on the left.

That door is always closed. Bob Stacey is the only other person who has a key to this house, stored in a small, steel cabinet in his office. But he never enters here, so no one else ever does, either. Since I never open the cellar door, it remains closed in perpetuity. There is a reason for this.

My mind is usually wandering when I come home. But today, I am just thinking about what is beyond the portal. And I am thinking about what I will hear – what I always hear – when I pass.

Music. The Music of the Spheres. The song of the Harpies. A soft, classical, unidentifiable melody; soothing, peaceful, comforting, and hypnotic. And inviting. And deadly.

I have no idea who may have lived in this home in years past. I only know that it was built in 1952, and inhabited by any number of people, including students, instructors and, for long periods of time, neither of the above. I don't know what happened within these walls, but once upon a time I am sure that something terrible did happen. Something violent enough to draw *Them*. Then, something that made Them stay.

Demons.

I know nothing of "haunted houses" or poltergeists, yet I hear these melodies. I don't know if anyone else can hear what I hear each and every time I pass this portal. I don't exactly know what is down there, and I will never know because I will not go there. I know it is something malevolent, something that wishes me nothing but harm, something that *needs* me to investigate the confines of its dark dominion. How I am aware of this, I don't know either.

I also know that these wraiths are impounded here. While they have the power to draw others to them, they are powerless to leave of their own accord. I do not know if their influence – even though exercised within the boundaries of this particular space – reaches to the ends of the universe, or if it extends to me alone. But these entities do have attributes common to all of their ilk.

They do not determine their existence. They are created and empowered by *us*, by what we *are*, by things we have *done*. I feel their presence as surely as they feel mine.

I do not fear them because they are contained. So, as I do each day, I note the harmonies that would draw me to the musicians that play them, living memories, things that were once *ideas* now taking unknown, unseen forms.

My small pad is just a few feet ahead on the right. There is a living room, a bedroom, and a smaller room where I keep an electric piano facing the street below.

The piano is a wonderful instrument, and I used to love to play. I developed quite a proficiency at one time, I am told. Through the piano I was able to channel both negative and positive emotions and turn them all into something beautiful.

But not anymore.

A kitchen, rarely used, is further ahead. Another, uninhabited, three-room apartment is on this level, and I seldom frequent it although it is open to me and available for my use. There are two more just like it upstairs, and I rarely go there either.

My place is sparsely furnished; the living room contains an old couch, an easy chair, a lamp on an end table, a television, and that is all. There is one window, facing an alleyway, looking out upon a brick wall which is the exterior of an adjoining house. The scant light that tries to make its way through is frustrated by dark curtains.

On the broad arm of the old fashioned armchair is a small ash tray. In the ash tray is a perfectly rolled marijuana cigarette, which I always roll first thing in the morning, and which is waiting for me now, along with a half-used pack of matches. The matches bear the emblem of the Dory Inn, a local Irish bar I occasionally frequent when I am in a less-than-reclusive state of mind. It is quiet, it is dark, and it is sparsely populated at any time. The bartender's name is Lark. I know him and like him. I like him because he leaves me alone and usually doesn't speak unless spoken to. He respects my privacy, yet he will talk to me if he senses that I am amenable to conversation. Or desperately need it.

The joint is usually lit within a minute of my arrival home. On the end table next to the chair is a half-filled bottle of vodka and a clean six ounce glass. These tools sometimes keep away bad thoughts and bad things and I do not hesitate to use them.

On the table is a phone. It rarely rings because I rarely call anyone, and I suppose I have made it known that I do not wish anyone to call me. These days, it is used to contact one person and one person alone.

I slowly sank into the chair, lit the joint and inhaled deeply. I filled my glass to the brim, drank a third of its contents, and leaned back.

Coming home from work, for most people, is simply the end of another day. For me, it is the beginning of a struggle. I typically do not prevail.

I tried to clear my mind and think of nothing. I prayed that this would be possible, but such prayers are rarely answered.

I tried to imagine that I was safe and calm and alone, truly alone, although I never feel quite safe, am rarely calm, and know that *they* will never let me be alone.

I closed my eyes and visualized a straight line moving across my mind's eye into infinity, like a flat line on one of those hospital devices measuring heart rates or brain waves or the like. When I found I could not sustain this image, I imagined a brick wall, much like the wall outside of my window. I imagined a wall that had no end on either side, and that traveled up, up, up; so high that I could neither see nor imagine its end point. When I could not sustain this image I took another drink, and another toke.

I tried to think of the line again, but this calming image quickly faded; I thought of the wall again, but the wall crumbled.

I finished my drink and my joint, and I was feeling the effects. I tried to close my eyes in the hope that bad thoughts would disappear with the light. I replayed the day's events in my mind to distract myself from what might now transpire.

My anticipation of their arrival is not always accompanied by fear, because they do not always bring pain and suffering with them. However, their coming is always preceded by anxiety, because they are always uninvited, and their entrance into my world always appears random. They carry with them the character of the unknown, and their ability to appear and disappear as they wish is a constant reminder of my unique and unqualified inability to affect anything that they do.

The day rushed into my thoughts and out again quickly, too quickly, and I was soon out of distractions. I reached into a small drawer in the end table and took out a cellophane bag filled with weed. I was clearly not high enough, so I rolled another joint. I closed my eyes again, leaned back, lit up and breathed deeply. I was really feeling it now; maybe this was going to be one of those lucky days; a peaceful late afternoon leading to a peaceful evening.

For no particular reason, I felt a sharp panic envelop me. I jerked my eyes open and took note of the bottle of Clonopan sitting on top of the television, facing my chair. The panic subsided as quickly as it came. I clenched my eyes closed and gritted my teeth. I imagined I was in a closet; a dark closet with the door closed, quiet like a womb, like a tomb, nothing inside, nothing outside.

But he came nevertheless.

He usually appears in the same manner, usually when it is warm and bright outside, when a steady breeze blows out to center field, at times of the year when simple air and grass combine to make a fragrance as compelling as any aphrodisiac. When little boys across this great land that is America feel a stirring in the air, and take wooden sticks of every variety and dimension into their hands, together with balls covered in white cowhide, and sprint to rocky fields to play the time-honored game that is the official pastime of our nation.

I opened my eyes, turned in my chair and faced the couch to my right.

He was sitting there.

His hands were folded in front of him on his lap. He was bent over, his head bowed; thoughtful, ruminating.

He rarely appeared in uniform. He was dressed as he usually was, in jeans and brown cowboy boots, with a thick leather belt adorned by a silver and turquoise buckle. He wore a white denim shirt open at the neck that revealed a gray-white mat of hair on his broad chest.

He looked to be about sixty years old, around the age he was at the time of his death in 1997. But he also seemed robust and fit, not at all the way he looked in '97 after cancer had disassembled his liver.

He doesn't talk about that much. I don't think he sees much point in it, as he admitted long ago – to himself and others – that 40 years of hard drinking and hard living had laid a neat and fertile foundation for the disease.

Cancer may have made the putout, but he had the assist. One was as necessary as the other to the final score.

But right here and now he looked as huge and as solid as a boulder, not misshapen or abnormal as so many bodybuilders look today. He simply seemed as big and as strong as a man could naturally be in the absence of steroids and the overbearing attentions of doctors, therapists, nutritionists, trainers and pharmacists. His body seemed ready to burst, his clothes barely able to contain the power within.

He was born this way. He was The Natural. A pure athlete with God-given abilities, trained from early childhood by a father obsessed by his own failures, and determined to have his son avoid his fate.

He was destined to become the best there ever was. The best there could ever be. But the errant choices he made over a lifetime, combined with the workings of a harsh and unyielding fate, caused this destiny to be averted.

He lifted his head to look at me with his deep blue eyes and all at once I realized how much of the boy the man had retained. He had a kind, innocent face. He really was that way in life.

That's what I loved about him. Of course, he could also be cranky and abrupt, even cruel, for no apparent reason. I kind of understand this. On the one hand, no one is perfect, without defect, foible or blemish. On the other hand, he had a grueling childhood and a hard life; a career dominated by debilitating injuries and pain that never went away. He died that way, and before his time. A long healthy life hadn't been in the cards for him.

Or for his father. Or his grandfather. Or his sons.

So it goes.

He spoke with his unmistakable Oklahoma twang:

"D'I ever tell you 'bout the time my daddy came out of the stands and beat my ass in front of four thousand people?"

His daddy had never 'beaten his ass' at all. I knew because he had told me – 'bout that time his daddy had come out of the grandstands' – the last time he stopped by for an unannounced visit.

"You told me about that time."

"I did?"

"Yeah."

"Oh."

"But you can tell me again."

"Ya sure?"

"Sure."

He hesitated, and then smiled. My tolerance flattered him, and he liked me for it, and I knew that he did.

And then he was back there in 1949, at the age of seventeen, in his final year of high school in Commerce, just a few miles from the "big" city of Miami, Oklahoma, and I was back there with him.

"There was this big ol' righty on the mound: wild red hair; a crazy, arrogant kid. He was strong, and he threw greased lightning. Few of the boys could keep up with him. I had faced him once before in pre-season; I bunted my way on the first pitch he threw, but he thought that was *cheating* or sompthin'.

"'Next time stand up there like a man and take your medicine!' he pouted as I stood on the bag. I was a little annoyed, you know; after all, I was the one on first base. But for some reason I felt like I *had* cheated.

"Anyway, I watched him warm up that day, and the more I watched the more I felt I could tag him good if I wanted to. But I wanted to make sure. I had a bit more power standing on the right side of the plate, but my dad was grooming me to be a switch-hitter; he was crazy in that way. I only hit both ways because he *made* me, always, every time I picked up a bat; left against right-handers, right against left-handers.

"I never understood why I had to do this. I could hit most any pitcher I had ever seen batting righty; I never saw the point in learning another way. Learning to hit from both sides of the plate was an effort, it was *work,* and I never thought baseball should be work. Hell, if I wanted to *work,* I woulda' stayed in the mines with Daddy. But I guess he wanted more for me; I guess that's what every father wants for his kid; more than he had, better than he had.

"So I stepped up against this big ol' boy, and damned if I

didn't want to smack that ball down the neck that held that big red arrogant head o' his. Hell, I *knew* I was going to smack it good; I was feeling the magic, you know, and when I was feeling that way I could do no wrong. I walked up to the plate slowly, smiling a little, not listening at all to his big mouth cat-a-calling me, not even lookin' at him, just staring down at the plate, hitting my spikes with the end of the bat, and smiling. I was gonna crush him.

"I took my place on the right side of the plate, where I felt the strongest. I looked up at him slowly, just looked him right in the eye, and he glared back kinda' strange, like he was worried a bit. I readied myself, crouched down and held my breath, because I was gonna swing at the first pitch he threw and crush that rock. I was gonna crush that rock, and it was going to go farther than anyone had ever seen a baseball go.

"Red peered in at the catcher but then, instead of going into his windup, he stood up straight and put both hands on his hips. Now that was kinda strange, so I straightened up out of my crouch, stepped back and looked at him. He seemed to be looking over my shoulder.

"And then I heard and felt the *whack* across my head. I turned around, and a second *whack* came straight across my face. And there he was, straight outta the stands, Dad, Pop, Father, Papa – Mutt, his friends called him – looking like an angry dog.

"'What the hell do you think you're doing?' he asked. I was confused for a minute, but just for a minute, 'cause I *knew* what I was doing. I had a reason, you know, but that didn't make a difference; Dad had caught me red-handed – *right*-handed, actually – on the wrong side of the tracks and the wrong side of the plate, defying his will, which was the last thing on earth any Mantle wanted to do."

He looked up at me dolefully and smiled.

"And that was the last time I ever did *that* again."

I asked him what happened when he finally got back into the

box against that red-headed right-hander.

"I went up there left-handed and bunted my way on," he replied.

I asked him why.

"Dunno. Guess I was punishing myself."

It was a cute, homey story, even if it was told a little differently this time than the last. But there was a purpose behind its telling.

The dead do not come to me without a purpose. They have something to say, a communication of particular importance to deliver at a particular point in time. This was a message from the beyond, a guiding light that could enlighten and counsel, if I could decipher its meaning and relevance.

This time I could. There's a right way and a wrong way of doing things, he was trying to tell me. The right way is always a little harder. You may get away with doing the wrong thing for a while; hell, you might have so much success doing the wrong thing, that as time goes on, you see no reason to change your ways at all. But one day it all catches up with you. One day you're found out. One day someone who knows better screams "the emperor has no clothes" and then your facade is stripped away, and you're seen for what you truly are: A man trying to take the easy way out. Then, you pay the price for doing so.

He was gone.

He rarely says goodbye. I guess the powers that send him here in the first place don't see much utility in that. He's here to say what he has to say, and he moves on.

And here I am, Meester Reechard Gooodman, taking the easy way out. Drugging and desensitizing myself until I can hardly feel anything at all. Thinking I can just make everything go away, as if I could push away for an hour or an evening the reality of what I am, and the memories of what I experience. But I can't push anything away.

"I yam' what I yam'," Popeye said.

I am able, from time to time, to peer into the souls of people and see exactly what is there. I perceive a secular truth, a distillation of their spirits, an essence meant for the eyes of no one. I ride a wave of compelled insight and I am swept away along with it as an unwilling participant, forced to follow where it leads. It leaves me alone and exhausted on a beachhead, but with a novel understanding I was never meant to acquire, but that I can use for the benefit of others or myself.

I am able, from time to time, to see through the clinging mist of the hereafter, and converse with the famous, the infamous, and the undistinguished, all of them long past gone. They come as uninvited guests, they intrude upon my life as they will, carrying with them no timepiece or datebook, ignoring all conventions and niceties, having nothing in common with each other, save that they have something to say that some higher power demands I hear. They care not if they are vague or specific, or if I understand anything they have to relate. They do not consider whether I will be mortified, bored, offended or horrified. I am the tablet, and they are the scribes and that is all. Their marks upon me are recorded with impunity. But I can take their words, and I can put them to use.

And I am compelled to witness still more, the horrors of a dark underworld curtained behind the veil of my dreams, whose denizens seek nothing but my harm, and whose very existence burdens me like the weight of a terrible sin. But even these terrors carry with them a chance for insight and greater understanding.

Yet if I could, I would face a mirror at night, strip myself naked, look into my reflection and claw at my body until I set loose what is raging within me; a fury in the form of a question that screams Why Why Why?

Left to my own devices I would hammer my head against a wall until my skull cracked, until I was released from my confusion, my fear and my pain, from my terrifying disconnect from the common man, from my inability to feel any kinship with those of flesh and of blood, from the feelings of loneliness and helplessness and unreality that accompany me, caress my hand and look lovingly into my eyes as we walk through this world: my constant companions, my alter egos, my shadows.

I grasped my head with both hands. I wanted to cry and I wanted to feel sorry for myself. I wanted to beg for an end to this all, to scream for an answer, a reason why...

and the phone rang.

I looked at it for a moment as if I didn't comprehend the sound.

It rang again. I picked the receiver up numbly, my hands shaking, and held it to my ear. I said nothing.

"Hello, lover."

I hesitated as if I did not recognize the voice. But, of course, I did.

Thank God for Kara.

I met her at the Inn one night after 1:00 a.m. It was her last stop after a night of partying in Manhattan with her less-than-sober girlfriends. While not by any means a habitual drinker, when she does imbibe she can drink most grown men under the table. Way, way under the table.

That night, she had taken the initiative. This was necessary because I do not go to the Inn to meet people or engage in mindless banter.

She dragged me out from under the glass cage I had placed myself in, excused my obvious rudeness, and refused to be put off by my less-than-sociable demeanor. Lark, behind the bar as always, gently encouraged what little conviviality was in me, and I was ultimately glad he did. She was encouraged rather than discouraged by my iron exterior, my refusal to engage in meaningful conversation, and my obvious disinterest in engaging her in any way.

It seems I was a challenge. No doubt, I continue to be.

She is a beautiful girl, slim and muscular with strawberry

blond hair, and just taller than me at five foot nine inches. This doesn't bother me, and it doesn't seem to bother her either, even when she puts on spiked heels and towers over me. She has piercing green eyes that see into my soul. She is joyful and rarely put off by my pervasive, dark moods. How she puts up with me, I do not know.

She is my lifeline, my anchor, and my savior. In my darkest moments, she has always been there for me.

We've been dating for three years, now. I see no one else, and I don't believe she does either. To the extent that I can love, I love her, but I have never told her. Half of me says I don't have to. The other half of me says I'd better before it's too late.

She has never put any pressure on me and takes me for what I am. Slowly, ever so slowly, I have told her about me and she has reacted as if I were describing a birthmark or, at worst, a dishonorable discharge. She has never judged me and, not unfairly, refuses to allow me to judge her.

She completed three years at New York's Columbia University and received sterling grades. Then, for inexplicable reasons, she dropped out. She did not let that stop her from recording on her resume that she had graduated from that school with honors, on the strength of which she obtained a position as a copywriter at Smith, Banner and Smith, a prestigious advertising agency. After seven years she became an account supervisor earning a salary deep into six figures. I do not understand how, or why, she continues to work under this terrible misapprehension, as it is inconsistent with her straightforward personality and honest character.

Otherwise, she is bubbly, confident, vivacious, wholly convincing when she wishes to be, and comfortable with herself in all ways. She attracts attention wherever she goes and would, I believe, whether attired in a low-cut sequined evening gown or a burlap sack. In other words, she is everything I am not.

"Good evening, my dear."

"Oh, Bela Lugosi tonight, is it?" she quipped. "Hey, listen to this."

She put the phone next to a speaker and nearly blew my ear off, treating me to a 1970s version of The Tubes singing "White Punks on Dope."

"Cool, huh?"

"The coolest."

The Tubes are an innovative hard rock band that originated in San Francisco in the mid-1970s. During one concert in Boston, a member of the band was observed running up the center aisle of the auditorium with a chain saw in his hands, waving it over the heads of enthused concert goers.

The lead singer went by the pseudonym "Quay Lewd." This was a lampoon of one of the more popular recreational drugs of the time, Methaqualone, sold under the trade name of "Quaalude." It was originally promoted as a sleeping aid and sedative, but was removed from the market when it was found to have addictive properties. Its general effects included euphoria and relaxation. Also, slurred speech and difficulty walking. Also – in the case of overdose – delirium, convulsions, and cardiac arrest.

"Tell me, Bela, are you taking your beloved anywhere this weekend, or do I just have to pick a place, break down your door and drag you with me as usual."

She read my hesitation and replied for me.

"Tell you what, Spiderman, I'll let you cool out today and tomorrow, but on the condition that you plan a day trip for us on Sunday; something fun, OK?"

"OK, sweetheart that sounds fine."

"'Sweetheart,' now doesn't that sound better?"

It was not a rhetorical question.

"Yes, darling, that sounds better."

"Sweetheart, darling, MY GOD, I can't take all this affection!"

"You deserve that and more."

"Well, I find it hard to correct you, particularly when you're so correct. But don't get mushy on me stranger; just pick me up early on Sunday morning, you plan everything and make it good. I've got a special announcement and I want to be in a fun place, DIG?"

"A special announcement?" I couldn't help being nervous.

"Yes, a special announcement, but don't get nervous, don't get crazy, just plan ahead and pick me up at 8:30, OK, Kemosabe?"

"Eight-thirty it is. What are you going to do till then?"

"Oh, you know, whore around with my friends, as usual."

"Don't joke like that."

"Oh, come on, Ricky baby, you know I only have eyes for you."

"Is that true?"

"Do you really have to ask?" There was a touch of annoyance in her voice.

"No, sweetheart, not at all, I'll see you Sunday morning."

She softened immediately. "OK, lover, I'll see you Sunday, and counting the minutes, OK?"

"Good night, sweetie."

"Good night, baby… Kisses…" She hung up.

V

The moon.

The milky white globe hung unnaturally, like a teardrop against the darkness of the beyond. Throughout human history it had persevered, much as it was today, slowly marking and measuring the moments of man's existence.

And watching, he thought.

Dayne Francis Dorio sat gazing from the window of his spartan dormitory room. It was immaculately clean, and he enjoyed keeping it that way, a symbol of an organized existence and an orderly mind. It was a representation of the man he was now, of the man he had always hoped to be.

He was not always this way. At a point in time, his mind was muddled by confusion, his spirit commandeered by wildly fluctuating emotions. His actions were not his own, but controlled by other things. Bad things.

Demons.

But those days were over, now. The therapy had helped. The drugs had worked.

But the voices; my God, there had been so many voices. For so long they had whispered words of nihilism and hopelessness into his all-too-willing ears. But they had been silenced. Shuttered by the force of his will. Foreclosed by the disciplined application of his own unique personal power.

He had remade himself.

He turned from the window to look at his compact surroundings. Not a spot marred the cork-tiled floor, not a speck of dust lined any surface. No pictures hung from any wall, and no television, radio or stereo equipment muddled the limited space. No books, mementos or souvenirs detracted from the stark emptiness. This place, like his mind and his spirit, had been swept clean of any distraction or commotion, purged of the mindless babblings and worthless musings of others. Here, in this place, his sanctum, the order was absolute.

Here, the voices were silent. Here, there was perfection. He sighed.

Ahh, but there was one thing: An artifact from the past. A reminder of where he had been and, therefore, by operation, a reminder of *what* he had been, what he was now, and what he might yet become.

This was permissible. After all, to indulge oneself in small ways is a healthy attribute, a sign of a smoothly functioning organism.

The small wooden object rested on the top of his narrow three drawer dresser. It was a simple thing: two parallel curved arcs composed of a rich, golden, African hardwood, each radiating upward on either end to form the shape of a broad "U". The arcs were joined by a decorative connector of solid silver. Each arc ended in a small, unusually shaped concave depression lined with a black felt. Beautiful in itself, it was not immediately obvious that it was designed to hold something.

Dayne smiled and approached slowly. He paused with his hand on the wooden handles of the top drawer of his dresser and closed his eyes.

The past was properly put away. But, now and then, it was harmless to relive certain past events in order to achieve a greater understanding of one's life. He could not, however, repress the shiver that went through him each time he did so. He did not dwell on this.

He opened the drawer.

He always wondered how heavy the instrument seemed.

At first. It always seemed lighter later on.

The handle was embedded with small triangles of turquoise that he had cut, polished and set himself within the thin, hand-hammered silver plate that covered the grip and secured each stone.

The blade was nearly six inches wide and over a foot long. It claimed an almost unnatural looking trailing point, curving upwards towards its end. Resting along its spine were eighteen razor sharp serrations that would rip and tear when removed from flesh. Along the center of the blade ran a cannelure – sometimes known as a blood groove. It was believed that this part of a knife's anatomy allowed a victim's vital essence to flow freely without the need to withdraw the weapon.

He ran his index finger ever so lightly along its edge. As he did, a thin red line appeared as if by magic. He raised the knife over his head with both hands. Crimson droplets ran down his hand to his wrist.

Satisfied, he placed the knife on its stand and stood back, bringing his injured finger slowly to his mouth. The taste was sweet and salty all at the same time. He allowed the memories to flow back to him as his finger continued to bleed. He did not notice the sweat forming on his brow or the quickening of his breath.

He did feel a slight breeze on the back of his neck, an errant current that passed silently through the crack he had opened in the window. The curtain rose and fell slightly. As he lost himself momentarily in thought, the urgent murmurings in his ear were almost imperceptible.

Sunday

A long festoon of electric light leaped from one side of the park to the other, followed by a second and a third. Then there was a perfect maze of them. Tall towers that had grown dim suddenly broke forth in electric outlines and gay rosettes of color, until the place was transformed into an enchanted garden, of such Aladdin never dreamed.

Albert Bigelow Paine
Coney Island, NY 1903

VI

It was the beginning of the fall, or the end of the summer; who is to say where one begins and the other ends? You tell the difference not by the marks on a calendar but by the transformations that take place in people when the time comes for the seasons to change.

I picked up Kara at precisely 8:30 a.m. She was looking lovely in blue jeans and a maroon halter top which exposed just the smallest portion of her tummy. Her hair was tied back behind her head in a ponytail. She looked happy.

She always looks happy.

She immediately asked where I was going to take her. Determined to surprise her I refused to say, and so began a largely silent hour and a half journey to the tip of Brooklyn.

One can see Coney Island from miles away as the Parachute Jump – that great old amusement area's stellar landmark – becomes visible long before one arrives. The 250 foot tower was built in1939 and delighted thrill seekers by carrying up to twelve of them at a time by cables to the top. There they were released and entered into a free fall until a parachute opened, permitting them to glide down the rest of the way. Patrons were saved from oblivion only by the silk chute and steel cable of the apparatus. The historic ride closed in 1964, yet the structure itself had been maintained and its red frame stands as the park's most enduring and visible monument.

"Coney Island?" Kara shouted, bouncing up and down on the car seat like a little kid. She put her arms around me and kissed me on the lips as I drove at a speed of 65 miles an hour.

"You'll kill us both!" I blurted out, but I had to laugh, as she was laughing. God, was she good for me.

Arriving, we parked the car and made our way past the New York Aquarium and the infamous Cyclone Roller Coaster.

Beneath the Cyclone was an equally infamous shack where, it is said, a proprietor still resided, with the pounding of the surf eternally facing him and the screaming thunder of the coaster as his backyard. We made our way to the boardwalk.

It was an unlikely place for an old Bronx boy to be, and I had not been here since I was a child. I was with my father, then, at a time when the old park had entered into one of its cyclical periods of decline, becoming worn and in marked disrepair. Families began to avoid it during the daytime hours; gangs roamed its streets at night.

In the past, Coney Island was not one amusement park, but a collection of parks rolled into one gigantic fairground. At one time, the rides and attractions extended for eight city blocks from north to south. Today, the park is bordered by Surf Avenue on the western side and three blocks or so to the east, by the boardwalk. Beyond the boardwalk is the beach, and beyond the beach, the Atlantic Ocean.

One hundred years ago the famous Luna Park stood on these grounds with its "Helter Skelter," and "Shoot the Chutes" rides. Steeplechase Park was here, too, its entrance emblazoned with the memorable visage of an animated character with a lunatic grin, much like Alfred E. Newman from Mad Magazine fame. This was "The Funny Place," a sign promised.

The hallmark of Steeplechase was the famous Steeplechase horses. Eight wooden horses stood on eight sets of steel rails. Patrons – typically a boy and his date – mounted the realistic equine replicas and, propelled by gravity, traversed a track one-half mile long. "Half a mile in half a minute," was assured.

Even during my early childhood, amid the park's decline, for block upon block one could see massive roller coasters rising above the beach, each surrounded by attractions of every kind and description. On the boardwalk, marking the outer edge of the amusement area, animal exhibits, freak shows, fortune tellers, candy apple salesman, and balloon vendors abounded. One could buy hot dogs or hamburgers from the famous Nathan's – an area attraction since 1916 – or clams, shrimps, T-shirts, sunglasses, silly beach hats, colorful balloons or cotton candy from a hundred other merchants.

Games of chance of every variety were also to be found. One could shoot streams of water through a gun into a hole, which in turn would move a small racehorse along a path. You could attempt to toss a softball into the spout of an old fashioned, three foot tall, steel milk can, or try to flip wooden rings around the neck of a Coke bottle. You could try your hand at shooting a basketball into a narrow hoop, attempt to knock down cloth "cats" or three stacked bottles with a hardball, or explode balloons placed on a board with darts. Always, of course, to the rare winner, went the "Kewpie" doll or, if you were exceedingly lucky, a massive Teddy Bear large enough to earn the undying admiration of your sweetheart.

A massive restoration would eventually return the aged park to respectability, clean up its famous beach, and cut the vast amusement area to a less spectacular but more manageable size. Today, decades after that restoration, Steeplechase Park is long gone, but Astroland Park is still here, with its bumper cars, go-carts, fun houses and kiddie land. The boardwalk, once pristine, then tattered and broken, then restored again to its former greatness, was showing its age once more. A step on any of the diagonally cut boards – each four inches wide and eleven feet long – might elicit a groan or cause the opposite end to move noticeably upward. Every stride along the walk was fraught with the real potential for minor injury of one sort or another.

Still, in ancient shanties by the ocean, as old and as weathered as the wooden pier itself, one could still find irresistible mysteries. One could still see remnants of grandness in some of the attractions that made the park great, such as the Wonder Wheel, the Parachute Jump and, of course, the great Cyclone. Ghostly memories of others seemed to linger in large square fields, between attractions containing only sparse grass, marked every now and then by jagged pieces of metal protruding from the dirt, like demons trying to force their way from Hell.

This was such a special place; everything so alive and so vibrant yet at the same time, all of it constructed on the ashes of the past, rising from the meager remains of the forgotten…

We walk past a sign promising "Freak Show" and I am not sure I want to be here.

I am holding Daddy's hand and looking around anxiously. I try to pull away, towards the light, towards the beach, where the air is clean and crisp, and the sun is bright and cheery, but he holds on tight. It is dark and quiet and musty inside and I am walking on dirt and hay and peanut shells and the wrappers of candy apples and those huge lollipops you buy from the vendors that seem to be everywhere. I look up at him and he is silent and distracted. He seems to be thinking but he's not really thinking about anything and I don't really know how I know this but I do.

All of a sudden I see a calf behind a low metal gate and there's a spotlight on it. It looks pretty and cute and we walk close to it. I reach a hand out to touch its wet nose and I notice a leg laying on its rear hindquarters across its back, a leg that will never walk, a leg that was never really supposed to be there. I'm little but I can read and pretty well for my age and I read the sign on the gate and the sign says "five-legged calf" and I look up at him to ask whether this is real or a joke and he has this far away look in his eyes like he's looking at something but not seeing anything at all.

We walk on and he leads me to a jar, a really big jar on a stand, and the stand has a light over it that makes the liquid in the jar seem thick and yellow and sick. He heads right for it so this is something he's interested in. Maybe it's something he really wants me to see.

There's a shape of something in the jar, but it's hard to make out. At first. Then Daddy brings me closer, much closer, close enough to touch the jar, and I do, and he doesn't seem to care, though usually he tells me 'don't touch' or 'watch out you'll break something' and he's looking at the jar, really looking, and now he's touching the jar, too, only in a weird way that makes me scared and makes me want to get out of here.

He looks down at me but doesn't seem to know I'm here. He looks back at the jar and I follow his eyes. Now I see what he sees…

There is a baby in the jar. Or, something that looks like a baby or that once was a baby or that could have been a baby but its head is way too big to be a baby's head and its eyes are not baby eyes. It doesn't have baby hands, either. In fact, it doesn't have any hands at all but things like flippers where there should be hands. I think I should be scared, but right now I'm not scared because I'm looking at him looking at the jar.

He starts talking to the jar but he's talking to me. And he's asking the jar and asking me 'where's this baby's father?' and I don't know if I'm supposed to answer and I want to say something really smart because I think I'm kinda smart and know some things but I don't have any idea where this baby's father is or even if it is a baby or if it had a father at all or if this isn't just a big joke, just a plastic baby in a bottle of yellow water, made up to scare little kids and doing a pretty good job of it right now.

He's talking again. He's saying that the baby is alone in this jar and will always be alone. He's not crying, but I see tears coming down his face and he asks me how he can get the baby out of the jar.

He's grabbing the jar with both of his hands and asking me how can he get the baby out of the jar.

Then he answers himself and says the baby is never coming out of the jar; it's just going to stay there, year after year, forever and for always, and people are just going to look and laugh and look and laugh, year after year after year and its always going to be here in this dark and dirty place and I'm scared, really scared, and before I can talk or cry or scream out he picks me up and runs away from the jar with me in his arms. I put my arms around his neck, and we burst out into the air and into the light and he runs down the boardwalk. We go that way for a while until he slows down. He's not saying anything at all. He's not thinking anything, either, but I don't know how I know that. My arms are clutched around his neck and my head is tucked against his shoulder.

The sun is not as bright now.

We walked hand in hand, with Kara fairly skipping along. We were enjoying each other's company as well as the cool, ocean brushed air, and taking advantage of the thin, post-Labor Day crowd. She seemed as wide-eyed as a little girl.

I gazed at her as we walked. How beautiful she was, and how blissfully happy. Couldn't I be happy with her? Despite my disabilities, couldn't we make a life together?

My past and my present collided here, and perhaps this was why I had chosen to take her to this place. By saying good-by to old memories, might I not usher in a new life, a better life with this sweet girl?

A long goodbye, then. A last brush with the past. And then?

Many of the smaller exhibits and businesses were closed or closing. Still others appeared just partially open, not wanting to stay open yet not willing to close, not yet, trying in a half-hearted attempt to extract the last of the summer income from the small crowds.

Up ahead, as we walked the planks of the ancient boardwalk, with the vastness of the sea to our left, we saw a small commotion, a slight thickening of the crowd. There, a hawker stood in front of a weathered and battered marquee and, in strangely subdued fashion, held a placard describing the mysteries therein. "Learn the future," it promised.

His age was difficult to estimate; he could have been between forty-five and seventy. He had that worn and tired look that one only gets from doing the same thing over and over again for too long and for too little. He hadn't shaved in a few days and his black cap and suit were worn and dusty. He was positioned to solicit or encourage the crowd, but he appeared to feel it was too late in the season to waste the effort. He looked tired and empty inside, with barely the energy to breathe. He looked like men I have seen who have dedicated too much of their lives to activities so unproductive and unfulfilling that it leaves them numb, with hollow hearts and vacant stares, strangely resigned and complacent, like wildebeest that stop struggling after a lion attacks on those National Geographic shows.

We were ten yards away.

The small crowd circulated in front of the hawker. As we approached, he appeared to look directly into my eyes, and in a normal tone of voice that somehow carried above the wind to my ears he said, "Learn the mysteries of your future."

I was experienced enough to sense something unusual, something too familiar and too personal in his tone. I was street-wise enough to sense something dangerous, something dark and forbidden, without needing an objective reason to justify so instant a conclusion.

The Wave rose quickly within me.

And something else came with it.

I am with my brother. I am back with him in New Orleans.

It was a bright and beautiful day in the Big Easy. I was on a side street deep in the French Quarter, at the entrance of a large storefront with no sign.

The front door was wide open, but the intense sunlight outside seemed to stop at the door, barely illuminating a huge, windowless space within. Without stepping over the threshold, I craned my neck to look inside.

It would have been impossible to see anything were it not for the glow coming from a large grouping of candles, placed upon a small round table in the rear of the space. Three people sat at the table. As we approached the doorway, they all looked up.

On the left side of the establishment, I saw a stand of unfinished wood shelves. There was row upon row of them, extending from the very front of the storefront to its rear, and from floor to ceiling. Large Mason jars of identical dimension lined all of the shelves. Each jar was clearly labeled. Each held contents of unspeakable design. The internal organs of exotic animals. Parts of insects and poisonous plants. Potions and elixirs, black liquids and dark powders, things of mysterious origin and sinister purpose.

I looked to the rear again. The three denizens within watched us attentively, waiting. I knew this was not a sideshow or carnival act. My brother stepped gamely inside. I started to do the same, but stopped with my foot suspended over the demarcation between inside and out as the Wave passed over me, choking me and freezing me where I stood. Standing on the threshold of the door leading into that shop, at the junction of where the light of day met the darkness, I slowly retracted my foot, removing it again to the bright sunshine.

There was something inside that I didn't want to know about, something that I knew I shouldn't toy with or take lightly.

The Wave surged again.

Now I am wandering alone as a child, through the ghostly remains of a deserted bungalow colony in the woods of upstate New York.

Such places are just collections of small wooden cottages, that time and the animals and the woods have reclaimed, interspersed through towns by the names of Hopewell Junction, or Goshen, or Monticello. The tiny homes usually surrounded a great house, or the concrete remains of a swimming pool or handball court. Once, fathers abandoned their families here for the summer, returned to their jobs in the City for the week, and then trekked back to the country to spend the weekends with their spouses and children.

This ritual repeated itself for eight weeks. Men were left to fend for themselves for five days each week, while their wives were deserted in primitive surroundings without cars, telephones, televisions, dishwashers, or air conditioners, or any proximity to malls, supermarkets, convenience stores or beauty salons. Children were left largely to their own devices and given the choice whether to perceive their condition as an exquisitely painful isolation, or an unparalleled opportunity for unrestrained liberty.

Which they selected depended upon how they felt about trees, I suppose: or mountains, or frigid summer nights, or orange salamanders that greeted the dew of each dawn, or frogs or mosquitoes, or giant brown toads the size of your foot, that stalked the grounds around midnight each evening. It would depend how they felt about campfires and hot dogs and marshmallows, and ghost stories, and weekly movies, and bingo games: or trucks that stopped by once each week, loaded with Entenmann's brand cookies and cakes: or tree houses, or Monarch butterflies snagged in huge nylon nets.

I began to ascend the rotted steps of a particular building when I froze without thinking, my left foot suspended in the air of its own unilateral volition, refusing to go farther before it compelled me to look down.

As I complied, I saw, just inches beneath my hanging foot a coiled Copperhead snake, one of only two poisonous varieties in the state. It was staring at me calmly. It was a copper-brown, perhaps four feet long, with a large flat head, from which the breed gets its name.

Copperheads are not particularly aggressive animals. They prefer to keep to themselves, but have little fear of humans and will not tolerate direct threat or attack without a powerful and immediate response. Their venom is as fast-acting as it is deadly, and there was little doubt that I would have perished – alone, rapidly, and rather painfully – if I had completed my step. Instead, I slowly raised my leg higher, lifting it slowly over the head of the beast, which serenely permitted me to continue on my way. My senses served me well.

And then, presto chango, I was back on the boardwalk of Coney Island, but no divination froze my step; no tide of sensation gripped my body or my mind.

"Oh, Ricky," Kara cried, "I want my fortune told!"

She pulled me along through the onlookers and into the exhibit.

The hawker looked at me without uttering a word.

At my first step inside something crackled beneath my foot.

Peanut shells.

A young girl no more than nine, with long blond hair and a dirty white dress, met us at the threshold.

"The Conjuh is this way," the little girl said in a forced stately manner. I barely noticed her guttural pronunciation of the word "Conjurer".

Kara giggled and looked at me, humming the Twilight Zone theme music.

The child led us down a short corridor winding to the left. Its walls were stained plywood and adorned with cheap electric lanterns and old posters of Coney Island, covered with the grease and sweat of a dozen summers.

The passageway emptied into a tiny room, lit only by three candles, placed in a candelabra upon a small round table. The table was covered with a multicolored cloth framed by tassels. Behind the table, facing an empty chair, sat an ancient woman wearing gypsy garb, with an array of cheap costume jewelry adorning her neck.

She appeared to be sleeping.

Kara immediately sat down and waited eagerly.

The woman opened her eyes, raised her head slowly and smiled at Kara, then looked directly at me.

"Five dollars, please," she murmured in a hoarse, throaty whisper. Her accent was vaguely Hungarian.

She extended a thin, wrinkled hand in my direction, and I placed the bill there. The light of the candles played across her features revealing a gaunt, bemused countenance. She smiled again without a word and shifted her eyes to Kara.

"Your hand, my dear."

Kara giggled like a schoolgirl and thrust out her hand. The

gypsy received it in her outstretched palms and gazed at it for a moment, then looked up and fixed her stare upon me once more as she spoke.

"You are innocent and kind, and never hesitate to help others."

"You see, Ricky, I am *innocent*," Kara feigned, giggling again.

The gypsy continued.

"You have talent and imagination, and display skill in your chosen profession." Kara straightened her back and looked fully pleased with herself.

"You have a small secret, my dear, that you keep from those with whom you toil, but it shall never be revealed and its keeping shall never cause you harm."

Kara shifted uneasily in her wicker chair, her look of wry amusement suddenly gone.

I heard – or felt – a low hiss of air, as if something was being released, like the sound one hears when a child releases the pressure of her thumb, held against the base of a blown-up balloon. The woman did not avert her eyes from mine.

"Is there anything else?" Kara queried.

"Yes," the gypsy replied.

She turned and looked deeply at Kara.

"You shall be happy until the end of your life."

Kara smiled uneasily. The gypsy did not.

"You go, Ricky," Kara blurted out, rising quickly from her chair, now all too eager to remove herself from the old woman's presence.

There are analytical and biological certainties in the world; mathematical rules and universal principles of physics that keep us grounded in reality, that hold the world together and that keep all things observable and linear, predictable and clear. Surely there are no such things as magic, or conjurers, or witches or dragons or hobgoblins or the black arts. Right?

Right.

I sat down in the chair with my hands at my side.

"This is a special day for you, my good man. You are the last."

The coincidental reference to my last name was just too much.

"The last what?"

"The last I *conjuh* for."

The back of my neck turned cold. I shivered and glanced at Kara. There were no windows and no sources of draft in the small enclave, which somehow seemed bigger now than when we had first entered. Kara's eyes were upon the old woman.

"Give me your hand," she demanded of me.

I sensed a hunger. I looked at the witch's two cupped hands thrust before me and resting on the small table. They lay open, inviting, tempting, just about two inches from my sternum. I looked down at her hands, unmoving. Disjointed thoughts and waves of indecision and confusion passed over me. I felt like a schoolboy being challenged to a brawl by the neighborhood bully. I could take up the challenge and fight, or decline the invitation, and be beaten up anyway.

"We came here for our fortunes," I stuttered pitifully.

"And you shall have them," she replied.

My gaze shifted from the gypsy's hands to her eyes. I looked at her with a childlike wonder. Was I taking all this seriously? I looked again at Kara. She returned my gaze with a small smile as if to say "it's your move."

A distant memory of a baby in a jar. A vision of a small shop in New Orleans. A dream of a dragon hiding in the grass.

Conjuh.

"Your hand."

Her hands lay in front of me, awaiting a response. I was a fool. There were no such things as witches or hobgoblins or dragons. I grunted out loud.

Purging doubt and suspicion from my mind, I placed my hand into hers. I looked directly into the conjurer's eyes, but she was looking at my hand resting in hers, as if she were relieved.

The posters on the wall rustled slightly. I noticed that the girl in white, who had been posting guard duty just outside the small room, had turned and quietly left.

The old woman closed her eyes and began to kneed my hand gently between hers.

"I am a Conjuh," she began. "The daughter of a Conjuh who was a daughter of a Conjuh. I see the last day of my life. And today I see yours, as well."

A poster of the parachute jump slipped from its place on the wall. Impossibly, the candles appeared to dim.

"I am a Conjuh," she repeated. "And you are the last I conjuh for. I give you the fortune you seek, and more.

"Two days, eighteen hours, fifty-eight minutes… And now…"

The conjurer gazed intently at me, and seized my hand so tightly that I winced in pain. Her lips parted without speaking. She gasped and threw back her head, but no air reached her lungs. Her eyes opened wide. She tried to breathe, but it seemed like there was no air there for her to breathe. It was like her head was in a fishbowl filled with water. She looked back at me, or through me, and it was the face of fear that stared back. Or of death. Or of the end of all things.

Her death eyes relaxed. Her hands loosened their grip. Out of the corner of my eye I noticed Kara looking down at her watch.

My eyes opened wide as the true meaning and import of her words sunk in. Words formed in my brain and fluttered out of my mouth, dribbling across my lips like drops of rain trickling down a slippery rock.

"Two days, eighteen hours?"

The witch did not respond.

"Two days?" I repeated. She responded.

"The time of your life on this Earth."

Memories, again; a passage from the Old Testament:

Turn ye not unto ghosts, nor unto familiar spirits, seek them not out, to be defiled by them.

This was an unholy creature. Was I under the spell of a witch, or under one of my own making? Was I under the influence of a supernatural force, or merely enraptured by my own superstition and fertile imagination?

The hag's silent gaze was deafening.

"Is that it?" I demanded. Even I did not like the urgency of my query.

"*Not* it," the Conjuh replied. "To the last person I conjuh for I pass on the gift. A gift that is with *you*. For one day."

She leaned forward. "Till the setting of the sun tomorrow. *You* the *Conjuh*."

She cackled. "*That's* it."

The shack had become dank and humid. A large black insect of some kind appeared from behind the witch's chair – or from under the hem of her tattered dress – and darted to a corner of the room, then skirted along its perimeter.

"Well all-righty then," Kara quipped, mimicking Jim Carry's comedic line. With a smirk on her face she looked at the witch, then at me.

"This has been fun," she said. "And we'll be sure to stop back next year, too..."

She grabbed my hand as if I were a child being ushered off of a kiddie ride. She attempted to tow me clear of the woman, looking over her shoulder as she did.

"...and tell all our friends."

Despite Kara's bemused look and manner, she gave the clear impression that she was no longer amused and that it was time to go.

I pulled back and looked at the witch again. She was leaning back in her chair, in no obvious hurry for me to leave.

"I have two days to live?"

"Two days, eighteen hours, fifty-eight minutes," she repeated.

Why was I still here? I fought the impulse to bolt and run. The shack appeared darker and more depressing with each passing moment. Although I longed to be in the sunshine and clear my lungs of the vile atmosphere of this place, I resisted the less-than-subtle tugging of Kara that urged me to follow her out.

"Can I change it?" I asked, disgusted by the weakness and timidity I was hearing in my own voice. The query apparently sounded perfectly sensible to the Conjurer.

"Course you 'kin change it," she replied emphatically. "But few do."

She no longer appeared to be a simple carny or charlatan.

"Let's go, Ricky," Kara said. She tugged at my arm once more. I grimaced and involuntarily jerked my arm away, recoiling from her touch without knowing why. I looked into her eyes and saw my own helpless gaze reflected back.

Conjuh.

"Let's go," she repeated. Her voice was more urgent now.

That hissing sound, again. Kara didn't seem to notice.

For one day. Till the setting of the sun tomorrow.

You the Conjuh

I rose to my feet, wanting to say more, ask more, know more, feeling confused and disoriented. But I could think of nothing to say, no question to ask. There was nothing left but for me to leave. I took Kara's hand and let her lead me slowly away, dazed, through the sixties-style glass bead curtain which separated the room from the antechamber outside and then into the cool September air. The light from the outside hurt my eyes. The sun looked strangely surreal and unfamiliar.

Outside was the man in black. He was closing up shop, fumbling with the meager remnants of his carnival show: tattered banners and placards weathered by a thousand days of sun and salt and sand and ill winds. He tarried for a moment as we passed and he looked at us with mournful eyes.

"She was a true Conjurer," he said.

He looked almost apologetic, and as if wanting to say more. He seemed so very tired. He must have spent a lifetime shouting of the mysteries within the small shack. Perhaps it was just the end of another season. He, too, appeared to be at an end of sorts.

We stopped. He stood in front of us, staring. He wanted to say something. He waited, and I waited, as if his words were sure to come any moment. But none did. For some inexplicable reason he put his hand on my shoulder.

Kara looked on curiously. She had no idea what could be going on between us. But in a few moments the bonding was over, and Kara and I were walking again along the boardwalk, only this time with me in the lead, grasping her hand.

"Well, that was really, really fun," Kara said after a while. I sensed she felt stupid the moment she said it.

"Gangs of fun," I replied. We continued to walk.

"Kara…"

"Yes," she asked tentatively.

I stopped and faced her, seizing both of her hands in mine. I squeezed them gently; my lower lip dropped, and tears came to my eyes. Tender thoughts I had never expressed to her began to take form; words of love I had suppressed for so long began to issue from my lips.

But none ever did.

It happened.

The sun melted away. The boardwalk disappeared from beneath my feet. The crowds vanished in a puff of mist in such a way that I thought I had become blind.

I was alone. I looked up into a darkened sky and saw clocks, dozens of clocks, as if I had stepped into a Dali painting. Some had wings. Others melted before my eyes, as if subjected to an infernal heat. Still others rolled around in the heavens as if propelled by some hellish vortex.

A hissing sound filled the air, arising all around me, getting louder, unbearably louder. I dropped to my knees, shut my eyes tightly closed and put my hands over my ears, seeking to shield them against the noise. But this action had no effect, as these sounds did not originate from *here,* but from somewhere else, somewhere *outside.* I began to gasp for air.

Neon-like signs, much like those that hung in the window of the Dory Inn, appeared out of nowhere, dancing in the air, advertising a group of words that were faint and blurred. They blinked on, and blinked off, begging me to see, daring me to see, tempting me to see what their meaning was. And I did see.

Two days, fifteen hours, fifteen minutes, the signs said. But it was my voice that I heard speaking the words.

I opened my eyes, and Kara was kneeling beside me, holding both of my hands in hers. I was on my knees, staring at the planks of the boardwalk.

"Ricky!" she exclaimed.

I looked at her, vision blurred, shaking, sputum dribbling down my lip. I looked down at the boardwalk and touched it as if to make sure it was really there. I ran my fingers over a rusty nail and a gray mass of bubble gum adhered to the weathered wood.

"Two days, fifteen hours, fifteen minutes," I repeated to the wood. I looked up.

"The time of your life on this earth," I said to Kara.

"Ricky..." Kara said again, slowly urging me – lifting me, really – to my feet. She led me to a nearby wooden bench facing the ocean.

Seagulls floated on the stiff ocean breeze. Sandpipers darted along the beach looking for small insects and crustaceans. The wind rustled through my hair and quickly worked upon drying the beads of sweat covering my arms and face.

Kara looked on, terribly concerned, saying nothing. I looked at her and tried to lift my hand to stroke her hair, but my arm couldn't move. I tried to say something, but my mouth was dry, my tongue as stiff as a dead man's, and what came out was little more than a hoarse gasp. With little option, I turned my head to the ocean again, trying to regain my strength.

She tried to hold my hand, but I pried myself from her grip and, in doing so, nearly fell from the bench.

"Ricky…"

I felt dizzy, weak, and physically ill. What I had experienced had not fully settled upon me.

It was impossible, of course, that I could now somehow predict the precise moment of a person's demise; impossible that such an ability could be bestowed by the squeezing of hands and the fluttering of eyelids; impossible that I could have mere days to live; inconceivable that Kara would somehow share my fate, and that she would die just hours before me.

Impossible.

Conjuh.

But nothing I felt said that this was so. There was no doubting what I had just experienced. It was extraordinary, even supernatural to be sure, but not caused by a drug induced haze or an epileptic fit; not the result of my psychic powers; not the consequence of a disturbed state of mind. There was no uncertainty about the words I saw dancing across the surface of my mind, or that had thrust themselves from my lips; no doubt about the admonitions of the sorcerer.

I had little over two days to live; Kara, a few hours less than me.

My strength was slowly returning. I could smell the fragrance of candy apples and peanuts wafting in the air. Kara was holding my wrists with both hands.

"Do you know what you said?"

"I know. What do you…?"

The words 'what do you think' seemed trite and foolish. I looked at her with eyes that must have appeared pensive and pleading.

"She was just a fortune teller," Kara said. Knowing me, she couldn't have believed her own words.

"We have just a few days, Kara. I don't know why or how, but we do."

"Then we'll change it," she said.

Course you 'kin change it...

"Then we'll change it," I repeated, hearing the lack of confidence in my own voice.

...but few do.

She put her arms around my neck and held me close. After a moment, I slid my arms around her exposed waist and held her tight.

And the world exploded.

Like a fireworks show for me alone, like some hellish LSD trip, splashes of color appeared across my eyes, appearing as words emblazoned across a crimson red sky.

And the words said this: *Two days, fifteen hours, four minutes.*

I lost consciousness.

VII

I awoke later, much later, in the back seat of my car, staring at the roof. I heard the hum of the highway and felt the gentle rocking of the vehicle.

"Good afternoon," Kara stated.

I looked at my watch. It was 3:45, some four hours after we had left the gypsy's shack.

"Don't ask how I got you here," she stated. "I'll only say that you're much heavier than you look. And you don't drag very well."

Had I not considered myself mad in the first instance, I certainly would have thought I had gone fully off the deep end by this time.

"What happened?"

"You lost it. You were screaming something about two days, and then you just went into a fugue state or something; hey, I don't know, you're the psychic here, not me."

"Two days, fifteen hours, four minutes," I repeated helplessly.

"You know, a few minutes before that you said I had two days fifteen hours and *fifteen* minutes; I simply won't tolerate a man who can't make up his mind about how long his girlfriend has to live."

"That isn't funny."

"Not funny? Well, how the hell else should I take it? Two days to live, three days to live, nag, nag, nag. Make up your mind, at least. No, no, wait; I got it… I'll kill you, then you'll kill me, then I'll kill myself, again; that'll work. Maybe we should just start planning now, this way we'll be right on time."

"Right on time," I repeated.

"Better yet, maybe we can make this a made-for-TV movie. I can sure as hell see the headlines of the Post: 'Man kills girlfriend twice, self.'"

Flat on my back, I looked out the car window. I could see the trees race by on the highway.

I closed my eyes and feel asleep again.

When I awoke I found myself staring at the front steps of my house. Kara had parked the car and was sitting beside me in the back seat.

"How are you doing?"

"How *am* I doing?"

"Well, you have a pulse, you're breathing, you're conscious, you're not predicting the end of the planet… all in all a considerable improvement, and the conclusion of a successful day. All that, and you're home."

I sat up. Every part of my body hurt.

"Oww."

"I would expect you'd be sore. Particularly after I had to tow your ass over three blocks of concrete and boardwalk to get you to the car." She was serious for a moment.

"How 'bout I stay with you tonight, lover."

"I'm all right."

"You don't look all right."

"I'm a big boy. Besides, you have work tomorrow."

"So do you."

"No, I don't."

Apparently I had already made the decision to isolate myself – at least for the next 24 hours – from any further psychic incidents. Under the circumstances, I considered this a sound decision.

"OK, sweetie, no sweat, we'll talk more tomorrow." She kissed me on the lips. "We'll talk, OK?"

"OK," I replied. I picked myself up to leave.

"Can you find your way home?" I asked.

"No big deal, I'm not that far away, remember?"

"OK." All of a sudden, I remembered.

"Your 'big announcement'…"

"It can wait; just take care of yourself, and we'll chatter in the latter."

"We have to."

She kissed my forehead. "Things may look different in the morning, OK?"

"OK, baby," I meekly replied.

I climbed up the stairs and entered my house.

The basement door was closed as usual. No skeletons popped out; no bony hands extended, beckoning.

And no music.

I let myself into my apartment and collapsed onto the bed. I soon fell asleep once more.

Remarkably, my rest was mostly uninterrupted. Amorphous entities did not plague my subconscious, nor use my mind as their personal playground, as they are gleefully wont to do. There was just one dream…

There is a man on the top of a hill. I am climbing towards him, and his back is turned to me. His hands are on his hips, and he is knee deep in snow. He is a large, powerfully built man, but he doesn't seem able to free himself. I want to help him, but I'm not sure he would take my help if it were offered.

I know this man.

I continue to climb. It's snowing, and it's getting colder and colder as I near him; the wind is cutting through the thin T-shirt and khaki pants I am wearing. The sneakers on my feet are ill-equipped for this task. I'm getting tired, so tired.

I'm nearing the top now, and the cold has taken its toll on my body. Each step is painful, terribly painful, but I continue to climb. I'm shouting at him, telling him not to be afraid. He doesn't appear to be, but God, oh God, he should be, because I think he's going to die right on the top of this hill, he's going to die right in front of my eyes. Hell, we're both going to die, and that's something I can stop, something I must stop. If I can only reach him in time.

Words spurt out of my mouth in short, hoarse gasps; I don't have a voice left, but I still try. I try to warn him he's got to free himself before it's too late, that he can free himself, that's he's not a prisoner up there, that he just thinks he is.

I'm almost there now; the snow is way above his thighs. He turns his head as if he hears me, but he makes no other outward sign that he does. Even in the blinding snow I can see his profile clearly, and it's one I've seen before.

I think I'm going to reach him, and finally, I do. I put a stiff, frozen hand on his arm and with a last burst of strength I spin him around. And the face that looks back at me is my face, the face of Richard Goodman. But not Richard Goodman.

He seems shocked to see me and he screams "what are you doing here?" He grabs me by both shoulders in his large powerful hands. He shakes me and roars over and over again: "You're not me you're not me you're not me…"

VIII

A terrible mistake has been made.

Mistake, mistake, mistake.

Daddy always said that if you didn't make a mistake, everything would work out perfectly. You just couldn't make a mistake. You had to work slowly, carefully, take your time. You just couldn't make a mistake.

Never make a mistake.

Daddy would be mad. Very mad. *Very, very mad.*

A glance in the mirror; a look around the room said it all. *All.* Blood everywhere. In smears, drops, puddles, splashes… *everywhere.* Parts of animals: everywhere. Skin, fur, bones, pieces, everywhere, on everything.

Open the door. Look outside. No one there. Look! On the floors, the walls… There! There!

Windex. Windex cleans everything. Scott Towel and Windex. The best. Get it! Cleans everything. There. There. Not so bad.

Open the door. Look around. No one here. Look again. Clean. Close the door. Quietly. *Quietly!* No more mistakes.

Back to the room. Breathing hard. Breathing *very* hard. Pain right here; right here in the center. Pain. Breathing hard.

Don't want to look at the room. Must. Must! Must correct the mistakes. Make everything perfect again.

Don't be afraid. Just dirt, really. Only red dirt.

Clean. Just clean. Can. Will. Just clean.

Head hurts. Head hurts a lot. Like it used to before.

Before. When the voices talked. All the time. Saying everything and nothing, all at the same time. So many different voices. *So many.* So many that there was no *me* anymore. No me, just them. *Them.*

Must clean. Don't think. Just clean.

Windex. Have Windex. Lots of Windex, and Scott Towel.

Wonderful products.

Wonderful.

Cleaning now. Throwing Scott Towel in the tall wastebasket. Full. Keep cleaning. Red, dripping red Scott Towel making mountains in the tall wastebasket. Like mountains of red mud.

Time. All that is needed is a little time. If you have time, all mistakes can be corrected. All things can be made perfect. If you just have time.

We have time.

No. *NO.* Correction. Not *we*. NOT WE. *I* have time. *I.*

Yes. I have time. I have time, Windex, and Scott Towel.

All the things we need to make things perfect.

Monday

Time is the teacher that kills its pupils.

Louis-Hector Berlioz

IX

For one day. Till the setting of the sun tomorrow.

One eye opened at 9:30 a.m. I was still here.

I cautiously sat up in bed and surveyed my surroundings. An armoire loomed in front of me at the foot of my bed, a clock and a small black and white television rested on a night table to my left. These days there are old Star Trek repeats on at midnight, and that is all I usually watch on this TV. I don't know why.

To my right was a pair of battered filing cabinets pushed against the wall. On the same wall there was a curtained entranceway, leading to a small room containing my Rhodes electric piano and ancient Ampeg amplifier. There was nothing else in that room, except a faded picture of an old dog playing in the leaves of fall. It is the only room in the house that gets any sun.

Too bad. I seldom used this space anymore.

I desperately wanted coffee but dreaded the physical labor necessary to brew a cup. I decided in favor of inaction. Of course, the corner diner was a mere half block away, and there was ample coffee available in the school right next door. Then I remembered it was Monday.

There was no way that I was going to work today. Hell, I wasn't going outside. No contact with people was the prescription. There would be no repeat of any of the events of the previous day, and I would make sure there would not be. Moreover, I wasn't going to listen to the TV, or turn on the radio, and I damn sure wasn't going to pick up…

…the phone rang. There was only one in the house and it rested on the end table in the living room. I looked at it from my bed, just fifteen feet away, totally disinterested. I let it ring five times, six times. I meandered in that general direction and yawned.

Seven times, eight times.

Maybe he would give up. Maybe he was a she.

Nine times, ten times. This was a persistent caller, whoever it was. I took a deep breath, flopped myself into the easy chair, looked in the ashtray for a joint that wasn't there, and picked up the phone.

It was Mathis C. Aputa, one of four senior administrators at the school, a plastic manager taking up valuable space that could have been used by a person with morals, or ability, or a trace of human feeling. At six foot six inches he was frighteningly tall. He was razor thin with a beak-like nose, the hollowed cheekbones of a corpse, the stoop of an elderly man, and the narrow countenance of a weasel. He harbored an intense personal dislike for me, as well as for the students he purported to serve. Everyone knew that he had worked as a parole officer for the New York City prison system and, before that, as a prison guard at the infamous "Sing Sing" prison in Ossining, New York, located only about forty miles north of the school.

Everyone also knew that he was licensed to carry a gun. Most believed he still did. This conviction discouraged the expression of any vocal opposition to his persistent callousness, perpetual sloth, and inveterate, slipshod omissions.

Aputa had been working at the school for over fifteen years, before Robert Stacey began his tenure as the school's executive director. He kissed Bob's ass with an unnatural enthusiasm that, with steady practice, became quite accomplished. He always agreed with Bob's decisions and propped up his ego whenever there was an opportunity to do so. He was eager to provide the school director with any information about anyone – whether student, faculty or staff member – and had proven over time that he would carry out any of Bob's commands with ruthless efficiency.

Stacey, for his part, began their association by merely tolerating him. His tolerance later became a grudging respect, and eventually their professional relationship turned into an unlikely friendship.

Just what Aputa's actual duties were now, I couldn't tell, although it was clear that his job description appeared to include the relentless denigration of those he perceived as violating school policy of one kind or another.

I was instantly sorry, deeply sorry, that I had picked up the receiver.

"Where the hell are you?"

I looked for a joint again, hoping I had overlooked one. I put the receiver on my shoulder and looked under the table, but there were no drugs there waiting for my lungs to burn.

Aputa was highly skilled at propounding questions that were either impossible to answer, or that had answers so obvious that his defensive, stunned victims were often left with both hanging jaws and exposed egos, the way he liked them. I refused to play this game, and I refused to answer his foolish question. No matter: Aputa posed another.

"What are you doing over there?"

"What am I doing?" I repeated stupidly.

"Yes, what the hell are you doing over there?" I considered this inquiry carefully before answering again.

"Well, Mathis, I'm waking up right now."

"You're waking up?"

This was too much. I was too weary to respond, so I didn't.

"Do you know what's happened over here?" Of course, I could not know what had happened 'over there' but at least his question now held some mild interest.

"No, Mathis—" He interrupted me. Apparently, his question was rhetorical.

"Get your ass over here." He hung up.

Now I was awake. It was enough that I was forced to suffer this imperious asshole on a near-daily basis. But calling me in my home – even if it was a home owned by my employer – and *commanding* my presence *anywhere,* as if I were a child, was an insult I would not tolerate.

I went to the bathroom and combed my hair, not bothering to brush my teeth or wash my face. I indiscriminately picked a T-shirt out of my dresser and quickly donned a pair of jeans. I put on a pair of sneakers, not bothering with socks. I walked to the standing wooden armoire in my bedroom and opened its twin doors. Located discreetly within was a smaller cabinet I had built myself, made of an exotic hardwood.

The cabinet contained a small, but rich variety of martial arts weapons: two short staffs, six pair of nunchaku, an axe, and ten, eight-pointed steel stars, each point sharpened to a razor's edge. All were specially crafted for a person of my size, weight, and strength. At one point or another in my life, I had mastered their use.

I paused, considered my choices, excluded those before me, shook my head, closed the cabinet door and turned and stormed out of my apartment; past the basement door, through the front door, down the stairs and up the wheelchair ramp leading to the dormitory. Crashing through the dorm's entrance door impressively, I strode through the connecting corridor gaining speed with each stride. Uncharacteristically, I barely glanced at Domingo who was at his station as usual. He was polishing the aluminum counter of his kitchen with downcast eyes.

I took the steps leading to the main classroom two at a time. At the top of the steps, a left led to the main classroom. The stairway continued up one flight, to my perch, overlooking that classroom. I made a right turn which led to the entrance of the school and a small, circular, waiting room, with a domed ceiling with a mural depicting the history of time. To the right of this vestibule was a huge room containing only two desks, the work stations of Josephine and Andrea, the school's secretaries. To the left was the office of the school director, my friend and protector, Robert Stacey.

I made a right.

A startled Andrea jumped to her feet – rather adeptly for a 68-year-old woman – unprepared for my disheveled condition and brisk arrival.

"W–where the hell is he?" I stammered.

Knowing me, and knowing Aputa, and certainly knowing of our contentious relations, it was not necessary for her to be aware of the latest incident between us to know that there had been one. She replied cautiously.

"He's in the main classroom… but Ricky…" She grabbed my arm in a firm but motherly way. "What do you think you're going to do?"

"I'm going to beat the crap out of him."

"No, you're not."

She continued to smile as sweetly as she held my arm tightly. She wasn't going to let me go until I concurred.

"No, you're not," she repeated, smiling broadly. She raised her eyebrows in an inquiring fashion. "Ricky…?" She fluttered her eyelashes.

Sheesh.

Andrea had worked at the school longer than anyone. Her official title was secretary but she was the unofficial den mother of the institution. Students found her warm and approachable, while staff and faculty found her charming and utterly convincing.

When she decided to assert herself she was difficult to challenge. Notwithstanding that she was Bob Stacey's right hand, she had worked under – and had outlasted – every director that the school had ever employed. She was revered by the school's ten trustees – all elderly males – who each made it a point to stop by her station and caress her hand or kiss her cheek before every monthly meeting. While she had no supervisory authority over anyone, no one ever seemed inclined to go against her wishes.

Besides, she wasn't going to let go of my arm.

I am not an inherently violent person. However, I refuse to be stepped on, and while I rarely find it necessary to interject my small frame into a physical confrontation, I will not run from a fight or a challenge to my integrity. It was clear that Andrea was pitiably unaware that her personal charm and charismatic allure were inadequate to divert a man infused with malice from obtaining the respect and retribution he so richly deserved and sought.

"OK," I replied meekly.

She had a soothing effect on most everyone, not just me. She tilted her head coyly.

"What did you say?" she asked, exhibiting a most delightful comportment, and smiling a smile that surpassed mere brilliance.

"OK, Mother, I won't do anything."

"Good," she replied, releasing her grip on me, obviously pleased. "Now go into the main classroom."

I hesitated, temporarily immobilized. She returned to her desk and her ancient IBM typewriter as if nothing had happened.

I had been worked over by one of the best. I exited through the portico, turned left and approached the main classroom. Stacey and Aputa were chatting in animated fashion in the middle of the room. There was a huge, empty area in the center of the floor where there should have been work desks.

As I entered I saw Henry Bojovian and Franklin Swank, the school's head instructors, standing bunched together on my right. Their shoulders touched as they conversed quietly. Both were great teachers, but they employed totally different teaching methods.

Swank, a Korean War veteran with a left leg shot to hell, was as tough and as gruff as his Marine background would presuppose. He would push students to figure things out for themselves, reasoning that one day they would be on their own with no one to guide them, and no one to answer their questions.

He was there to train them in the art of watchmaking, but his principal objective was to teach his pupils the virtues of self-reliance, perseverance and creativity. He had never been babied in his life, and he wasn't there to be anybody's friend or daddy. He showed students what to do only if they couldn't figure things out for themselves. He was a hard guy to approach and a harder guy to get used to. But he was a brilliant craftsman, and if you bought into his method, you might become one, too.

Henry was just the opposite. The only disability he possessed was a lovable eccentricity, and he wore it on his lapel like a clown wears a flower that squirts water when you get too close. He was funny and fun loving, and never took anything too seriously. He spent hours with his students discussing fine points most instructors would overlook. He made sure they thoroughly understood everything he said, and gently guided his young and often compromised charges through the sometimes treacherous waters of the craft.

I was quite friendly with both of them, but neither looked at me as I entered.

On my left stood – well, sat, really – Bobbie Meyer, another instructor, and my best friend in the world. The first time I met Bob he was holding a gun to the throat of the man I had been hired to replace.

Dean Spencer – the unfortunate recipient of Mr. Meyer's attentions at the time – was a genuinely nice guy. He later went on to become the director of media relations for the National Football League, and ultimately the president of the National Hockey League.

Then, he was just a very scared 25-year-old with a gun to his throat. Bob started out as a student at the school and, upon his graduation, was made an instructor, and he was a good one. He was a small man of slender build and he seemed even slighter sitting in his wheelchair. He had kind, deep blue eyes which could turn wild at a moment's notice; like a half-dog-half-wolf, that doesn't know what it is and can act like either depending upon the circumstances. Like everybody else at Waterman, Bob had a story.

He was raised on the streets of the Lower East Side of Manhattan in the late 1950's. He was the son of a construction laborer, and later on became a laborer himself. He was also a Jew, an anomaly in a trade that, at least in the old days, was dominated by people of Italian descent.

But Italians disregarded his religious beliefs and accepted him, and he always felt right at home with them. He also became accustomed to the regular presence of the Cosa Nostra, a close-knit fraternity commonly referred to as the Mafia, which exerted a pervasive influence on New York's construction industry.

When he was just 14, he was lucky to get a gig as a "job clerk," working on a high rise project with Pop, at the site of the old Rheingold Brewery on the Upper East Side. His primary undertaking was to report the number of trades on the job, how many men they used, where they were and what they were doing. He took his duties seriously and everyone on the job liked him.

One day, he decided to sneak across the street around 10:00 a.m. to get some coffee for himself and some steamfitters. Coffee breaks weren't provided for in the union contract – no one quite understood why – and if anyone wanted coffee *someone* had to "make the run," a mad, blind dash across First Avenue to the local coffee house, hopefully under the radar of the assistant superintendent, whose job it was to catch *that someone* in the act.

Bob was small, and he was fast, and he became quite adept at this task. The guys would pause from their labors each day just to watch him accomplish it. A few dollars and a few words of praise ("fucking unbelievable") were the typical rewards he received for his efforts. In any event, he needed the money, appreciated the crew's admiration, and was glad to do the job. And, he had a method to his madness that he proudly referred to as "patented."

First, he would sprint twenty-five feet from the edge of the job site to the corner of 93rd and First. Then, he would hunch down low at the street corner, behind the aluminum base of a street light. He would wait for a break in the traffic and then cross trying to use a passing bus to camouflage his movements.

This day, like any other day, he was lucky to benefit from the cover of a southbound 36 heading down the avenue. It was excruciatingly hot, but people who do physical work outside quickly learn to ignore the heat – or at least get used to it – and Bob was no different. Shirt soaking wet, sweat streaming down his face, he blazed across the street on a diagonal just as the bus passed. He was two-thirds down the block when he lost the cover of the jitney, but neatly ducked into the air conditioned coffee shop at the corner of First Avenue and 92nd without being discovered.

He barely got to take one elated breath of the cool air inside before he realized that the boss of all bosses – the construction superintendent, Simy Tezari – had gotten the same idea and was waiting at the counter for his coffee.

Tezari did not benefit from the advantage of a union contract and could get coffee anytime he was thirsty for it. Bob thought of turning about and running for his life, but that would have attracted Tezari's attention immediately. With few options at his command, he stood petrified, staring at the boss until the inevitable occurred and the boss turned around on him, coffee in hand.

Simy never smiled or raised his voice or showed any other outward sign of emotion. But people usually reacted to his words as if he had screamed them.

"You were going right back to work, weren't you," he said as he sipped his beverage.

It wasn't a question. Bob mumbled a few words, turned around and disappeared out of the store.

While he certainly desired to keep his job, Bob had also assumed the duty of quenching the thirsts and appetites of the masses that relied on his morning trek. Besides, even at 14, Bob found he needed a cup of Java around this time. So, instead of going back to work, he simply slipped around the corner at 92nd and decided to wait until Tezari left the store. He planned to boldly sneak in behind the man when he left the shop.

He would return with the prize. He would become a hero. He would become famous. The minstrels would sing of his triumph. Bob waited.

His patience would earn him more than he bargained for.

Tezari was a huge, overweight, giant of a man, with a crew cut composed of wiry black hair, and a razor-thin mustache deliberately manicured to make him resemble some ancient silent movie screen character. His lips and nose seemed to come to a point at the center of his face, making him look like a ferret. Nobody liked him, but everyone respected him, not only because he could fire them in a moment, but because his links to organized crime were well known.

The big man paused at the threshold of the coffee shop door, sipping his coffee from a wax-lined paper cup. He seemed to be waiting, too.

In truth, something was waiting for him.

Later on, Bob would ask himself why he never noticed the man who walked right past him, turned the corner and approached Tezari as he leaned against the frame of the door of the coffee house. This man was five feet ten and of medium build, with short, dyed, blonde hair and a black five o'clock shadow. He wore khaki shorts, a clean white T-shirt, the V-necked kind, and open-toed brown sandals that looked as if they had seen rosier days.

He looked like a man who liked to be comfortable when he worked.

He approached Simy slowly, smiling. The .38 caliber revolver that he held in his left hand was pointed down at his side.

The .38 is a reliable old gun. It rarely misfires and will fire flawlessly even underwater. Or so they say.

The gunman approached Tezari and stood within a foot of him, staring, saying nothing. Tezari's face held no emotion. He looked at the man, sipped his coffee, looked down, and saw the gun. He sipped his coffee again. The man took the gun, placed it against Tezari's forehead and held it there. A second or two passed. Tezari's coffee spilled over his hand. In another second, it would be a dead man's hand.

The man fired, dropped the gun, and walked away. Tezari fell, killed instantly.

There wasn't much blood, really. Bob had heard quite a bit about people getting shot and it was no surprise that sooner or later he would get to see a killing himself. And sneaking past the superintendent was no longer necessary.

Bob took a quick turn around the body and a step towards the door of the coffee shop, but quickly realized that there would be little served at this establishment for the next few hours. He ran across the street and back to the job site, still instinctively using the cover of the buses.

The buses traveled by as if it were just another day. The cars moved down the avenue as if nothing out the ordinary had occurred.

In fact, this event had not been particularly unusual at all. Three more people would be shot in New York City that day, four the next, and two the day following.

Nobody saw anything, of course, but that wasn't exactly true. Of those people there were a) those who really didn't see anything; and b) those who saw everything but refused to say so; and c) those who saw something but couldn't remember what. Perhaps these three groups of people make up the entire world.

Nobody back at the job asked Bob what he saw, and everybody knew better than to ask. Bob hadn't seen a thing, anyway, just like everyone else.

Although Bob never thought much about that day, it made a

big impression on him. He wanted to feel bad about his former boss, but he couldn't. He wanted to feel scared and shocked because of what he witnessed, but he didn't.

Maybe there was something wrong with him.

Or, maybe it was because he was just a kid.

Yeah, that was it.

Five years later, Bobbie Meyer would still be a kid, only with an M-16 rifle in his hands, a sergeant leading his five-man platoon through the jungles of South Vietnam. His story was an old story, but a true one, and one that rings no less true because it is constantly replayed in different lands, with different actors.

He was at the center of his team. His men fanned out around him when they hit a clearing just before a small village. They didn't know who was in the village, or whether the residents might be friends or foes. It rarely seemed to matter.

A woman approached from about 25 yards away, smiling, holding a baby. The men relaxed and lowered their weapons.

Bob did not. Kids from New York City don't relax.

Bob shouted a warning to his troops, but there appeared nothing for him to warn them about. One soldier raised his rifle halfway. The others proceeded at a slower pace. The woman smiled again as she slowly reached within the folds of her clothing. Bob sounded a more urgent warning that took the form of an order. All stopped, except the woman, who kept approaching.

How many seconds passed between the time he saw the grenade emerge from her rags and the time he acted, he could never recall. It did not matter, but only because he acted.

Bob was a kid from New York. He had guts, and he had speed.

It took both to kill a woman and her child a second before you were to be blown to bits.

The rifle was set on full-automatic. He screamed and pressed the trigger, fanning the weapon horizontally from left to right and back again as the mother raised the bomb behind her ear. It looked as if she was about to toss him a baseball.

"Always make sure the ball passes right by your ear as you throw," his dad used to say.

He fired until the ammunition in his gun was exhausted. The mother caught two in the throat. The baby's head came clean off and tumbled high into the air as the mother fell away. In the end, no one but Bob had moved. Later, none of the others could accurately recount what had occurred.

Bob guessed they had seen *something*, but couldn't remember what.

They gave him a medal for that. He stood at attention among a row of soldiers, in his dress uniform, while a full bird colonel pinned it on his chest and shook his hand. He smiled and thanked the officer. He then marched to a nearby barracks, into a bathroom, and flushed it down the toilet.

In much the same way, this is where our civilization has gone. To a place where a man is rewarded for killing a child. Or, if you prefer, to a place where an infant must be sacrificed to save your comrades. This is where our God has placed us, you and I.

Just who the Hell does He think He is, anyway?

Probably just an Asian woman with a tricolored Mohawk haircut watching a cosmic television set.

It was ironic that after surviving two-and-a-half years in the jungle without suffering a single scratch, he would seriously injure himself some years later in a car accident. Driving without a seatbelt, he was thrown through the windshield of his car and his back was broken. After months of rehab, doctors told him he would never walk again; meaning, that it was medically impossible for him to do so, and that he was to be in a wheelchair for the rest of his life.

But Bob was a kid from the Lower East Side of New York. He had guts. In seven months, with the use of a cane, he was walking again.

But his mobility came at a price. His spine was no longer

equipped to carry the weight of his body; the pain in his back never left him, and soon became unbearable. He couldn't work and was often doped up; at least five or six hours during the day, and then all night.

His wife divorced him, taking his son and everything else with her. That's when he decided to get "the operation." He never understood all the medical lingo, or what the surgeon was going to do, only that he was promised that the chances for relief were great, and the chances that something could go wrong were insignificant.

Right.

That was how Bob ended up in his wheelchair for good. Something about the use of an alcohol-based solution when a saline-based solution was called for; something like that. Anyway, there was this something injected into his spine by the doctors; his nerves shriveled up and they died soon thereafter, and that was that.

No more speed for Bob. No more walking the dog, no more softball games, no more sex, no more walking up stairs, no more nothing at all that required anything at all below his waist. In the end, he was alone, at the end of his rope, and virtually unemployable, with an ache in his gut to match the anguish in his soul.

Facing this oblivion he mustered the will to make a decision that turned out to be the most important one of his life; he decided to re-train himself for a new career in an attempt to rebuild what remained of his life.

Which brought him to the Waterman School, and which brings us back to the gun at poor Dean Spencer's throat. Bobbie felt naked without a firearm since coming back from the war, and considering what he had been through, he was a bit paranoid anyway. So he kept a snub-nosed .38 strapped to his left ankle.

He knew, from past experience, that the .38 was a pretty reliable weapon.

Normally, when his body wasn't contorted in pain, he was a pretty quiet, amiable guy who wouldn't start a confrontation unless challenged. He put a big emphasis on the word "unless." As Bobbie later described the event:

"....one day this pencil pusher started mouthing off to me, and so I kept asking 'what did you say, I can't hear you?' and the pencil pusher got closer and mouthed off some more. I asked again 'what did you say, I can't hear you?' and the pencil pusher got a little closer and bent down. I grabbed him by the throat with my right hand and reached down to my ankle with my left. I pushed my rod against his throat, and in a second or two the pencil pusher was saying stuff like 'please God' and 'Jesus help me,' and 'Jesus Christ Almighty,' and shit like that.

"As I sat there watching him squirm and beg, I realized that I was enjoying myself; hell, I was *loving* this, and all of a sudden I started to think about this guy I used to know, Simy Tezari. I started to think really hard about that guy, and the more I thought about him, the more I was OK with blowing this prick's head right off his body right then and there.

"And then, someone came up behind me and put his hand on my shoulder; he just put his hand on my shoulder, just like that, and I turned and there was Ricky, who I didn't know from Adam. And he smiled like he could read my mind or something, and for the life of me I couldn't figure out why I didn't turn and blow this guy away, too, but I decided not to, at least not right away. Ricky smiled again and said, 'why don't you leave this pitiful prick alone, he's too stupid to realize who he was talking to,' and I said 'who the fuck are you?' and Ricky said 'I'm the one replacing this little prick,' and I said 'no shit?' and Ricky said 'no shit!' and that was that."

Anyway, we've been the best of friends ever since.

Of course, the last card that a random fate would deal Bobbie was the cancer that even now was slowly disassembling his body. He told me about it once, and we never talked about it after that. Soon, everybody else knew, too, but no one talked about an early retirement, or about "enjoying your life while you can" or any such rot. Bobbie was going to stay at his post until he couldn't any longer; he wasn't a crap cook like Domingo or a drunk like Nurse Emily. He was an experienced craftsman and a talented teacher, so sure as hell Bobbie wasn't going anywhere just because he was a dead man walking.

Or rolling, as it were.

So, by the by, there Bobbie sat, across from Franklin and Henry, and he nodded to me as I walked into the classroom. He didn't look so good today. He started shaking his head from side to side.

"How are you doing, Bobbie?"

"Bad scene, Ricky-Boy, bad scene."

He wasn't talking about himself. I looked at him quizzically. He simply nodded towards the center of the classroom where Aputa and Stacey were jawing.

For some reason, it was only then that I noticed that the contents of the entire room had been destroyed. Most of the fifty-two watchmaker's work benches located there, each specially designed to accommodate wheelchairs, and each complete with thousands of dollars of high precision tools and hundreds of parts and supplies, were upended, pushed from the center of the room to the sides, as if some kind of bomb had been dropped in the middle of the space. Many of the hard oak desks were completely smashed, as if someone had taken a sledgehammer to them. The floor was littered with wooden shards and metal parts. The unique cork floor, installed to last for a hundred years or more, had been ripped up in places, bit by bit, in strips two inches wide and a foot or two long. Someone had taken their time, patiently taking the place apart.

"Any ideas, Bobbie?"

"I always got ideas, Ricky-Boy."

"Let me know if you get any good ones."

"You got it."

I began, reluctantly, to work my way towards my superiors in the center of the room.

"Don't take any shit, Ricky-Boy," Bobbie advised.

"Never, Bob," I replied. But I knew I was sure to get some.

As I approached, I saw that the destruction was not confined to mere wood and metal. There was more than that, oh, so much more. My nose should have given me a hint, but I guess my eyes had secured priority over my olfactory organ. I got closer and closer to the mayhem, ignoring, for the moment, the two administrators and their impromptu meeting.

I approached what was left of one particular bench. Its two rear legs had been removed and it leaned backwards, like some animal on its haunches. Built into its structure were sixty or so compartments of various sizes. One, about six inches square, was open, and the body of a small animal had been crammed into it. It was a squirrel, and it appeared to be sitting up, looking out of the drawer. Around its neck was a red, woman's watch band. The watch attached to the band hung like a medallion from the center of the squirrel's throat. Its mouth was open unnaturally wide and as I got closer I saw that the squirrel wasn't the result of a taxidermist's work.

It seemed to have been executed for the purpose of making this specific display. Cotton balls had been stuffed in gobs down its throat, and a two inch shard from one of the desks held its mouth open. Blood had colored most of the cotton, and coagulated blood coated the drawer and the animal's body. I gagged as I got still closer. The lower third of the animal had been neatly sawed off so that the rest of its body could stand erect in the small drawer. That third section was in another drawer, forced shut, with its legs hanging out, giving the illusion that the larger part of its frame was somehow within.

I looked around and saw that within this ruin had been placed a veritable menagerie of dead animals – cats, dogs, squirrels, and mice – none of which, I wagered, had died quickly or easily. Feces and blood were everywhere.

I put my hand to my mouth and looked up. A huge, stately, brass and crystal chandelier had illuminated this classroom for fifty years. It had been removed from its location, and was now on the ground directly behind where Aputa and Stacey were standing. A panoply of wires hung from the ceiling. The end of each wire was wrapped around the neck of a small puppy. God, they couldn't have been more than a few weeks old. Six in all, hung like macabre Christmas ornaments, each one just a few inches higher than the next, demonstrating that they had been placed there with patience and care. I choked back tears.

The next thing I saw was an old mechanical clock wedged between two broken benches. The glass crystal that covered its face had been removed. The two hands of the clock would have shown that it was two minutes before six, but you couldn't see the hands themselves. Now, they impaled two white mice whose red eyes stared into nothingness and whose tiny pink noses pointed out the time. These were not wild animals and must have been purchased somewhere.

On the floor facing this appalling display was another clock, but you could only recognize it as one by its four brass legs, which protruded from the remains of a full grown cat. The paws of the gold, white and black calico were outstretched as if frozen in an attempt to grab the mice it faced. Impossibly, its body had been sliced from its tail to its belly and carefully retrofitted over the timepiece that sat in a pool of blood.

I tried to swallow, but I couldn't. I held my head, turned my back on the mayhem, and closed my eyes.

"Where've you been, huh?"

Aputa's voice cut sharply through the air. I ignored his question and walked – in something of a dazed state – towards the two administrators.

Bob looked at me circumspectly, saying nothing.

"This was on *your* watch," my nemesis blurted out.

So eager was he to assert blame and thrust responsibility upon me that he overlooked his obvious pun.

"Where were you?" he demanded.

For some reason, Bobbie wheeled behind Aputa unnoticed, and stared at the floor.

I ignored Aputa once again and approached Stacey.

"Does anybody know what happened?"

"We were hoping you could shed some light on this, Richard," Stacey replied.

I could only shake my head back and forth once. "I'll see what I can find out; I'm so sorry, Bob," I added helplessly.

Now, Meyer appeared to be surrounding the three of us by wheeling in a rough circle around the area we were standing in.

"Well, you better turn up *something*, Goodman. This place was *your* responsibility. That's why we pay the mortgage on the house you're living in. This happened on *your* watch. *Your* watch."

Aputa got in his last two cents and stormed out of the room, glaring at me, muttering to himself and shaking his head.

"Hey, it's not your fault, Richard," Stacey said.

I hoped that he meant what he had said. I also hoped he was right.

"Talk to the kids in the dorm and see what you can find out."

"I will, Bob." I turned to leave.

"Richard?" Stacey asked quietly as I looked around.

He motioned with his head towards the rear of the classroom. This was code for 'I need to talk with you in my office.'

Aputa was thoroughly versed in all of the school's administrative procedures. He was also familiar with all of the secret passwords and clandestine gesticulations shared between me and my boss.

With one foot out of the classroom, he jerked his head around as if blessed with super hearing. His face lit up in a bright smile that accentuated his truly impeccable bridgework. For once, at least, he had nothing more to add.

I looked back to where Bobbie Meyer had been, but he was gone.

X

Waiting for me in the office of the school director was Carol Kane, not to be confused with the very talented and truly funny actress by the same name.

Carol was an Asian woman in her early 30's with a perpetual smile plastered upon her face. She enjoyed steady employment as the school's resident sign language interpreter, serving for the benefit of the school's deaf students. She is genuinely pleasant, dedicated, and a pleasure to work with, although I rarely have a need for her services, as I have little problem communicating with hearing-impaired people.

This is not so much a function of my unique abilities, and I do know a little sign language. To really understand a deaf person you must first eliminate all mental preconceptions of what you *believe* language *should* be from your mind. However they may choose to do so, whether by sophisticated hand code, grunts, gestures, puffs of exasperated breath or prolonged eye contact, they are merely employing a different language.

When you understand this, you realize something else, a simple truth that I have been privileged to acquire: That people of all disabilities are just people like everyone else. We're all just trying to get by in this often complicated world, trying to figure all of this out, trying to hang on and survive, making do with whatever we have, playing the game with whatever cards we have been dealt, and trying to be understood by each other.

We are all in this together, all of us so small and insignificant in the grand scheme of things, all of us just ants, crawling around on different hills of dirt.

Carol didn't talk much, and this was understandable. Her clients didn't either. We smiled and nodded to each other as I entered Stacey's plush office.

I was struck, as I always was, by the spartan order of my

boss's office. Three picture frames, linked together by a bright silver encasement, adorned the right corner of his huge, stately, hardwood desk. A "banker's lamp" with an emerald green shade cast a colorful tint upon the surface of the furniture. The carpet was a plush royal blue that masked the sounds of the footsteps of all who entered, and appeared to magically absorb the muck and soil brought in upon the wheels of the thousands of wheelchairs that had rolled into this room over the years. Two huge leather armchairs sat in front of the desk. Between them was a large empty space, reserved for disabled students. The chairs looked as if they hadn't been moved in years, probably owing to their sheer size and weight.

Carol sat in the chair on the left, with her back to rows of black file cabinets that consumed an entire wall of the spacious office. I took a deep breath and found my seat on the right. As I did, I felt a twinge in my stomach, like the tiniest hairspring of a watch that had just snapped from overuse. I looked back at Carol. Her countenance had not changed, but her feelings had.

"I'm so sorry," they whispered. We waited for Stacey to arrive.

The heavily oiled, immaculately polished, cherry wood door opened silently a few moments later. Advancing just as silently upon the two inches of cushioned carpet beneath his feet, Stacey soon took his place behind his desk.

"How are you, Carol?" he asked. Carol smiled broadly without uttering a word. He turned to me and lifted his eyebrows. I took this as his acknowledgment of the morning's strange events and our shared role in them. He was now prepared to discuss a subject completely unrelated to the mayhem that had taken place in the main classroom.

Through the windows in the office, filtered a soft panoply of red and blue lights that signaled the arrival of the first police car.

I was taken aback, as I often was, by his regimented intellect and personal discipline, by his marked ability to sort and partition events and conditions from one another, and deal with each separately as if one or the other had not occurred at all. This is actually a wonderful personal attribute that I, thus far, have been woefully unable to acquire.

Stacey looked back at me and shrugged his shoulders as if I already knew what he was going to talk about. Unfortunately, I did.

"Rena…" he said.

Rena Vance was one of the school's deaf students and a dormitory resident. I was aware that she had been on academic probation for the past two semesters. As this semester's grading and evaluation period was now coming to an end, I assumed that she had once more failed to meet the school's minimum academic requirements.

"She's done," Stacey said.

For a guy who was essentially kind hearted, Stacey could be surprisingly brutal on occasion. I suppose that just as an officer had to get use to losing soldiers on a battlefield, a school director had to get used to the fact that some students simply couldn't cut it and had to be thrown out of school.

"Nothing you can do?" I asked.

"Nothing I can do," he replied.

A school director is empowered to change a student's grade. Under the right conditions, he can pull a student back from the dangerous precipice of failure and expulsion. This was a discretionary power, however, and infrequently employed. Robert was clearly of the opinion that this student could either not be saved or was not worth saving.

"She can't be salvaged, Rick."

"She's a person, Bob, not a shipwreck."

This was a completely uncalled for remark. It was also a testament to my lack of discipline, an example of my unfortunate habit of talking first and thinking afterward, and the reason why some people considered me insubordinate and a smart ass.

While he wasn't always correct in his conclusions, Stacey was a good guy and an extremely competent administrator, who genuinely cared for the students in his institution. He often had tough decisions to make and he had both an obligation and the wherewithal to make them. And now, I had gotten him mad.

"I know what she is; she's a failing student, and she can't make it, and she's got to go and that's it, and that's not your job to determine, that's mine. Do you have a problem with that?"

Although typically soft-spoken and amiable, Stacey was anything but a wuss.

I bowed my head in submission, wanting to say more, but knowing I had said too much already. Carol bowed her head as well, as if in a prayer for the dead.

"I can tell her, or you can tell her," he said.

He shrugged his shoulders again with his hands outstretched. This was his way of asking "what do you want to do?"

"I'll tell her."

"OK. Take Carol with you."

"Now?"

"Now."

I nodded. I looked up at Stacey, angry and hurt, as if I was the one being expelled. Bob had a broad smile on his face. This made me madder, but it was a sign that he had quickly forgotten my impertinence and that all was forgiven. I turned to leave and Carol followed closely behind.

I was about to begin my "dead man walking" routine, one that I had executed many times before. On occasion, Carol had taken this walk with me. When she did, she always walked behind me with downcast eyes. I don't know why she does this, and as annoying as it is I have never asked her why. I suppose this is her way of coping with the task at hand. She might as well be holding a bible, because she looks like a preacher escorting a prison warden, who in turn is escorting a condemned man to the gallows.

When I am sent to inform a student that he or she has been

terminated, there must be a certain look upon my face, because invariably the students who see me immediately stop what they are doing. Faculty and staff grow quiet and look at me with pitying eyes. Passersby I may come upon in a hallway, part and respectfully let me pass.

Dead man walking. Sean Penn handled this really well in one of his movies. James Cagney didn't handle this well at all in one of his. I am closer to James Cagney. I needed a moment to compose myself.

"Can you wait here for a minute, Carol?" I said as we exited the office.

Carol nodded her head silently.

As soon as I stepped away, she raised her head and spotted Andrea in the secretary's workspace just outside Stacey's office.

Carol and Andrea are great friends. They see each other frequently, but each time they do, they greet one another as if years had passed since their last gathering.

Carol's face changed to one of great delight and she opened her arms wide. Andrea squealed like a schoolgirl, and they embraced each other. The erstwhile mute whisperer beginning to talk up a storm.

Carol would be distracted for a while.

I climbed to my perch wearily and stood on the balcony surveying the damage. The police were conducting interviews of staff and students. I would make sure that I was not one of those interrogated.

Someone very powerful and very angry had been at work here. But who? As I mused, I heard a voice coming from the bottom of the stairs.

"Eliminate the impossible," Bobbie Meyer said quietly, making sure his voice wouldn't carry too far. I stared back at him not comprehending.

"Eliminate the impossible," he repeated. "When you've eliminated the impossible, whatever remains, however improbable, must be true."

I realized he was quoting the words of the noted writer Conan Doyle who, in 1887, introduced the character of Sherlock Holmes, the famously inscrutable detective to whom the phrase Bobbie employed could be attributed.

"When you determine who *couldn't* have done this, Ricky-Boy," he explained, "…you'll know who did."

"And how did you come to this sweet pearl of wisdom?" I inquired.

"Elementary, my dear Ricky-Boy," he replied, nodding to the foot of the stairs leading to my office. I met him at the bottom.

"You've probably figured out that the person who did this lives here – he shits where he eats – and there's only a handful of people living here at any one time, not counting you and anybody living with you."

Bobbie was right, of course. While all of the staff had keys to the school, it was hard to imagine any of them having the motivation, let alone the strength, to accomplish what had obviously been done overnight while I slept. All students living in the dormitory had unfettered access to the main classroom at any hour of the day or night. This had been an inside job. Someone I knew, and likely brushed arms with most every day, had been responsible.

"Figure out who couldn't have done this, and you'll figure out who did," he repeated.

"What next?" I asked.

"What next?" He laughed. "That's your fucking job. I'm a watchmaker, you shmuck, not freaking Kreskin."

George Joseph Kresge, Jr. – more commonly known as The Amazing Kreskin – was a world-renowned mentalist and magician who made predictions ranging from the contents of a person's wallet, to the winner of the next presidential election. He claimed he had once hypnotized an entire room of people into believing that Martians had invaded New Jersey.

Bobbie winked and turned his wheelchair toward the exit. "I'll keep an eye on you, Ricky-Boy."

"Thanks, Bob." He had been right about one thing. My answer was in the dormitory.

Only ten individuals occupied the dorm these days. Laura Kroc was wheelchair bound and way too fragile to commit the kind of havoc that had been wreaked in the main classroom. Leon and Eddie Tulvay were on self-prescribed leaves of absence. Buddy Seacourt was in the hospital. Angelito Cortez and Dayne Dorio were fairly beyond suspicion by virtue of their sparkling characters and even demeanors. It was hard to imagine that either Celia Turata or Rena Vance, utterly and perpetually occupied with each other to the exclusion of all else, would have had the time or inclination to commit such an act. That left two.

One of those two, Marty Rodriguez, was in the main classroom now. He was working at one of the very few desks – *his* desk among them – that had been spared destruction. He appeared to be studiously laboring, with a magnifying loop over one eye and tweezers in one hand, carefully lowering a mainspring into a movement.

Marty was simply not this industrious and it was difficult to believe he would be working amid the tumult around him. More likely, he would have taken this incident as an easy excuse to beg off. He was the only student in the main classroom right now, and he labored as if oblivious to the obliteration surrounding him.

I approached him slowly. He must have seen me coming, but he didn't look up.

I walked right up to his desk; he continued working.

Watchmaking is a delicate profession. Watchmakers work with parts that can sometimes barely be seen with the naked eye. It is an art requiring a steady hand, dexterity, superior eye-hand coordination, and patience. One simply does not interrupt such a craftsman under any circumstances, and I did not. I didn't have to, as Marty spoke first.

"You know this is messed up, Rick."

I found both his words and mannerisms strange under the circumstances. I replied.

"That it is, Marty."

He realized I was staring at him and that I had unvoiced questions. He finished his work and put it aside.

"You know who did this." This was a statement, not a question.

"Is that a statement or a question?"

"No; you *know* who did this."

"I'm listening."

"You're playing stupid, now." Marty picked up his tweezers and started working again.

"Mart, I don't know what you're talking about." Rodriguez stopped working and stared at me as if to determine whether I really *was* stupid.

"Are you kidding me?"

He repeated his rhetorical query, as if I was deaf as well as blind.

"Are you kidding me? Who's crazy in the dorm? There's only one crazy in the dorm; Vander. *He's* the one who did this; he's the only one strong enough and wacky enough to do this; the only one *dangerous* enough to do this and you God damn well know it. You're just lucky that there was no one *in* this room when he decided to nuke it."

He put down his tools, looked around, and gestured for me to come closer.

"Look, Rick, I live right next door to the guy, and I'm telling you there's something wrong with him. I hear him getting on and off his bed late at night, and there're voices coming from his room, weird voices, and I can't even tell if they're coming from him or not. Hell, he's a psychotic, he's a convicted criminal and he's built like a tank. What else do you need?"

"He's not a psychotic, Marty." I didn't sound too convincing.

"Not a psychotic?" Marty laughed. "Hell, Rick, you're the only thing keeping him from going totally off the edge. I don't know why he's here in the first place. Look, now you know, and now you know what to do. Rick, I tell you, I'm scared; he's had his coming out party, and this is the beginning, not the end of the crap he's going to pull. I'm telling you, I live next to the guy. I want a friggin' bodyguard."

"Marty, did you *see* anything?"

"Did *I* see anything?" He guffawed. He started working again then stopped just as quickly. He opened his arms wide and looked around the room.

"Do *you* see anything, Rick? Well, do you?"

"I hear you, Marty… I'll look into it."

"You'll 'look into it?' Boy, you better do something more than 'look into it,' and *pronto hombre*." Rodriguez muttered an inaudible phrase in Spanish. "Look, that boy's been cruising for a breakdown for a while. And now he's *broke*. And Rick…"

"Yeah, Marty…?"

"He's gonna break some more."

"OK, Marty, I hear you." I turned to leave and Marty got in his last words.

"I'm scared, Rick, I'm not kiddin'. This is bullshit. You gotta get that guy outta here before something *really* serious happens. Rick!"

I looked at my student over my shoulder.

"Soon, Rick."

XI

The cleanup of the main classroom began. Raymond and Enrique, the two maintenance men under the employ of the school, were on the job. Raymond worked silently.

Ray was the product of a black woman and a white man, and had characteristics of both races. His skin was taut and coffee brown, and his delicate features were without blemish of any kind. He usually had a smile on his face and was always pleasant.

There was a reason for this. Two years before, Ray's seventy-year-old mother-in-law had won eleven million dollars in the New York Lottery. Realizing that she had a winning ticket, she assembled her family around her, sending cabs and limousines to the surrounding boroughs and suburbs to retrieve them. Without so much as an explanation to anyone, she then retained a security force of five armed men who stood watch over her house and family for the remainder of the night.

At daybreak, she dispatched her daughter and her son-in-law, Ray, to a lawyer's office. Ray and his wife returned with counsel in a limousine. With two of her guards, she joined this contingent, and they proceeded to Albany, the state's capital. By the end of the day she had verified her winning status and arranged for the appropriate funds to be directly deposited into her checking account.

She cleared just over seven million after taxes. She deposited five million in her savings account and then dedicated the remaining years of her life to spending the rest on her children and grandchildren. And Ray.

She wasn't frivolous with her newfound wealth, but her good nature did often get the best of her. Without asking, Ray got a brand new Cadillac Eldorado, the only new car he had ever owned, and which he proudly drove to work every day. While it occurred to him that he might parlay his mother-in-law's bonanza into a life of ease and luxury, he found the possibility of total financial security at some point in his future sufficient. So he kept his $17,000 a year job with no regrets and with a renewed, positive outlook on his station in life.

Enrique, a middle-aged refugee of Castro's Cuba, cursed under his breath as he labored. Enrique didn't talk much, and when he did talk, he talked to Raymond exclusively, usually so quietly that no one else could hear. Enrique was positively unapproachable. His likeability was not enhanced by the fact that Raymond had happily nicknamed him the Butcher.

No one dared to ask for an explanation, and probably only Raymond was aware that Enrique had worked as a butcher in Cuba.

I didn't envy them their work; the place was a mess.

I nodded to the pair as I passed. Raymond stopped, beamed me a glorious smile and saluted me with his right hand, his typical greeting. Enrique barely raised his eyes from the floor and grunted.

Soon, Carol returned in a scurry from the secretary's station and we continued our trek to the dormitory. We walked downstairs into the deserted dining room and past the vacant pool table. Domingo's kitchen space was closed off by a sliding aluminum panel, which hung from the ceiling and rested on the counter upon which his tempting delights were usually placed.

The long corridor leading from the dining room to the dormitory was eerily quiet. The sounds of our footsteps echoed. Spooked, I stopped to ensure that the echo I heard came from our feet. Carol stopped as I did without questioning why.

The smell of chlorine filled the air and irritated my nostrils as I passed by the pool. I peeked through the twin portholes of the pool's two doors and saw no one and nothing. I saw no reason to check the saunas to the right of the entranceway, hidden from my view.

Past the pool, and now immediately ahead of us, was the end

of the hall and the double doors that were my preferred entry and exit points into and out of the building. To the left was the corridor leading to the residential section of the facility; five rooms facing five rooms – odd numbers on the right and even on the left – and one at the end of the passage. I was convinced that within one of these rooms dwelled a very annoyed person, capable of committing the havoc I had witnessed upstairs.

And maybe more.

We walked slowly down the hall linking these rooms. We passed by Laura Kroc's room, room number one on the right. She was a petite, pleasant, soft-spoken girl of nineteen from New Jersey, and a distant relative of the McDonald's founder, Ray Kroc. She was also the victim of a horrific car accident that had killed her boyfriend and had left her confined to a chair. She was a good student and kept to herself. As usual, there was nothing but silence emanating from her room.

Across from her, room number two was the domicile of Angelito Cortez, and he carried with him a remarkable story. Angelito was born in the city of Tancol on the east coast of Mexico. By the age of eighteen he was married with a young daughter, unemployed, without marketable skills and penniless. Yet, he was not without ideas, and not without the courage to implement them; he decided to emigrate to the United States. The plan was to find work, send money back to his family, and find a way to bring them to America.

Of course, there was no way for him to do any of this legally. To this end, he said his goodbyes to his wife and infant child, enlisted the help of a friend, and hid in the trunk of a car for seven days and seven nights, making a long, dangerous and ultimately successful trip to New York City. Once there, he was able to find himself a job as a dishwasher earning four dollars an hour. With this cash he was able to buy food and send money home to his family.

"I am working and happy," he wrote.

He was unable to afford any decent place to live, so he made a home with a group of similarly affected men and woman in an abandoned tenement in the Bronx. All went quite well until immigration officials busted the joint just six weeks after he had arrived. When they did, he sought safety on a window ledge six stories above the ground.

It was a very bad decision.

He shifted his weight on the aging concrete of the shelf and it crumbled beneath him. As he fell the sixty feet to the pavement below, he wondered if his wife would ever find out what happened to him. The question was remarkably irrelevant, as Angelito was not killed in his fall. However, the seventh through tenth vertebra on his spinal column were crushed, and he would spend the next thirteen months of his life rehabilitating in Montefiore Hospital. It was there that he learned English, word by word, while mentally grappling with the idea of life in a wheelchair.

He was also amassing incredible medical bills, and attracting the attention of those happy people at the United States Immigration and Naturalization Services, who, fearing a possible lawsuit over his accident, decided to take the offensive and instituted proceedings to have him deported, wheelchair and all.

Angelito's future might have been nothing more than a one-way ticket back to Tancol, had it not been for a friend of Bob Stacey's who worked at the hospital. Hearing of his plight, Bob monitored both his medical and his legal status and when he was well enough, granted him a full scholarship to attend the school, including free room and board.

I had contributed my own small chapter to his story. Angelito was a wonderful kid, soft spoken, well mannered, and photogenic. My unique powers of persuasion yielded multiple news stories and television interviews. INS soon looked like the devil on earth, and Angelito, like a hard working kid in a wheelchair just looking for a piece of the American dream. It wasn't long before a sympathetic congressman was sharing the TV screen with Mr. Cortez, promising to write a bill that would make Angelito a legal resident. INS backed off, the hospital forgave its six-figure charges, and all ended well.

Except for the condition of Angelito's back. His injuries were severe and every six months or so he would find himself back in the hospital for a "tune up," as he called it. That's where he was right now; but he was expected to return shortly.

Room number three was unoccupied. Across the hall in room number four was Buddie Seacourt, who aspired to be the world's second one-armed watchmaker.

The first, Darien Phillips, had been a veteran of World War II and had graduated from the school some forty-five years earlier. Despite his disability he mastered his craft by ingenuously incorporating the use of a metal hook that functioned as his left hand. It was powered by Bowden Cables, a system once used as a part of bicycle hand brakes and later used extensively in the aircraft industry.

Phillips eventually became the sole proprietor of his own repair shop in Dayton, Ohio, earning both a nationwide reputation and a good living.

Buddie lost his limb in a motorcycle accident. He was a highly motivated student, but wasn't doing well. At this rate, I doubted whether Buddy would earn either a reputation or a living. I would have to keep my eye on him.

Rooms five and seven belonged to Vander and Rodriguez. Rooms six and eight belonged to the twins, Leon and Eddie Tulvay.

The pair were the product of rich, doting parents in Los Angeles, where they were currently on a self-declared holiday, totally oblivious to the school's schedule or the academic requirements of their enrollment. They were also the product of a rare, genetic birth defect called Larsen's Syndrome. The disease manifests itself in various ways, producing deformed limbs and curvatures of the spine. Its sufferers are gravely susceptible to fractures and dislocation of the major joints.

In Eddie's case the syndrome had resulted in paralysis. Multiple surgeries had kept Leon out of a wheelchair thus far. He possessed the prominent forehead and wide-spaced eyes sometimes found in sufferers of the ailment.

The aberrant proclivity of the twins to avoid their studies was enthusiastically ignored by all staff, including Bob Stacey, who saw in their parents the next generation of charitable benefactors, who could no doubt be properly groomed by practicing an extreme indulgence of their children.

Dorio's room, number eleven, was sandwiched in between numbers nine and ten, belonging to Celia Turata and Rena Vance, respectively. Rena had been referred to us by New York State's Office of Vocational Rehabilitation, which was paying a reduced rate to board her while she studied here. Both were deaf and they communicated with each other by means of American Sign Language. While they were permitted to have interpreters with them, who would have been paid for by the State, both refused the accommodation.

Rena and Celia had formed their own personal club to which no one else had been invited to join. While relationship building was always a part of the rehabilitative process, this pair had taken the idea to an extreme and remained aloof from all other students and staff, including me. One of their rooms was always empty because they were always together.

Rena had been born deaf, and was profoundly so. She could not, or would not, read lips. Celia was another story.

A large woman – over six feet tall and weighing 175 pounds, if not more – she had been a brilliant engineering student at the Massachusetts Institute of Technology, with double minors in Theatrical Studies and Applied Logic. By her sophomore year, she had won three state awards for her amateur theatrical performances; the school's chess club had won two consecutive national championships with her as its president. From all accounts, she had been industrious, highly disciplined, and singularly accomplished.

Her one detriment seemed to have been her taste in boyfriends. After a brief affair with a young man who turned out to be a methadone addict, and apparently prone to random and spontaneous acts of violence, she performed her own spontaneous act and dumped him.

His ability to withstand this rejection was severely limited. He broke into her college dormitory room on an early Sunday morning. She awoke, sat up in her bed, bleary- eyed, and took his first blow squarely on the left side of her face. His hand had not been empty. He had picked up the first available object in her room; a heavy brass lamp that her father had given her some years before. Her eardrum collapsed immediately, and he was able to hit her three more times before she was able to rise to her feet. But she did rise.

While the ensuing skirmish was reportedly brief, the effect on them both was devastating. She attempted – somewhat successfully – to rip his throat out with her teeth. He survived, although his voice box did not. She left him bleeding in the room and without calling the authorities drove to the hospital.

The hearing in her left ear was gone, and her right eardrum had been punctured. She was left with 20 percent of the hearing in that ear, but that soon disappeared as well, and in a profound irony, she found herself as deaf as her assailant had been left speechless.

Celia was unable to adjust to the aftermath of the attack. Soon after, she dropped out of school and disappeared. The police could not find her, the private investigators hired by her loving family could not find her and after eighteen months she was presumed by most to be dead.

But she was not. She emerged three years after her trauma,

having mastered the arts of signing and lip reading, and having spent two of those years studying exclusively with a Zen Master. What metaphysical plane she had been able to ascend to, or what dimensional veils she had been able to part as a result of her studies was unknown, but it was clear that the experience had left her better adjusted and in fabulous physical shape.

The multiple scars on her face remained, however, as a living testament to the ordeal she had endured.

She had met Rena some years before – no one knew exactly how or when – and when her friend was admitted to Waterman, Celia simply followed along. Unlike Rena, however, Celia excelled in the art of watchmaking. The precision her highly ordered mind was capable of seemed to link directly with the uncanny dexterity and sensitivity of her hands and fingers. To say that one worked like clockwork with the others was a pun, but a truism nevertheless.

Celia could speak and be understood fairly easily. She acted as interpreter for Rena, who could not verbalize beyond unintelligible grunts. They felt more than comfortable having formed their nation of two within the confines of the school and no one felt inclined to breach its borders. While I never hesitated to attempt communication of one sort or another with a deaf student, I had never felt it necessary to walk to the end of this hall while they were in residence. Today, I was compelled to do so.

I knocked on the door to Rena's room. Carol stood patiently behind me, kindly declining to criticize this pointless formality. I realized my mistake, turned the knob and opened the door slowly, hoping that this would properly announce our presence.

Celia and Rena were sitting on the floor, on the opposite side of the room under a window, facing each other with their crossed knees touching. The window looked out to the narrow alleyway separating my residence from the dormitory.

They stared at me as I entered the room. I was not greeted.

Celia's already less-than-friendly eyes soon turned hard and cold when she realized that Carol was with me. She glared at her as she entered. When I started to talk and Carol prepared to interpret my words for Rena's benefit, Celia pointed at Carol and then slashed her right hand violently across the air in front of her chest. While I did not know if this was official sign language or not, it was clear that Celia would not tolerate Carol in Rena's room.

Though she was familiar with Celia's proclivities, Carol was nonplussed nevertheless. She shot a quick glance at me, took a short breath and abruptly turned and strode from the room, leaving me there by myself.

Celia turned to look at me. I felt I was facing a lioness. Whether she was a lioness protecting her cub, or looking for her next meal, hardly seemed to make a difference.

All was silent. I began to speak. I directed my words towards Celia, as I knew she was Rena's communicative link to the outside world.

I corrected what would have been my second *faux pas* almost immediately. As is the case with most people, deaf people consider it rude if you don't look at them while you're speaking to them, even if your words can only be understood by the interpreter.

Rena had black, short hair, cropped in a page boy style. She sat there on the floor, cross-legged, eyes half-closed. She had a small frame, holding just a few more pounds than it was meant to, and she would not have been altogether unattractive were it not for the thick bags under her eyes and the expressionless, nearly blank look on her face. She looked as if she was in some kind of trance and there was no visible sign that she was breathing at all. I hesitated, waiting for an indication that I was imagining this, or for some other sign of life. Finally, I spoke.

"Mr. Stacey sent me, Rena," I said. I allowed myself this small out which I thought forgivable under the circumstances. "It's about your grades."

Showing no emotion at all and without moving her head, Rena jerked her eyelids open and fixed her stare upon me, and then Celia. I found this absolutely creepy and shifted uncomfortably.

"You've failed three consecutive quarters, Rena, did you know that?" I wanted to glance at least at Celia, but didn't dare.

"Listen, we don't think this is the right place for you. You've had a hard time here, haven't you?"

Although I wasn't looking at Celia, I could hear her breathing hard, snorting and heaving, like a racehorse behind a starting gate.

"Rena?"

I looked at Celia now to make sure my words were being conveyed. Celia's swift, almost vicious hand motions indicated that they were.

"There's nothing I can do, Rena."

We hadn't had much contact, but I was hoping she was at least aware of my reputation as a friend to all students.

Uh, no, apparently not.

Rena looked at Celia, questioningly. Celia was obviously distressed and was communicating nothing to Rena at that moment; at least not with her hands. Celia slowly turned her eyes to me.

"You."

She jabbed her index finger in my direction, using it like a rapier. I could swear that I felt her finger contact the center of my chest.

I had seen emotional reactions from students at times like this and knew how to handle them. The problem was that I had to resolve, in my mind, the fact that some students simply couldn't make it here. What might happen to them after they left the sheltering environment of Waterman was something I couldn't control and shouldn't dwell on.

Celia uncrossed her legs, slowly rose to her full height and leaned her considerable girth towards me. Rena looked on silently. I tensed without meaning to, and there was a logical explanation for this. I am neither a huge physical specimen nor a betting man, but I felt at that moment that the odds of Celia pummeling me within an inch of my life were quite good.

"Don't," Celia said, softening only slightly.

The word was carried by a soft lisp, and in other circumstances it would not have been an unpleasant sound. A lock of her thin, sandy hair fell down across her forehead.

"There's nothing I can do, Celia."

"This is the second time something important has been taken from me," she said.

One wouldn't have known that she was deaf at all.

"If there's anything I can do for you – either of you – I'll do it; just ask. Otherwise, tell me when she can be ready. I was addressing Celia directly and it didn't seem to matter. She was both of them, now, I guess.

"Tell me how much time she'll need and I'll tell Stacey and get it for you."

Celia was frozen with both hands balled into fists at her sides. I did not need the assistance of my own heightened intuitive abilities to know what she was feeling.

"I'm not your enemy, Celia," I said. I turned to Rena.

"Rena, let me know what I can do for you." Celia hesitated, and then translated my words back to Rena using American Sign.

Once a student was terminated from attendance at the school, dormitory privileges continued only for whatever period was absolutely necessary. I realized that Rena was losing not only her education and her future, but also her home and her best friend. I waited for a response that was not forthcoming. Then Celia began to sign again. But this time, her message was meant for me alone.

She locked the forefingers and thumbs of both of her hands

together like links on a chain and thrust her hands at me twice. She then extended the forefinger of her right hand and traced a circle in the air in front of her chest, ending the circle by touching the middle fingers of both of her hands together.

I accessed my somewhat limited database of American Sign and was able to discern her meaning.

The links formed by her fingers signified her relationship with Rena. The outline of a circle combined with the joining of her middle fingers signified perfection. Together, she was saying, they were perfect.

I turned to leave and as my fingers touched the doorknob, I heard rounded words roll slowly from Celia's lips.

"Be stirring as the time; be fire with fire; threaten the threatener and outface the brow of bragging horror."

That she was quoting Shakespeare was clear; her exact meaning, for the moment, escaped me.

She took two steps toward me and from her impressive height glared down and grimaced cruelly, the corner of her mouth flaring to show an abnormally pointed canine.

I didn't think there was a sign for that.

XII

Outside the dorm room, I put my back against Rena's door and exhaled deeply. This ordeal had left me drained.

More than the mere stress of the confrontation was the realization that I had changed the life of not one, but two individuals, and certainly not for the better. This was not what I was meant to be and not what I was meant to do. If my life meant anything at all, it was to be a source of some good in this world. It was not my function to be an agent of injustice, to use John Locke's words, to create unhappiness, or to spread pain to others, much less to those already compromised in body and spirit. But this was exactly what I had accomplished.

That someone had to do what I had just done, and that I had been ordered to do it, were only convenient axioms, pretexts employed by humans since time immemorial to excuse all manner of deeds, from forced segregation, to mass extermination.

Of course, I could not predict the future. I had no way of knowing whether my actions, in the end, would ultimately be destructive or beneficial for Rena or Celia. Many of life's experiences that initially appear negative and detrimental, turn out later on to have been necessary or even helpful. Personal, intellectual and even physical growth is often preceded by pain and suffering. Failure can be the foundation upon which success is constructed. Life can take the form of a sadistic taskmaster, viciously prodding you along a rocky and broken path leading to knowledge and to change, and to whatever it is that you were always meant to be. Perhaps, to what you *must* be.

Yeah. Right.

I took a few steps down the hall and something caught my eye. I knelt down and picked up a thick wooden splinter, not more than two inches in length. I looked up. I was facing the door to Vander's room.

I looked at Vander's door, then at the splinter again. And then…

Then, it was as if someone had tightened a plastic bag over my head. What followed was an avalanche of agony pouring over me, carrying with it the terrible weight of hatred and singular aggression.

The Wave came as never before; overwhelming and devastating, blocking out all light and life and hope. I fell to both my knees and grabbed my head, screaming in shock. I couldn't open my eyes. Then the pain increased.

Words came to me, but not from any human larynx, not through the air and into my ears, but like a spike driven into a cow's brain, employed as a weapon, not as a means of communication.

Hatred for all that is weak; hatred, revulsion and loathing for the imperfect.

I thought I heard someone shouting my name.

Hatred for the weak, hatred for the imperfect; hatred for all those who touch their lives.

"Richard!"

Hatred for me, pure, blind hatred for me, hatred for Kara…

"Richard!"

I managed to open one eye and saw Cook trying desperately to lift me up from the floor.

Pain as passion, suffering as pleasure, Death as God, as Lover, as Release…

I grabbed Cook with both hands as hard as I could, trying to hang on, God help me, just trying to hang on…

The world changed.

The tile floor disappeared, along with the fluorescent lights suspended on the ceiling of the hallway. There was darkness, then light, then darkness, then light again. I couldn't feel my extremities.

There was a buzzing in the air, an incessant, piercing sound, as if the very fabric of existence was being ripped and shredded. And there was a smell; a sickly sweet smell, like candy apples, but not candy apples.

Numbers flashed by in the air. Huge numbers, small numbers, three dimensional and two dimensional, numbers of unknown dimension, thousands and thousands of numbers, fleeting across a sky that was not of this world. I stiffened, as if I was experiencing some kind of rigor mortis that occurs before death, not after it.

Three numbers stopped and swelled as all the others continued to swirl around them. The trio of numerals bulged and grew larger, until they blocked out the others, until they blocked out the light, until they filled the space of all existence; everything that is, that was and or will ever be.

One, seventeen and one.

"The time of your life on this earth," I heard myself say. But the voice was not my own.

And then the numbers were gone – they were all gone – vanishing as swiftly as they had appeared. The hallway returned, and the fluorescent lights returned, and I was clinging to Cook's arms as if I were attached to him, as if we were Siamese twins that could never be separated, as if he were the only thing keeping me slipping from off the edge of this world to whatever is beyond this earthly plane. The silver Bulova watch on my wrist told me it was 11:00 a.m.

I looked at Cook: painfully, slowly; at his innocent, concerned face, and I knew.

I pushed myself up against the wall parallel to Cook's room, as the door to Derrick Vander's room opened. Derrick's hulking frame filled the doorway.

He stood there in shorts, shirtless, veins bulging on his muscled body, the tattoo of a cobra etched on his breastbone, with its tail trailing down from his left shoulder to his arm. There was a dagger etched on his right arm, and the dagger was splitting an image of the earth. The dagger was dripping blood, and the drops covered the world. He looked down on us both with contempt, as if he controlled our lives, as if he could will us to live or to die, all in his choosing. I recoiled instinctively and could barely meet his gaze.

"What are you doing outside my crib white boys?"

I looked at Vander, then at Dayne, and the force of my realization choked out whatever air remained in my lungs.

Dayne Dorio had one day, seventeen hours, and one minute to live.

At that precise moment in time, Derrick Vander was going to kill him.

XIII

The moon.

The ghostly sphere cast a narrow finger of pale light through the curtains of my music room that trailed across my feet. It added meagerly to the light coming from the single forty watt bulb burning in the lamp by my bed.

I awoke to Kara's eyes shining through the shadow of the lock of hair that tumbled wistfully over her brow. She was hovering over me with a terribly concerned look on her face. To her left was Cook. He was supporting her with one hand and holding my hand with the other.

"How are you, Richard?" Cook asked.

"How are you, sweetheart?" Kara asked with a whisper.

I sat up with some difficulty and looked at them both, and then, at the stark decor of my bedroom. And I remembered.

"I'm OK."

I touched Kara's forearm and tried to be a bit more convincing.

"I'm really OK, but I could use something to drink."

"I'll get something for you," Kara replied, with a look of some relief.

As soon as she left the room Cook leaned over and spoke softly into my ear.

"You had me a little concerned, Richard."

Cook stared at me without blinking, genuinely concerned, his hand still holding mine. Such a good kid.

"I'm fine, Cook, and thanks for your help."

Cook beamed a movie star smile.

"You were in quite a bad way, Richard. I had to carry you over here." Cook grinned proudly, but then his brow furrowed. "You were actually quite disturbed, and making some rather odd statements."

"Like what?"

"Well, frankly, Richard, you seemed quite worried about my future well-being."

I didn't remember what I might have said and looked at him hesitantly. Cook paused, his eyes probing, seeking answers and explanations.

He looked over his shoulder and then moved his face very close to my own. His perfect lips whispered into my ear.

"You said I was going to die."

"Did I?"

"Yes."

"Did I say anything else?"

"Well, yes, in a manner of speaking," he replied. "You said I was going to die in one day, seventeen hours and one minute."

Cook kept his eyes fixed upon me; he straightened his back and cocked his head strangely. "What did you mean, Richard?" he asked.

This was reminiscent of a Mathis Aputa question; a query for which there could be no cogent response. But Cook repeated it anyway.

"What did you mean?"

He looked a little weird and quite serious. His heavy, Midwestern twang appeared to have faded. I blinked my eyes twice. He cocked his head in the other direction.

I opened my mouth as if to respond, for what purpose I could not begin to guess, for I had no reply whatever in mind.

Kara returned with my drink. I sat up in my bed a bit more; every muscle in my body felt sore. Cook adjusted my pillow to account for my change of position. The cool water tasted delicious. I swallowed with some difficulty then looked at both of them hesitantly.

"Vander?"

"What about Vander?" Cook queried.

"Where is he?"

"I guess he's still in his room, Richard. Where else would he be?"

I had no answer for this question either.

"Listen, Cook, I want you to be careful with him."

Cook cocked his head in that strange way of his once more. I sat up abruptly.

"Just watch out for him, stay out of his way, keep your eyes open, you know what I mean?"

Other than for the strangeness of my recent behavior, Cook had no reason whatever to know what I meant. Yet, I had to warn him, protect him, somehow, someway, and I wasn't doing such a great job of it.

Cook took my half finished glass from my hand and gently pushed me back against the pillow. He looked at me intently and smiled, speaking softly but with an emphasis on each word. "You never, ever, have to worry about me, Richard."

Kara looked at Cook, then at me, then back at Cook.

I closed my eyes and prayed Cook was right and that I had no reason to worry. But I suspected – no, I *knew* – that my real worries were just beginning.

XIV

Is he mad by now?

Perhaps just a tad. Perhaps he's caught just a *whiff* of madness, like a late winter cold that disappears when the seasons change.

Perhaps he has stepped just a bit over the line; perhaps the demarcation separating sanity from madness has become obscured; maybe he's been working with percentage points, playing with small numbers, morphing from black to white and hoping to stay in the gray long enough to retain a fragile hold on his skills, and his job, and his dignity.

And his mind.

He wondered if he was always this way and whether it is only now that his mental state was becoming oh-so-much-more noticeable. He wondered if he had become a coward, whether he always was, or whether the terror of a lingering and painful death would whip him to the brink of insanity, as if he were a stallion with Death as his rider, a mount being driven wildly toward the edge of a cliff.

No. It was just the pain.

It was greatest in the evening. Without the distraction of daylight it descended upon him like a putrid fog, engulfing and strangling him, his own personal demon.

It usually began with a sickening feeling in the pit of his gut, an agony that seemed to branch from this epicenter along tributaries that spread throughout his body. His useless legs were not spared, as phantom suffering invaded these parts of him as well. This always made him chuckle.

Morphine was his only ally now in the face of his disease and its aftermaths. The pill form was handed to him at first, and then the injectables, representing the final front of relief at his disposal. Now he was permitted unlimited access to the drug. His doctors had advised a certain dose within a prescribed period, the last advice given him. He would be the only one dispensing either pharmaceuticals or advice from now on.

He had never shied away from pain. After all, pain was a wake-up call, a defense mechanism that could save your life. But what he experienced now was a different kind of agony, one without purpose, without benefit of any kind, and without end. It qualified him to play for the grand prize in a random game of chance.

Winning the grand prize ended the game.

It helped to remain occupied, but this was difficult given his chosen profession; the intense concentration and steady hand required to practice the craft of watchmaking often eluded him. He had all but ceased the watch repair business he successfully operated out of his home, in his spare time, for the last nine years. At the school, he was now relegated to tasks requiring less effort. He had supervision over an ever shrinking number of students. Nevertheless, he found that his work, his friendship with Ricky, and his love for his wife were more than enough to keep him going.

He was watching television. Jean Luc Piccard, the captain of the Starship Enterprise, was attempting to divine the nature of a deadly alien creature that had invaded his ship. Nae Tong, a South Vietnamese National, sat by his side holding his hand.

Bobbie brought her with him to the States after the fall of Saigon. They were among the last few who retreated, by helicopter, from the roof of the US Embassy in that city. Once here, he provided for her in every way; his romantic intentions remained unannounced for a period of years. He prayed that any attraction she might develop for him would bloom naturally and that nothing she gave him would be out of gratitude.

His affection for her was never the issue. By the time they left Vietnam together, he had already killed two men for her.

For her part, she saw him not as some transient savior, but as her knight in shining armor, a Prince Valiant, who had swept her away from the hell that was her life, to a land where, together, they might live happily ever after.

They eventually did. Even Bob's subsequent disability, two years after their marriage, did nothing to dim their love for each other.

"How about a beer, Nay-Nay?"

"Of course, Bobbie."

She was so good to him. He didn't deserve her, and she deserved better than him. Perhaps it was too late in the movie for either of them to change the channel. In any event, the final scene was approaching.

Captain Piccard, aided by the brilliance of his android sidekick, Mr. Data, reasoned that he might expose and ultimately defeat the unseen aliens by subjecting them to particle beams, powered by his ship's warp engines. Of course, he was right.

A burst of pain coursed from his right hip to his right knee. He gasped and grabbed at his leg. He grimaced at the fact that the only purpose it served now was to torment him.

Pain. An unseen foe.

Nae Tong returned with his drink.

There were two things particularly unusual about the events in the main classroom; other than the fact that dozens of dead animals had been employed as macabre furnishings in the re-decoration of the school.

Of the fifty-odd watchmaker's benches located in the classroom, seven were permitted to remain standing, apparently untouched by a marauder that had otherwise ransacked the room and everything else within it. Why? The number of benches coincided exactly with the number of individuals Ricky had reported as actively occupying the dormitory. A quick glance at a floor chart of the benches confirmed that those of dorm residents Rodriguez, Vander, and Dorio were left standing. He was sure the other four intact benches also belonged to dorm residents.

At first glance, the destruction appeared to be of a random variety, violent and wholly haphazard. But upon closer examination, he determined this was not the case.

A watch is primarily a circular mechanism. A balance wheel and a hairspring are the principal time-keeping elements of the machine. The former is a circular piece of metal, often less than one-half inch in diameter, fitted with a dozen or more screws around its perimeter. These are adjusted as necessary, providing the balance associated with the wheel and that gives it its name.

In the center of the wheel is mounted a thin, cylindrical, metal staff no more than one-eighth inch long, which holds and supports the wheel. The ends of the staff rest upon jewels smaller than pinheads, lubricated by minute amounts of oil. A fingerprint or a grain of dust upon a jewel will interfere with its proper utility.

The hairspring – a metallic ribbon – rests within the balance wheel and powers it. When a mechanical watch is wound by its owner, the hairspring is coiled, and the balance wheel oscillates under its power.

If a balance wheel is bent just a fraction of a millimeter -– a deviation too small to be seen with the naked eye – its function is altered. Correcting a defect in a balance wheel, called "truing," is sometimes performed under a microscope. An exquisite coordination of the hand and the eye is required. A watchmaker must innately possess this ability, but must develop this skill as well. As he does, the dimensions of his world change forever. Such a craftsman works long and hard to adapt himself to existence in a truly Lilliputian universe.

Perhaps that was why Meyer had noticed a balance wheel of one design or another, stuck into a piece of cork tile in the center of the havoc that was the main classroom. Bob had wheeled over to the tile while the talking heads were doing what they did best. With the thousands of watch parts strewn around the room, this particular part had apparently drawn no notice. It appeared to have been carefully impressed upon the center of a tile so as to be made flat with its surface without breaking it.

On a hunch he counted the tiles, proceeding in a westerly line from the balance wheel. Nine tiles later, he encountered the remains of two, thoroughly smashed bench drawers.

He retreated to the wheel and counted in the other direction. He counted nine tiles before he met with a lathe crushed into the middle of a high back, upholstered chair. A substance of unspeakable derivation had been smeared along the armrests of the chair. He found the same symmetry in the northerly and southerly directions; the destruction seemed to originate nine tiles from the balance wheel that formed the eye of whatever storm had affected this area.

He wheeled to one side and then to the other. All of a sudden the destruction appeared less random. A near perfect circle – measured from around the balance wheel of a mechanical watch – seemed to have been purposely constructed from the mayhem.

"Another beer, Bobbie?"

"No thanks, sweetheart."

A watch is a mechanism with a clear logic and purpose. But it is more than that. It is orderly. One part melts seamlessly into another; all parts work together toward a singular goal.

A watch is also a machine that presupposes the presence of a higher power; it is an instrument that demands the existence of a watchmaker. But for the limitations of its hairspring or power source, its revolutions would be without end, like the circumference of a circle. But it is yet more than that.

In many ways, it is perfect.

Except that a watch occasionally requires the steady hand of a technician: to oil a jewel, repair a staff or calibrate a balance wheel. To correct what would otherwise be a faultless mechanism.

That was what was accomplished by the students of the school, with a notable distinction. Here, the watchmakers were far from perfect, far different in form from the logical and orderly mechanisms they labored upon.

They were decidedly imperfect.

Perfection-imperfection. A higher power. The watchmaker labored to correct an otherwise perfect mechanism. He restored order.

The aliens had fled from the Enterprise and Captain Piccard had prevailed once more.

Bob Meyer – Marine sergeant – watchmaker – paraplegic – wondered and worried what aliens he worked among, and what chaos they might unleash next.

XV

Derrick never slept very well and tonight was no exception.

A guilty conscience never kept him up, because he had never felt guilty about anything he had ever done in his life. The horrors of his past acts were not sufficient by themselves to disturb his rest, not even, for instance, when his thugs took the head of that little prick who owed Johnny B. money – what was his name? – anyway, when they took his head and held it against the curb and he stomped on it until red and white stuff came out of the kid's ears like he was some kind of overripe tomato. That even kept La Shawn up nights, and he told Derrick so, and La Shawn was never there to help Derrick out again.

Derrick was uncomfortable with that. Once you'd seen him *do* shit, well, he had to feel comfortable with you; comfortable enough to feel that you wouldn't go blabbing to the first pig who sat you down in a cold dark room and started asking you questions. He had to be able to rely on you just a little; just enough to know that you'd always keep your mouth shut, even if a priest put you in a closet with a screen separating his space and yours and did the same.

To Derrick, talking was talking. He made no distinction between talking to God, or the people who worked for Him, or the law, or the people who worked for it. All in all, he had to trust you, just a tiny bit.

Just enough to know that he wouldn't have to kill you.

It was *all* about trust, you see.

No. What kept Derrick up nights was something he couldn't quite put his finger on, something formless, with no name, something that took wing and flew around and around in his head each night, and picked off little pieces of brain matter and flung them against the wall of his skull, and did it over and over again.

Flying things; dark things with hard, leathery wings, going round and round, that whizzed past his head, that left a cold, vacant space where they passed, and that whispered things in his ears as they went by; weird things; funny things.

Sometimes they made suggestions. Sometimes he liked what they suggested.

But it didn't make a difference what these things said, because whatever they said, whatever they were, and whatever they did, they always came uninvited; they came and they went whenever they wanted. They stayed as long as they wished and they did whatever they liked for as long as they liked.

That was the sick thing, the really sick thing; he couldn't stop them from coming. They kept him up all night, they kept him on edge, and they didn't let him dream. He tossed from one side of the bed to the other all night long, as they talked to him in one voice or another, in the voices of people he knew, or never knew, or thought he might have known; in the voices of people he had robbed, or beaten up or killed.

Worse, sometimes he woke up in the middle of the night and didn't know where he was; hell, sometimes he didn't know *who* he was. When this happened, he had *ideas* in his head; there was something he had to *do*. Only it wasn't *him* that had to do it, it was someone else, because *he* was someone else.

But later, if he thought about it long enough, he'd realize that it was those *things*, those *things* in his head that made him feel that way. Then he would become afraid and he'd start shaking and sweating, and that's when he would feel this little itching behind his ear, or hear a noise behind him, or under his bed, or in the hallway outside.

Only nothing was ever there. Nothing he could see, nothing he could touch, anyway.

But he knew that *something* was there. Something.

Or someone.

XVI

It was their feeding time.

Richard Goodman tossed and turned again and again in his lumpy bed, in his three-room apartment.

He was in a deep sleep, at the very point when his conscious mind was at its weakest and when a different and more terrible reality began to unfold and take hold.

All vestiges of what is real slipped away. What remained was only an outline, an empty shadow of the world left behind.

It was a vacuum that nature abhors. So into that vacuum they came.

He was sometimes unsure of the nature of what attacked him on nights like these. Many times he would awake, remembering nothing, his body visibly bruised, his muscles stretched and tortured as if he had been in a boxing match or had run a long distance marathon.

At other times he would be jerked awake as if tethered to a vehicle that had suddenly begun to move, gripped by a paralyzing anxiety and a numbing fear that he could neither explain nor understand.

But no matter how deeply he slept, he would always remain somehow aware, as if he were in some kind of semi-conscious state but still helpless, as demons invaded his thoughts and his soul.

Sometimes, the previous day's events replayed themselves in his mind. Unseen specters whispered in his ears, gleefully noting his missed opportunities, his casual mistakes or his outright blunders. Worse, they would take him a few steps into the future and show him the terrible, long-term implications of the errors he had made and the effects they would have on those he loved. Sometimes they seized upon a single negative event – that might otherwise have remained unnoticed in the passing of a typical day – and magnified it, making it appear as if it was the only significant thing that had occurred.

When he closed his eyes he lost control; he no longer resided in the world of air and light, but in a nightmarish existence, embellished by a wildly imaginative fiction as real and powerful as anything one could experience. He existed on the outer limits of a distorted teleplay, and he was not in control of the television set. All that he experienced – all that he saw and thought and felt – was controlled by entities that had no form and that existed on a plane without dimension of any kind.

Demons.

He alone empowered them; he gave them their lives and their powers, he breathed existence into their putrid shadows and gave them what substance they had. He imparted to them the power to alter his beliefs and his feelings, his body and his soul.

He was an active participant in his insidious torment. He was an enabler. His weaknesses and faults were what truly plagued him; his psychic abilities – presumably bestowed upon him by some benevolent power – were the feedstock of the wraiths that invaded his nightmares.

When he entered their world he was like a caged animal tormented by sadistic zookeepers. All he could do was throw himself against the bars of his psychic prison and scream and suffer and scream again. Every expression of his agony fed and strengthened his tormentors.

Cutting through the harsh winds of his malignant thoughts was the realization that a real, flesh and blood monster was at work. He was tempted to believe that he had somehow created this person as well, but he knew this could not be true. This demon had a more significant birthright and drew his power from a well that was dark and deep.

Dorio was a walking dead man, his time on this earth measured as starkly and precisely as that of a cow being forced down a slaughter line. There were only two men on earth who knew this and Richard Goodman was one of them.

His demons breathed gently into his soul, telling him he was a powerless bystander, a mere observer, that regardless of what actions he decided to take, or not take, Dorio's death could not be prevented. He could watch, and that was all.

And then, there would be more.

Richard Goodman, psychic, do-gooder, madman, twisted and turned in his bed. He knew that the demons mixed fact with fiction. The question was, which was which? The greater question was, what was he to do next?

XVII

They are together. They were apart, and now They are together.

From now on, They will *always* be together.

A large, oval mirror in a brass casing rests upon the floor. It swivels on its frame, and it angles slightly downward. All that is visible is the reflection of their body, and it reminds them of a decapitated corpse.

Funny.

They look at their reflection. They like what they see. This is not unanticipated. What They see, after all, is perfect.

Perfect.

Their neck is long and lean and pale. It looks like the neck of a woman and this pleases them as well. Beauty is not specific to any one sex, it either is or is not, and They are delighted that They might be thought of as one or the other or both, a hybrid of both sexes. They sigh, breathe deeply, and smile.

They drop their eyes and stare at their left arm, and then their right. Their fingers are long; their hands are smooth and delicate. There are no calluses or bruises that might reveal the complexity or difficulty of their work. They are always so careful when They work with their hands. Theirs are dexterous hands, flexible and strong.

They move them back and forth, turning them over, this way and that, as if They are conducting a soundless symphony before an invisible orchestra. They glide silently through the air like wings. They are perfect hands, uniquely equipped for their diverse purposes. These are their gifts.

They pull the fingers of their right hand into a fist and turn its knuckles up and flex. They roll up their sleeves to reveal their forearms. The tendons and muscles there ripple. What appear, at first glance, to be delicate and smooth surfaces reveal undulating metacarpi, communis digitorum, carpiulnaris. Decidedly masculine.

Breathtaking.

They bend their knees slightly, so that their face comes into view. Delicate, silken hair falls lazily across their forehead. Every hair is spaced close together, like a lush lawn. It is so fine that the slightest breeze will cause it to blow way back against their brow. It is an angelic reflection They see, reflecting hope and innocence, purity and purpose. They know it merely mirrors what is inside of them and They are glad and grateful for this. They hope They are worthy of these gifts, too.

They swiftly cross both arms against their naked chest. They pout and glower at their reflection. They open their hands with fingers outstretched, bend their head slightly and peer intently at themselves. They are a bird, a free spirit. They are Mercury, an ethereal envoy brought to this earth not only as a messenger, but as a Wave, a tide of cleansing, of rebirth and regeneration, sweeping away the diseased and the dying, the ragged detritus and refuse of this planet, purifying air rife with the contamination of the imperfect.

Who offend us.

They hug themselves. They raise their head to the ceiling and breathe in as hard as They can, filling their body with life giving air. They slowly exhale through their nose until all of the air has left their body. They stand quietly there for a moment, without inhaling or exhaling; this is what it is like to be dead They think.

They close their eyes and listen closely for the slightest sound, for the slightest indication that They are not alone. But They hear no sounds at all. The silence is deep, and absolute.

Still refusing to take oxygen They look into the mirror once again and ask themselves how long They might stay in this state. They wonder if one day They will no longer be bound by the restrictions of this earth, forced to breathe and eat and defecate. Their work is too important to be limited by the margins of this life. Somewhere there is a force that knows this as well. They do not call it God or the Devil or anything else. They know these are foolish, pitiful connotations created by those without faith. They simply know that It *is*, and that is enough. It is unnecessary for them to understand, because there is nothing *to* understand.

They sigh.

They are so very, very happy.

They know there was a time when clear direction eluded them. This was a time of much unhappiness and confusion. They doubted themselves; They were vulnerable to suggestions that They were faulty and broken. They were easily bruised and damaged by others. Thankfully, those days are over.

The chrome plated, hollow, tubular aluminum rod lies on the bed. They fashioned it from the arm of a wheelchair.

How ironic.

They pick it up and caress it gently, kneading it between their palms, turning it over and over. It is about three feet long, but it is light, strong and durable. It has a purpose, too. It reflects their visage, even though it distorts it. Their face appears misshapen. Their forehead and lower jaw seem stretched to the breaking point along the curvature of the instrument, and it seems as if they are looking at their reflection in one of those Coney Island fun house mirrors.

But this is only an illusion.

They have used a fine toothed, metal hacksaw to carve eight jagged teeth along the edge of one of the ends of the tube. With a metal file They have carefully, painstakingly ground each point to a razor thin sharpness. Now, it cannot be touched without drawing blood.

They turn sideways before the mirror and raise their left arm as a fencer might, their right hand outstretched, holding the smooth end of the tube. They take a quick step forward and thrust and twist. And again. And again.

They are prepared.

XVIII

Vander was screaming again.

Marty Rodriguez lay on his bed with both hands over his ears, and then sat up abruptly, jerking himself upright like a puppet on a string. This movement was made possible only by his powerful abdominal muscles. His legs, as always, remained motionless on the bed. Every time he awoke, his unconscious impulse was to simply swing his legs onto the floor. Every time, he was reminded that this simple capability was denied to him. A deep sigh always accompanied this realization. Tonight, there was a greater distraction.

"You're fucking screaming again, Vander!"

He hit the wall separating their respective rooms three times with the heel of his hand. But not too hard. First, because the wall was made of cinder blocks. His lower extremities were invulnerable to pain, but this was not the case with the rest of his body. Second, it was one thing to live next door to the Devil. It was quite another thing to incite him into paying a visit.

"Madre de Dios, nunca en mi vida."

His room was pitch-black save for the sharp sliver of moonlight piercing the space between his window curtains and painting a thin line across the floor.

He turned on the light resting on a small night table to the right of his bed. As always there was a white towel placed over the shade. He didn't like bright light – never did – although he seemed to spend half of his life bathed in it these days, laboring in the main classroom.

Bright light showed everything. Everything that *was* there and everything that *wasn't* there that *should* be. Every involuntary tremble of his legs. Every fold of slack skin covering limbs that looked smaller and smaller day by day.

Every imperfection.

He stared intently at his two legs, lying there like matchsticks. He seemed to do this a lot these days. He would stare at them with a kind of disbelief, as if he had never seen them before. Then, the disbelief would turn to frustration, the frustration to anger, and the anger to fury. He would beat them with hands balled into loose fists, trying to drive the anger away, and the paraplegia away, and trying to compel himself to feel physical pain. If he could feel something on the *outside*, maybe, just maybe, he could make himself feel something on the *inside*, too. Maybe, then, he could start to have some kind of life.

Instead, there was this dark, black hole, this paralyzing, vacant emptiness in the center of his chest, this sickening, formless void that substituted for a soul.

He would never feel anything in his legs. They were dead. He would never feel anything in his spirit, or his heart, either, because they were dead, too.

As soon as he thought this, he wondered if it were really true.

A muffled groan seeped from the block separating Vander's room from his. It chilled him, distracting him momentarily from his dark thoughts.

He chuckled. Sick.

He chuckled again. *Sick*. They put him right next to a big, black, berserk *puta.*

Another groan. Right through the damn cinder blocks. Jesus. It was like he was being tortured, or something. A spark of an idea pierced through Marty's forehead like a dagger; there might be worse places on earth than the place *he* was in right now. Losing your body was one thing; but losing your mind…?

A moan, again; then, an almost pitiable whimper.

Marty held his head and then hit it with the heels of his hands.

"Fuh-kin Mur-ray!"

This guy was killing him. *Killing him*. The heel of his right hand came to his forehead again, only harder.

Killing him. And Rick: Rick was killing him too. Leaving a

Looney-Tune in the same space as nearly normal people like himself.

"Fuh-kin Ric-kee!"

Too loud. Remember where you are.

He fell silent quickly, listening next door for the slightest reaction. In the particular *barrio* he hailed from – 168th Street and Freeman Avenue in The Bronx (the "old BX") – you listened a lot. You listened even when it seemed you weren't really listening at all.

You filtered out the drone of the elevated trains and the roar of souped-up cars, the clash of the garbage trucks, and the blast of the boom boxes. You disregarded the screams of the children, the protests of their mothers losing their minds with their tempers, the barking of Dominican vendors hawking sugar-flavored rainbow colored ice and the occasional yelps of punks getting a public ass whipping.

You listened to the *subtext* of the streets, a rolling, dark, almost unnoticeable undercurrent, slinking along the cement floor of the urban jungle like a gray mist; an ether that without notice or warning could become tangible in a moment.

Things had a way of changing quickly on the streets of the old BX and it paid to be aware of your immediate surroundings at all times. This small accommodation often produced dividends that were not paid in cash or currency of any kind, but in time.

As in more time on earth.

Time. His stock in trade. Something he seemed to have less and less use for these days.

Closing his eyes for a moment and placing his ear up against the block, he listened again, intensely now, at the growing silence next door.

When he was convinced that nothing demonic was going to ooze through the concrete separating him from his neighbor and capture what small portion of his black soul that remained, his thoughts turned inward again.

He wasn't very good at this watchmaking stuff. He knew it, his instructors knew it, Ricky knew it; hell *everyone* knew it. He was just *passing* time in this place, like he had in all the other schools he had attended and where he had similarly failed to master the skills all the other well-intentioned Anglos had attempted to teach him. It would have been easy for him to conclude that he just wasn't good at anything. While he *mostly* believed that this was the case, just the tiniest kernel of doubt remained.

People did seem to like him; this was true. He was quick-witted. Everyone seemed to think he was funny – a riot in fact – and fun to be around. He had no lack of friends and wherever he went he was the center of attention, the life of the party, the cripple with the lampshade perpetually hanging from his head.

Marty Rodriguez. Crippled spic. Funny guy.

That was *something,* at least.

He closed his eyes and listened again for the slightest sound from next door.

It was strange that in this hyper attentive state he did not hear the shuffling of feet outside the door of his dormitory room.

XIX

Demons.

He called them demons. That was his name for them. It was a particularly funny name, because that's what some people in the neighborhood called him: A *Demon*. He liked that; he looked at it as a compliment. It meant they were afraid. It meant they respected him. It meant that he was doing his job of making people afraid and earning their respect.

But tonight, he woke up and no demons were rattling his brain, no voices in his head were crying out with brilliant ideas or suggestions.

At least, he didn't think so.

No… it was quiet, dead quiet inside and he realized that what woke him were these sounds from next door, where Rodriquez lived, and

"…there's that piece of garbage spic waking me up again, robbing me of the little rest I'm able to get. Commotion follows the little prick wherever he goes. He's always doing something to rattle my cage and he knows it 'cause I've told him and you'd think he'd have the common sense to save his own life; like I thought even animals knew enough to save their own lives."

Marty's disability would not serve to insulate him from Vander's wrath. Vander didn't see his disability. All he saw was a Puerto Rican who had woken him in the middle of the night. Rodriguez had made a very bad decision.

Derrick sat up in his bed and looked around, surveying his room carefully as his eyes adjusted to the dark.

What would he hit him with?

Another sound from next door, like liquid being poured into a vessel from a height. It sounded like someone pissing into a plastic bottle held up against the wall.

Rodriguez was fucking with him now.

Derrick put his lips up against the cinder block wall and whispered.

"I'm coming for you, you little spic. We're going to see just how much piss you have in ya. I'm gonna squeeze it all out of you."

Nothing.

"Rodriguez!" he shouted.

Silence greeted his bellow.

He swung his feet out of bed and slowly onto the floor. He carefully placed weight on one leg, then the other, then rose to his feet. A wheelchair rested in the corner of his room opposite his bed.

He chuckled to himself. He had taken it from the nurse's office, not because he needed it, but because he wanted it. It was like a decoration. He laughed.

He had been in a wheelchair. He remembered that he had the strength to walk out of it. He also remembered some of the great fun he'd had putting people *into* them. He chuckled again and sighed.

Those were the days, my friend. We thought they'd never end.

He walked over to the chair and pushed it across the room. It silently glided until it struck the side of his bed and stopped. He limped over, turned it around, and gently pushed it back to its starting point, then walked over to it again.

On each side of the wheelchair was a tubular, stainless steel arm shaped like a broad, upside down "U". Each end of the "U" fitted into slots located on the body of the chair.

A black, cushioned armrest about one foot in length was secured to the top of each "U" by steel screws. Derrick lightly touched each armrest, then grabbed the edge of one, ripped it from its place and threw it on the floor.

He lifted the arm from the slots in the chair and held it in his hand. It was ungainly and ill-equipped to be used as a weapon, but it made Derrick chuckle even more. He would bloody

Rodriguez's head with a piece of a wheelchair. The lightweight tubular steel would take a couple of swings to be effective and he might even miss him a couple of times.

But, all in all, it would be great sport.

Derrick suddenly forgot why he got out of his bed in the middle of the night.

Oh yeah; Rodriguez.

He began singing quietly to himself: "Rodriguez, Rodriguez." The melody was that of an old show tune called "Chicago."

Derrick put on shorts and sneakers and quietly slipped out of his room. He closed the door behind him and leaned against it. It was only a few feet down the hall to Marty's room. He looked to the left, and then to the right, and listened.

Derrick was good at listening.

It was silent in the hallway. He took the few necessary steps and edged up close to Marty's quarters, putting his left hand on the silver doorknob. He put his left ear up against the door.

Nothing.

He looked down at the knob again and gripped it tighter. As he did, he checked the hallway for life again. All he had to do was turn the knob, turn and turn and turn with all his strength until the lock broke off in his hands. He had done this many times before and he considered it to be an unusual skill that distinguished him.

Slowly, ever so slowly, the doorknob began to turn, except that at the point that he expected to meet some resistance, he felt none at all. The knob turned all the way and Marty's door popped ajar by an inch or so. It wasn't locked.

He laughed. Rodriguez was an idiot who couldn't empty his catheter bag correctly much less remember to lock his door. Derrick placed his lips against the crack in the door.

"Rodriguez, you fuckin' little spic, your daddy's here to teach you shit."

He opened the door and crossed the threshold; his hulking

frame filled the doorway entirely. Curtains covering the window located at the far end of the room rustled in anticipation as he entered.

The door swung open, bumping silently on a gray, rubber cushion installed at the base of the wall. He took a deep breath and thrust out his chest. He twisted his neck around and around, flexing and stretching the considerable muscles located there. He lowered his head and tried to snarl but tonight the snarl just came out as a smile. He always did something like this before he worked.

Proper preparation after all, was the key to success.

As he stepped into the room he saw the commode isolated on the left. There were two silver grab bars on each side of the bowl and these reminded Derrick of the amusing contrivance he had brought with him tonight. Outside the bathroom was a sink and a mirror, both lowered sufficiently to allow their use by a person in a wheelchair. There was a small night light plugged into a socket next to the mirror. Derrick could not resist shifting a little to catch a view of himself. His head appeared for a moment in the reflection. For the benefit of his image he smiled gamely.

This, his daily bread.

A dull glow greeted him at the end of the room.

Rodriguez's bed was on the right side of the room, situated lengthwise against the wall, the wall he shared with Derrick. Two small chairs were against the wall opposite the bed. A poster hung above and between the chairs and advertised the 1981 Mardi Gras in New Orleans.

New Orleans is, of course, a famous American city, known now, and probably forever, for the devastation it received at the hands of Hurricane Katrina in 2005. During this disaster, eighty percent of the city was flooded, due to the breach of levies designed to hold in parts of the Mississippi River. The poor and the elderly, and those without the means to evacuate were primarily affected.

In what was to become the greatest failure by government in the history of the nation, tens of thousands of "refugees" sought shelter in a football stadium, without food, water or medical supplies and left to fend for themselves. For days their pleas were heard on radio and television stations as a stunned nation looked on, and a federal government did nothing.

One of the more memorable aspects of the disaster was reported to have occurred when several hundred survivors attempted to flee, by walking over a bridge connecting New Orleans to the neighboring city of Gretna. Local police undoubtedly had their reasons for setting up a roadblock there, refusing the refugees sanctuary and ordering them back to their devastated city.

They threatened to kill them if they didn't comply.

Derrick spent ten days once in the French Quarter of that great town, drinking and screwing and eating, and drinking and screwing some more. He had a wonderful time and always looked on it as the one period in his adult life where it had never occurred to him to hurt someone or commit a crime. Coming home after this revelry, he thought that he might sustain these feelings.

Not.

Marty kept a lamp on the night table adjacent to his bed but it had been removed to the floor. The light was on and towels had been placed over the shade, painting that area of the room with a dull yellow radiance. Something loomed in that soft, ember-like glow.

"Rodriguez?"

Vander took another step closer.

Marty Rodriguez was by a radiator, under the draped, half-open window opposite the entrance.

There was something else. Rodriguez was doing something he had never done before. He was standing upright.

Well; kind of.

He had been propped up against the radiator, his useless legs buttressed by two, thick, jagged pieces of wood that looked like they had been ripped from a watchmaker's bench. These had been secured to each pitiful appendage with knotted pillow cases. Rodriguez's former inability to stand had been horribly rectified. His head was bent at an unnatural angle and rested against his left shoulder.

His eyes, however, were open.

As Derrick approached, he noticed that Marty's pants had been removed, that his useless, shriveled legs had been spread and that he was balanced over a bedpan into which a liquid was steadily dripping. He saw that the bedpan had overflowed and that the liquid covered the surrounding area.

Blood.

For some reason he hadn't noticed the addition to his dorm mate's chest. It came in the form of a hollow shaft sticking a foot out of its center. From it dripped a steady rivulet. Derrick looked down at the wheelchair part he had brought with him. The rod in Marty's chest looked like the same type of tubular steel. He chuckled nervously at the coincidence. Someone had gotten here before him, and someone had stolen his idea. Of course, his original design had been somewhat expanded upon.

Derrick hunched down in a crouch to take the weight off of his legs as he observed. He wasn't particularly sorry to see Rodriguez in such a state. But he was curious as to how he had gotten there.

Demons

As he edged closer still, he could see that the end of the steel tube protruding from Marty's chest had been carved into eight sharp teeth, which dripped blood like the mouth of a carnivore after a kill. It had been inserted through his back; this was messy work that required significant strength. But who…

Derrick heard the slightest squeak. The curtains rose and fell abruptly, and all of a sudden it appeared quieter. This probably meant that the door to Marty's room had closed behind him.

Derrick looked down at his feet and took a deep breath. He smacked his lips and shook his head slightly. He rose slowly. It hurt, of course, as it always did, and the bones in his knees cracked from the effort. He stood erect, perfectly still, and grasped the arm of the wheelchair tightly in his right hand.

He looked at the one section of the window facing him that no part of the curtain covered. What appeared in front of him was behind. He gripped the metal arm tighter and smiled. It appeared he would have work to do tonight after all.

He froze as he felt the ill current of a stale wind brush against the back of his ears.

XX

Gloopey.

Gloopey, Gloopey, Gloopey.

The eight inch long, red and white Oranda Goldfish with its genetically swollen body and silly name swam lazily in its 25 gallon home. Its graceful, elongated white fins undulated back and forth, moving like a flag in an underwater breeze. It was a fearless fish that didn't move as the fingers of Kara's right hand touched the aquarium glass closest to where the fish noiselessly lingered. Her other hand gently caressed her stomach, just barely exposed by her pajama top.

As far as one can foretell a fish's mood, the animal seemed happy in its underwater environment. But it was also alone. Kara had long thought about getting it a companion.

Nothing, she thought, should be alone.

She had found herself totally unable to fall asleep and had tossed and turned for hours until she had just given up. It was Richard, of course, who was the source of her restlessness.

He was a complicated boy, to be sure, way too complex for the typical young woman to have to deal with, or want to. He was moody and prone to depression. He was driven by some desire or need to isolate himself, physically and spiritually, not only from her, but from everything. He wasn't ambitious; he didn't seem to have any plans for the future. He was attractive, but whatever physical attributes he possessed – which would normally work to make him appealing – were often overwhelmed by the many negative aspects of his personality. He sometimes seemed to be just hanging on, tip-toeing on a ledge, merely trying to get by one day at a time.

Just trying to survive, some might say.

Yet, he was kind and sweet and sensitive. He cared deeply about the kids he worked with and dedicated himself to their happiness and well-being. He was selfless and altruistic, intelligent and a deep thinker, filled with thoughts and ideas that she had never seen in anyone else.

Add to this that he had super powers.

She rose and walked to the single narrow closet in her large bedroom, which also functioned as the living and dining room of her studio apartment. She opened the door and looked at herself in the full-length mirror installed there.

Still perfectly pretty; for a little while longer, anyway.

The things he claimed to experience! Remarkable, supernatural things.

Demons

He had visions of ghostly entities that inhabited his mind, invaded his sleep, and sometimes, actually paid him a visit.

Preposterous.

Messages from the beyond. Spirits floating up the stairs of his basement on the wings of haunting melodies. Waves of uncontrollable sensation – a sixth sense – that purportedly revealed to him the essence of a person's spirit, their beliefs and intentions.

Unbelievable.

And now, she was not only supposed to believe that he was the unlikely beneficiary of a death sentence, delivered in the form of a prophecy from an ancient Coney Island carny, but that he also acquired – for twenty four hours – the conjurer's ability to predict the exact moment of a person's death.

More particularly, her own.

Two days, eighteen hours, fifty-eight minutes.

According to the old woman, the time remaining in Richard's life. It had been eleven o'clock on Sunday morning.

Two days, fifteen hours, fifteen minutes.

The time of *her* life on this earth. That was what Richard had said. It had been eleven thirty. She had checked the time without knowing why.

Two days, fifteen hours, four minutes.

Ricky's second prediction, announced no more than five minutes after his first, and just before he passed out on the boardwalk. Two prophesies, predicting her demise not once, but twice, and approximately six minutes apart.

Ludicrous.

Gloopey.

A silent filter recycled the water of the fish's home, pushing it gently across the surface of the tank. A pirate's treasure chest filled with plastic baubles opened and closed, each time releasing a bubble of air that rose to the surface of the watery enclosure.

Her eyes roamed from the fish tank to her elaborate, antique writing desk, the one legitimately beautiful piece of furniture in her apartment. It rested against a wall, shielded from direct sunlight. To its left was a large picture window. When she sat at the desk and looked to her left, the window neatly framed the upper branches of the trees lining the street below. The morning sun pierced gloriously through these tree tops, splaying long fingers of light across the hardwood floor of the room.

This was where she was happiest.

She sat down. Facing her at eye level was a calendar suspended on a bulletin board. On the calendar was a picture of a puppy with its water bowl balanced comically on its head.

She removed a small, yellow tablet from a side drawer and placed it on the surface of the desk. She inscribed the three time periods on a piece of paper and next to each wrote the time of the prediction. Using the calendar, she computed the date and time each period corresponded to.

Richard was scheduled to die at 5:58 a.m. Wednesday morning. She was scheduled to predecease him at 2:45 a.m., or six minutes before that time, depending upon which of Richard's two premonitions one believed.

In just a few hours.

This is the end, my friend…

There was a clock sitting on the sill in the center of the picture window. It was old and terribly worn, with a mechanical movement that required winding each day.

It had a metal casing adorned with black paint which was chipped away in many places. Plastic substituted for crystal exterior covering its dial, with a crack that ran all the way from the "8" to the "1". It had belonged to her grandmother, who had died when Kara was nine. Her name had been Alegra, but Kara had always called her "Nona."

Nona fancied herself a mystic. Her relatives believed she possessed a "sixth sense." She seemed to "know" things about people that sometimes turned out to be true. You also couldn't throw surprise birthday parties for her.

This small timepiece had rested on her Nona's night table for as long as Kara had memories of her. It ticked loudly and there was always an audible click each time a new minute was added to the day. The eternal background noise provided by the clock always seemed to resound throughout the home.

When Kara asked one afternoon if the sound ever bothered her, Nona just smiled. The sound of the timepiece, she said, reminded her that life's moments moved by relentlessly, and that the passage of time was something one should pay attention to. Paying *attention* to time was her way of *grasping* time, of slowing it down, like putting a saddle on a horse. She believed that if you could slow it down, then you could *control* it. If you could do that, you could control your entire life and everything in it.

The clock stopped the moment Nona died. Kara knew this was so because she had been there. The mechanism had faithfully marked and measured the span of her grandmother's life, and when that life concluded, the clock was done, too.

Kara had taken it that day as her sole remembrance of her Nona. It continued to keep good time and she rewound it faithfully each evening. It was bruised and battered and out of place by the window, but that didn't matter.

Somewhere, for each one of us, she thought, a clock is ticking.

Somewhere, in some place, there was a timepiece measuring and marking the beginning and end of each of our lives as accurately as the clock had for her Nona.

Somewhere. Somehow. Sands in an hourglass, slowly slipping away, leading to the moment when there would be no sand left at all. And that moment would be the end. The finish line. Finito. Fini.

Her time was to run out at either 2:39 or 2:45 Wednesday morning.

Or whenever.

She stared at the clock on the window sill. This time it did not make her smile.

She and Richard were alone, walking along the boardwalk, when he was stricken by his prophetic wave.

First, they were just walking, hand in hand; then, sitting close to each other, and nothing more.

That there were two different predictions, made so close to each other in time, could not be reconciled.

First, just walking. Hand in hand. Holding each other.

Then, the second time, sitting close together. Holding each other.

The second time.

The second time his arms were placed around her waist.

She rose from the desk and circled around the room. She passed the closet, her reflection gliding over the glass of the mirror. She stopped.

Why…

Why would that make a…

Unless…

No. He didn't know. He couldn't *possibly* know.

Her breath caught in her throat and she could feel her heart pounding against her ribcage. Her thoughts raged, her vision blurred. She felt like she was going to…

A knock at the door; two clicks of the brass knocker she had installed herself, mainly for decorative purposes.

Visitors normally announced themselves using the intercom system downstairs. Her apartment had an electric buzzer located to the right of the front door.

Everyone used the buzzer.

Richard had keys to both entrances and would let himself in on the rare occasions he stopped by. But she always knew when he was coming.

Curious.

Probably Richard.

"Yell-oh," she proclaimed loudly.

Silence.

Curiouser and curiouser.

In six steps she was at the door. Her right hand sought the doorknob as she screwed her right eye into the door's small circular viewfinder.

She heard a subtle *click* from the window sill. She stepped back from the door and looked in the direction of the sound. The second hand of her Nona's clock had ceased its circular journey.

Kara cocked her head uncharacteristically, as if she was confused, like a German shepherd that doesn't understand the command of its mistress.

One more knock at the door, from the knocker again, only this time louder. She jumped without knowing why.

She shook her head dismissively and peered into the peephole.

What she saw was a strange, yet familiar face, but one whose strangeness was not altered by its familiarity.

The face smiled. The visitor could not see her, but Kara reflexively returned the smile.

The goldfish broke the surface of the water with a splash as Kara opened the door.

Tuesday

…At the heart of prophecy
you find your own.

M. John Harrison

XXI

I was sitting down to speak with my father when a phone rang in my dream and I woke up. I fixed a bleary, one-eyed stare on the real, honest-to-goodness-in-this-dimension phone on the cocktail table, just visible through the sliver of open curtain that separated the living room from my bedroom.

I waited, but was greeted only by perfect silence.

Every part of my body hurt. I turned to the right side of the bed; Kara was absent. I sat up and sighed, then walked slowly into the living room. I picked up the phone and the number came easily, trickling gently from my brain to my arm, then to my fingers. Her phone rang, but she didn't answer. The voice mail didn't pick up either.

Strange. But she was at work, of course. Where I should be right now.

I returned to my bedroom, lay down and closed my eyes.

No prophetic current tugged at me, no otherworldly transient descended to tap me on the shoulder or whisper in my ear. Nevertheless, I sat up abruptly.

The left door of the armoire facing my bed was wide open. On the inside of the door was a small calendar hung at eye level. Each month of the calendar featured the picture of a puppy. A German shepherd pup with its water bowl balanced comically on its head was this month's featured star.

It was the 23rd of the month.

For many years, I circled this date on many calendars. Today was not circled on this one, but this was of little consequence, as I cannot forget the day my father died.

Richard Goodman, Sr. chose to end his life by hanging himself with an electrical cord suspended in his bedroom closet. The cord had been scavenged from a table lamp I bought him as a birthday present; a heavy, bulky, antique-looking metal and glass thing; a blue and bronze colored, iridescent glass fish resting on its chin, mouth wide open, with the apparatus for the light bulb arching from its uplifted caudal fin.

It was strange, to be sure, unusual, even unique. But it was his taste, I imagined; hell, I thought he would like it. That he used a piece of it to murder himself I never took personally. Maybe it was because I thought that, in his own way, he was trying to say something to me. Not a bad something; not a sinister message of any kind. It was like a nod of his head, an acknowledgment that he shared a connection with me.

I don't think this conclusion so strange. That he would have said anything at all to me of any substance, any time, after a certain point in his life would have been special. That he chose the instrument of his death as a small means by which to communicate was better than nothing. He must have tried other ways to do so over the years, but I don't remember too many attempts. I never gave him many opportunities in the first place.

It was hard for him to express himself to others. When he did speak to me – I mean *really* speak to me – well, I just wasn't listening.

As much as I really did care for him, maybe I wasn't interested in what he had to say. I was always so selfish and self-consumed by my projects and problems. Maybe I just thought we were communicating in other ways, easier ways, ways that didn't require words. Maybe I thought everything important had already been said, or didn't need to be.

I just don't know.

Anyway, by the way, Dad was a meticulous carpenter and a gifted woodworker, possessed with a natural talent that provided him significant joy throughout his life and that often produced remarkable results. We used to say, my brother and I, that he could build a Boeing 747 with a stone knife and three scraps of wood.

He used this skill to fabricate the means of his demise,

securing a decorative oak support he had constructed with some care, directly into two wall studs so that it would sustain his weight. He hung the support a mere five feet off the floor; he did not avail himself of the traditional step stool or chair as a launching point. I imagine that in his condition he didn't trust himself to climb furniture. It had been necessary for him to bend his knees throughout the process in order to complete the job.

I try not to dwell on the perfect horror of this. I try not to imagine the suffering he endured in the exquisite silence and loneliness of his last moments on this earth, nor to speculate as to what thoughts, if any, raced through his dying brain, or even why he had done himself exactly as he had. I do sometimes marvel at the discipline that was required for him to accomplish the task.

There was no question he had been highly motivated. I have neglected to mention that he had been diagnosed with terminal cancer. He sought medical care infrequently and he was too far gone at the time of his diagnosis for any effective treatment to be rendered. My sense is that he knew he was sick long before this, and finally went to the doctor out of curiosity alone, merely to confirm what he already knew.

It was true he hadn't been feeling well for a while. He seemed to have lost a few pounds, and he looked more tired than usual, but other than that he didn't appear to be suffering any overt symptoms of disease. He called me one day and asked me to come with him to the doctor's office. That was unusual; hell, that he had called me in the first place was a downright phenomenon.

I thought he just wanted to hang out, I guess. But the Wave blew formless whispers into my ear from the moment I picked up the receiver that day.

I guess I wasn't listening even to myself.

To my surprise, the trip was to a specialist and not his regular doctor. To my further surprise I learned he had been to this specialist on several recent occasions.

He was escorted into the physician's office, not his examination room. No nurse or attendant hesitated as I accompanied him.

My father looked up and smiled gently as the physician entered his office, closing the door quietly behind him. I looked from the doctor, to my father, and back to the doctor again. The doctor's demeanor said it all. So did Dad's. Apparently, I was the only one who was going to be surprised.

So much for super powers. No supernatural deity waltzed out of any parallel dimension that day to tap me on the shoulder and kindly tip me off to what was going to be the biggest shock of my life *and by the fucking way have you brought your valium with you today Ricky-Boy?*

In essence, Dad was given two choices: First, he could writhe in agony for weeks or even months, wasting away gradually until he died, and as a bonus

…well, Phyllis, you can take that six month supply of toaster-pops home with you today as a bonus, or you can show this studio audience what heavy balls you really have and trade for that black box filled with lingering horror and death just behind curtain number...

and as a bonus he could slowly crush the souls and sensibilities of those friends and relatives as could be convinced to witness his end, all of us victims of a pious society so civilized that it will mercifully avoid a dying animal's suffering with a momentary injection but insist that another animal, blessed with a brain slightly larger and the ability to perfectly comprehend his demise in advance, bear personal witness to his own agonizing end as the purported condition of his birthright.

His second choice was to dope himself up until he became a vegetable. Little pain would accompany this alternative; except at the very end, of course.

Then, God, or the Devil, or Death or the World, or the Truth or the Random, or Krishna or Gaia, or whatever the fuck it is that is responsible for all this shit in the first place would make itself known in such a way as to open his eyes so fucking wide that he would have no choice but to see.

There would be no eloquent last words, no final goodbyes. And, following all of this, he would also be dead.

A red pepper, I believe it was. Or was it a fruit? Did they say he could be a fruit? Perhaps it was a banana. Dad always liked bananas. Consistent with his rather strange culinary tastes, he used to mix one inch pieces (*always* sliced with a plastic knife) into a green salad and combine that with Spanish rice. None of us knew precisely why he did this, except that this had been his favorite meal as a kid. I wondered who had thought up this kind of dish, just as I once wondered what thoughts went through the mind of the man who ate the very first squid.

Extreme hunger, and limited choice, I imagine. Extreme hunger for something drives us all. Limited choice just drives us harder.

Eventually, he decided he did not want to become any category of produce. The way he explained his view was that he was given a choice between dying as a human being and dying as something else, and had simply selected the former. To him, it was the only logical choice.

It didn't seem quite so logical after the excruciating misery of the first few weeks, as he lived with the practical results of his reasoning. So, always one to admit when he was wrong, Dad quickly altered his decision, availing himself of a third option the doctors had neglected to mention.

I visited him every day, at first, as he slowly passed; why, I'm not quite sure. Maybe there was something I wanted to say. Maybe there was something I needed to hear from him. But I never said much and never heard much of anything from him, except low groans accompanied by the soft rustling of bed sheets.

Even these wordless exchanges didn't last very long. One night, in the small hours of the morning, he simply left the hospital. That he was able to gather the strength to remove himself from his bed was remarkable. That he made it home unassisted and undetected was nothing short of magical.

There was a nurse's station on his floor. A security guard was posted at the elevator on the ground floor, and a manned receptionist's desk was situated just before the hospital's main entrance. He was haggard, terminally ill, and unimaginably weak, and for any exit he might have chosen he had to pass someone. He never bothered to dress in street clothes; I'm not sure he even had any in his room. It's not as if anyone ever expected him to leave that place. Except in a box.

Notwithstanding, he escaped from the facility unnoticed and traveled a mile to his house in his hospital bedclothes, which is how I found him in the closet.

Yes: how *I* found him.

Maybe it *was* magic. Dad always had a knack of making shit *happen,* you know? For a guy who was basically quiet, humble and unassuming, he had this way of forming ideas in his mind and then imagining them into existence. That was how he explained his success in the world. He said you had to imagine stuff in your head before you could make it real. He said that everything that we see, and hear, and do, and know, and touch, are just the end products of ideas that were in the mind of someone or something, somewhere at sometime. The universe itself, he believed, was nothing more than an idea conceived in the mind of a divine spirit, the ultimate consequence of a God's imagination. This was not an original precept, he was always careful to mention, but it was a true one.

Is it conceivable that he *wished* his way out of the hospital, then? Is it rational to believe that a dying, bedridden man might breach the confines of our physics using the force of his mind? And do what? Make himself invisible and walk on currents of air? Disassemble his molecules like some Star Trek character and beam himself into a clothes closet? And for what purpose? To murder himself?

I guess to believe all this you'd *have* to believe in magic.

I appeared at the family home in Westchester at 3:00 a.m. that morning, using my little-worn key to let myself in. That I already knew precisely where he was might appear to some as sorcery, too, particularly if they were to consider that I had to walk through Dad's spirit – posted like a guard dog outside of the closet – to retrieve his body.

He seemed to be trying to say something to me, but I walked right through him, just as if he wasn't there at all.

Hah hah.

I guess I wasn't listening to him even then.

In any event, to me, there was no real magic to any of it. That even an ordinary man can summon forces within himself that appear superhuman or other-worldly, I have come to believe. That there are spheres of existence other than this ball of dirt, water and rock we currently exist on has been made clear. That some of us decide to *come back* after we pass from this earthly domain, and somehow violate the inter-dimensional levies of whatever place we have been situated in, I understand. That there exist inexplicable forces in this world, most of them wholly beyond the ken of the common man, I get.

I, after all, am Richard Goodman. Without regard to my oh-so-human form, I am inimitable. Although I breathe, and feel, and cry, and bleed, nevertheless, in all of this world I am unique; the only one of my kind.

* * *

A little while later, without the benefit of breakfast or shower, Richard dragged himself out of the house and up the soft incline leading to the dorm. The electric doors swept open as his feet touched the rubber pad at the threshold.

As he passed the portal to the dorm rooms a flicker of

fluorescent light caused him to pause. He backed up three steps and looked to his right.

Nothing.

The gray tile floor was waxed and buffed. He smiled because he knew Ray took pride in these floors and kept them gleaming. The passage was completely silent. This was to be expected, as all the students in residence would properly be at their workstations by now.

He turned and walked down the dead-end corridor. That he did not know why he did was inconsequential, as he rarely questioned his own impulses. In any event, a short stroll to nowhere was preferable to going directly to work.

He traversed the corridor to its natural end and turned to face room number ten, Rena's room. That this simple act required him to turn his back to the door to Celia's room made him only slightly uneasy.

He grabbed the doorknob and froze. A sensation of hospital-like sterility passed through him. He turned the knob and entered.

There had never been very much by way of *stuff* in this room in the first place. It always reflected a kind of emptiness consistent with the disability and character of its occupant. Rena possessed few things that could fairly be said to reflect her personality. A small, oval, fuchsia-colored rug lay alongside her bed and a large black and white plastic clock sat on her night table.

As our senses are constrained by our genetics and our environment, our ability to perceive and understand the world is similarly restricted. We lose some of the capacity most of us have – and take for granted – to understand ourselves and everything around us.

Some find a way to use their physical limitations to expand their senses. Much as the hearing of a blind man may sharpen as a result of his sightlessness, some deaf people, wrapped in the perfect silence of their disability, begin to perceive another voice those who can hear cannot recognize. With the perceptual barrier of language and words removed and the clamor of the world silenced, some begin to perceive the *subtext* of our reality, a barely perceptible whisper, floating along that vague border separating the *now* from the edge of forever.

Some find truth balanced along that distant boundary. Others discover the wellsprings of personal power. Still others learn later, too much later, that darker waves surge along this subtextual periphery.

But for some, a lack of hearing produces a prison without bars, an invisible barrier they can neither articulate nor conceptualize and which separates them from everything and everyone. Their worlds are constrained by their senses, and they grow into an interrupted reality. Such was the case with Rena.

Her rug was still on the floor. But other than that, her room was completely empty. Her closet was empty; every drawer of her dresser was open and bare. Rena was gone.

Richard Goodman raised his head and sniffed the air, as if he could somehow pick up Rena's scent, but nothing – subtextual or otherwise – traveled along the still air of the dormitory room.

XXII

The streets of Pleasantside were too quiet. Bob didn't know why this was, but he knew that it was so.

It was Tuesday afternoon – four bells and all was well – school was out for the day and he sat in his wheelchair, on the street outside of the dormitory. It wasn't raining but the sky was dark. It was unseasonably cool and a small breeze lifted the hair falling across his brow.

It was only a harbinger of fall, he thought.

He had his gloves on, the easier to push his wheelchair with. The hard calluses on his hands made them largely unnecessary but since he didn't know where he might have to go today, he had brought them along. A strange thought, because he really didn't intend to go far at all. These days, he never did.

The several steps leading to the dormitory were before him. A ramp that led to the entrance to the dorm – the route he traveled – was to the right of the stairs.

He looked to his left. There were no people walking down the sidewalk, no cars traveling down this street. The cross street about five hundred yards ahead – Woodside Street – was usually a busy thoroughfare. Today he saw no cars, although he waited several moments to see if this was his imagination.

He looked to his right – the long way down 93rd Avenue – and saw a similar lack of activity. Time appeared to have ceased here. He looked up.

He saw the gray, two-story brick home that Ricky lived in, located immediately to the right of the dorm. A yard of sorts was in front of it – a postage stamp approximately one hundred feet square, fenced in on three sides. It was filled with tall weeds. Why didn't the fucker put some flowers in it or something? It was a silly question, because he knew why.

Between the two brick structures before him was a space

approximately twenty feet wide, running the length of the two buildings. He didn't know why this gap should exist, with real estate being as valuable as it was, but he guessed that this was not the case when the buildings were constructed a half century ago.

He stared at this empty space, not knowing why it captured his attention. He was confused, as if something important was there for him to see that he couldn't. A sharp breeze cut across the skin of his face; he felt

somewhat numb in his Air Force greens with three stripes on each shoulder, and three rows of medals on his chest, and looking upon that lot like it was some kind of

He shook his head violently as if to dispel a sinister voice whispering in his ear.

Yeah. The voice of his imagination.

Connecting the two buildings and permanently closing off this area from the street was a tall, iron fence. It was the old-fashioned kind, composed of thick vertical bars, with connecting rods near the bottom and at the top. It was nearly eight feet high, and each bar ended in an intimidating point. He was still young enough to remember a time when his legs worked – he could still recall climbing stuff as a boy – and he knew that a fence like this was nearly impossible to negotiate.

Its thick, black paint was worn and chipped in many places, exposing wide areas of orange rust that seemed to hint of the existence of an entirely different universe, slumbering just below the surface. This deterioration had done precious little over the years to weaken this formidable barrier. It was designed to endure, to permanently deter trespassers, and it continued to perform this function admirably. He wheeled closer for a look.

Mounted on the exterior brick wall of the dorm were three pairs of casement windows, spaced approximately fifteen feet apart from one another. Each pair belonged to a room in the dormitory facing this side of the building. Bob thought he could match up each resident to their windows if he needed to.

The dirt floor of the passage became higher as it moved deeper through the rubbish-filled alley and further from the street. A remarkable array of trash had accumulated there: Bottles – lots of bottles – with their labels worn off ages ago: beer cans, twigs, leaves, newspapers that had somehow survived the ravages of water and wind: pieces of cardboard boxes and bricks, partially exposed by soil that held them fast in place as if frozen in time, or as if captured while trying to escape from some subterranean dimension. He peered closer still.

There, a catheter bag. A used condom, there. A faded rubber ball; a tattered paper bag with half a can of *Schlitz* spilling out of it; the front page of a newspaper heralding a new NBA champion. He leaned forward in his chair until his forehead touched the metal bars.

Halfway up the alleyway he saw what looked like the remnants of a hundred Tootsie Roll pops, scattered in a group near the center of the space, lying in shadows and difficult to make out clearly. They looked like those little white sticks that were left when you finished the candy.

Just like the candy, but somehow, not.

He stared, transfixed, perplexed by this small mystery, one he would be unable to solve without getting closer. He considered what to do.

Our destiny is made of nothing more than narrow trails that linger before our every step. We do not create these pathways; they already exist as the *maybes* of our existence. Their importance cannot be measured by their size and their potential impact upon us can only be determined long after the first stride upon them has been taken. These pathways are events that alter all subsequent events; moments that change the very nature of eternity. The initial effect can be as subtle as a baby's breath, nothing more than an imperceivable click initiating a circular revolution, the beginning of a deviation in time itself that, when completed, will constitute what *was*.

And how is it that we choose any particular path? Is it our free will that makes it so? Or are we compelled by something deep within ourselves, an ancient force of which we are unaware; the strictures of an abandoned gene pathway perhaps, or the effects of trace chemicals in our blood stream?

All of these questions seek the same answer. There is just one query, really, and it is the greatest question of all. Greater than the question of whether there is a God, or life on Mars, or whether Santa Claus is real, or why the sky is blue, or which came first, the chicken or the egg, or where Judge Crater, Amelia Earhart and Jimmy Hoffa now reside. It is this:

Why do we do what we do?

Bob retreated from the iron fence and proceeded to his right, down 93rd Avenue. There was a decline to the street and he moved swiftly, rolling, more than pushing the chair along.

He passed a few row houses like Rick's and then came to the open air parking lot that the staff and faculty used. His old Ford was parked there now. Ricky locked the lot up each evening but the local kids liked to play ball there, particularly because it boasted two large, halogen lights that bathed it in a bright glow all night long. They had sliced an opening in the far corner of the wire fence that surrounded the lot, to ensure their easy access at any time. It was repaired frequently but each cure was only temporary, and did little to stop the bolt cutters apparently employed to re-establish the opening after each fix.

Pretty soon, this makeshift entranceway had become tolerated as just another doorway. It was at the top of a dirt incline of about four feet, that rose from street level. For a seventeen-year-old boy – even one with a glove, bat and ball in his hand – this span was just a hop, skip and a jump. For him, it was a nearly impossible ascent.

He didn't know if there was another way to access the alley from the rear, but he didn't want to arouse any attention searching for one. A trek across the parking lot would allow him access to the 92nd Avenue side of the school, near the main entrance. Although the south side of the main classroom faced the lot, the huge windows there were all located on the second level of the classroom, where Ricky's office was, and well above eye-level. Only Ricky might notice his furtive roll across the lot.

He checked his solid gold Bulova Accutron watch – the one with the tuning fork movement – and glanced in the direction of his friend's office.

Nothing… but that was not a surprise.

Ricky was somewhat slight of frame but fully capable of performing tasks requiring significant physical strength. He lugged around wheelchairs and their partially functioning human occupants on a daily basis. On more than one occasion he had dragged fully inebriated, partially functioning men and women in and out of them. He was often called upon to be an unwilling referee in the surprisingly frequent, and less-than-friendly, disabled tag team wrestling and boxing matches that spontaneously erupted in the dormitory from time to time. He could be both industrious and diligent and he was more than willing to perform tasks that required considerable spiritual fortitude and mental resilience: such as counseling suicidal paraplegic men at three o'clock in the morning.

However, "burning the midnight oil" was a phrase completely lacking from his lexicon. Ricky, in his own words, did not 'do' long hours in the office and could be depended upon to be absent from his desk any time after 4:00 p.m. each day.

Bob gripped the wheels of his sports wheelchair tightly. It was much lighter than the typical chair and narrower; its wheels angled outward, affording the user greater mobility, speed, and maneuverability.

He leaned forward in the chair with his head down. He had done a little racing himself before his body got as bad as it was now and he knew the drill. He pushed hard and ascended one foot up the short hill. Immediately, his wheels began to retreat, seeking gravity, and he swiftly slid his gloved hands backward along the circular chrome rails that attached to each wheel and held on. The chair stopped, but the price to pay was an intense strain to his upper body. He slowly pushed-pulled the rails counter-clockwise and the chair moved as he did, just a few inches this time. He blew out a sharp breath, chuckling darkly at his physical weakness. Six strenuous push-pulls later, he reached the opening and grabbed an exposed end of the fence with one hand. The chair slid backward but he kept his grip on the fence and with one hand pulled himself and the chair up and through the opening.

The firm, level surface of the lot's paving was welcome but he was gasping air hard and his chest hurt. It took him ten minutes to catch his breath, but he resumed his journey to the opposite end of the lot that led out to 92nd Avenue. Just before the entrance, he made a quick left turn along a narrow grassy trail that paralleled the lot.

Among the many amenities available to the students was a regulation size, indoor basketball court. The school had a renowned wheelchair basketball team – arguably the first of its kind in the nation – and the court was housed in a separate building, right next door. The structure contained an underground passageway that connected to the dining and conference area at the lower level of the school.

The trail cut between the parking lot on the left and the sports complex on the right. This building also had windows, but like those in the main classroom, they were designed to provide light, not views and were situated on high, out of the vision of anyone inside. Fairly invisible, his trek along the path was unobserved.

The trail led to the end of the lot and then along the rear brick exteriors of the houses Bob had passed. It seemed to terminate in a dead end, which appeared to be the brick face of the dormitory itself.

As he continued to push, he realized his arms were aching. His fingers were stiff underneath his leather lined sports gloves, the kind with the sticky surfaces that receivers in professional football used.

He had obtained this pair from Dean Spencer a while back. He chuckled.

A tight end from the New York Jets had placed his signature in ink on the right-hand glove. Now, just a faded patch of blue remained on the top of his hand. Bob didn't follow football, didn't give a shit who had signed it and he accepted the gift only because he needed a pair at the time. They had been Spencer's way of saying that there were no hard feelings between them.

There were no hard feelings. Fuck you, Dean.

He laughed out loud and stopped as he reached the exterior wall of the dormitory. The alley – just a moment before hidden from his view – loomed in the shadows to his left. An iron fence, as seemingly impassable as the one at street level, rose from those shadows to bar his entrance.

He was on higher ground on this side and the dirt beneath the fence had eroded considerably. Rainwater had inexorably washed it away over the years, carving a broad trench a foot deep and three feet wide underneath. He also noticed that each picket of the fence began and ended in a wicked point, one reaching to the sky, the other plunging towards the earth.

Beyond the fence, on the right, were the windows of the dormitory rooms facing this side – they had an idyllic view of the brick wall that was part of Ricky's residence. From this vantage point he could see the small grouping of white Tootsie-sticks, but no clearer now, halfway down the alley, than they were halfway up.

Just like the candy, but somehow, not.

"Why do I care?" he thought to himself.

He shook the thought from his head. He didn't know why he did this, but he was conscious that he had.

The formidable barrier facing him prevented a closer inspection. He looked again at the intimidating, downward pointing spires of the fence and the rain-sloshed dirt underneath.

"About a foot clearance between the two, maybe less," he mused to himself. He looked around; he was still alone, and it seemed preternaturally quiet.

He wheeled down the incline to the fence until his wheels touched the cold iron. He stiffened both arms and prepared to leave.

This was going to be dirty. Dirty and stupid and pointless. He would be covered in mud by the time he returned from this quest. The mud would be transferred from his clothes to his wheelchair, to his car, and his wife would be the one to clean it up. His stupid crap creating work for her, like always.

He assumed he would have no trouble returning to his chair; but everyone knows what happens when you assume – you make an ASS out of U and ME.

He moved himself to the very edge of the chair and it began to tip slightly. As it did, he grabbed an iron picket securely and slowly lowered himself off the chair and to the ground. He pushed the chair away a bit and positioned his dead legs straight out in front of him, pushing them each to their place a few inches under the fence.

Look how easy.

He grabbed the fence with both hands and pulled and his legs slid further underneath, further, until the points of the fence moved dangerously close to, what at one time, had been the most treasured part of his anatomy. These days, of course, it was an entirely superfluous part, but the effect was jarring nevertheless. Old habits, he thought, died hard, and he snickered to himself darkly.

He began to slide himself under the barrier. He was surprised by a wet, cold sensation; he was never quite sure how much feeling remained below his waist. His lower half was generally uncooperative in this venture and seemed to stall with every piece of debris that lay in its way. But in a few moments most of his body was through and the iron tips of the fence remained just a few inches above his neck. He realized it would be necessary to push his head into the mud, in order to maintain an acceptably safe distance between the fence and his eyes. These still operated admirably and he very much wished to keep them intact.

When the points of the fence met his vision, he stopped and considered those several inches separating his eyeballs from oblivion.

This was like an Edgar Allan Poe movie he saw once. What was the name of it? With Vincent Price or someone like that. Some device was moving back and forth across a guy tied down to a table.

He felt like having a cigarette. Yeah; a cigarette. He could smoke a cigarette while he stared at this pointed piece of rusted fucking metal hanging over his eye. Great idea, Bob; fine thought.

Better to keep moving. Yeah. Better.

He tried to slide further underneath, but he couldn't.

Strange. Strange brew. What you gonna do? Doors' song. Or was it Vanilla Fudge? Funny he should think of it. Like the Poe movie.

The Pit and the Pendulum. THE PIT AND THE PENDULUM. That was the name of the movie.

He chuckled again. Now; what the fuck was he doing here again? Oh yeah, that's right; Crawling around in a muddy alleyway, risking his eyesight.

That's the ticket.

Whose line was that? Jim Carrey. JIM CARREY. Crazy mother-fucker. Hey, he was getting good at this. No doubt, he was a witty man.

But now, on with the show.

He arched his back a bit and slid and pushed. And went nowhere.

This is fucking stupid. FUCKING STUPID.

Let me concentrate. CONCENTRATE.

He closed his eyes. He was concentrating (*CONCENTRATE*).

There were numerous parts of him that didn't work too well; more precisely, they worked day to day and from time to time, just like migrant farm workers. He was like an employment agency offering part time jobs to arms, limbs, and organs and every other component of his once reliable human form. His body parts were now just day laborers, working when they could, and rarely all at the same time.

Now concentrate…

…screamed and pressed the trigger for about a second

WHAT THE FUCK.

He jerked his eyes open.

The points of two iron spikes were touching his eyes.

TOUCHING HIS FUCKING EYES.

Something laughed. He gasped.

Now the rusted points hovered several inches above his head.

WHAT THE FUCK?

His heart pounded audibly with dull rapid thuds. He closed his eyes tightly and hugged himself while his fists clenched into tight balls across his chest.

Fear. This was fear. He was afraid. AFRAID. Shit, he hadn't been afraid since

"Always make sure the ball passes right by your ear as you throw," his dad used to say

since

abruptly jerking the weapon horizontally about a foot, from left to right just as

just as

just as the bomb was raised

the mother

The mother caught two in the throat.

The baby

came clean off and tumbled high into the air

In the air

Corpses

The mangled bodies of my friends hanging in the air…

high in the air

But in another place… at another time…

…the mother fell away.

The fucking baby

They gave you a medal for that.

They gave me a medal. I killed a fucking baby, and I took a medal for it. I took it and I flushed it

But you took it.

But I took it…Yes, God help me, I took it.

When he finally opened his eyes his face was wet with tears. It was darker outside and colder. The dim light of the setting sun did not reach this part of the alley. Encroaching shadows enveloped him and seemed to press against his flesh, groping at him, pulling at him like something from

Like something from

Demons

Jesus. JESUS CHRIST.

JESUS CHRIST ALL MIGHTY.

XXIII

I left work at 4:00 p.m. and went to the pet store. No one looked up from the main classroom as I walked quietly down the stairs from my lofty perch, slid past the nurse's office, through the dining room and connecting hallway, past the pool building, and out the double doors opening up to 93rd Avenue. I made a right on 93rd, then a left and a quick right, and wound up under *the El;* the elevated train leading directly into the heart of Manhattan Island. I walked east, away from the City.

There was only one pet store in the neighborhood and it was three blocks away from the school. A few blocks past the store there was a Columbian butcher, where you could buy any number of live fowl for purposes of consumption but other than that, it was the only place where quantities of live animals could be easily procured.

Including dogs. I loved dogs, but hadn't owned a pet of any kind for years, at least not since Ludlow.

A Greyhound-Great Dane mix, with a dash of shepherd somewhere along his line, I found him starving to death at a train station in Westchester County, the suburb just north of New York City. The stop was called Ludlow Station. He was 125 pounds once I fattened him up, fast as the wind, loyal and intelligent. He was also remarkably empathetic. Whether this latter quality was a function of my abilities or his or both of ours together, was always unclear.

Crystal clear was the fact that when the dead came to me, Ludlow saw them too.

A picture of him playing in the leaves on a fall day, so many years ago, hangs in the anteroom to my bedroom. He passed away, on a similar autumn afternoon, years later. At the relatively ripe age of twelve, no longer able to walk or to eat, he found himself in a veterinarian's office at the wrong end of a hypodermic needle. I cooed to him and stroked him gently. My body filled his vision; my eyes were the last he saw.

As I watched him gradually fade away, I was conscious of a large clock hanging high on the wall behind him. It had a sweeping, black, second hand that moved silently across its white dial. I imagined for a moment that I could muster the will, and concentrate hard enough to slow down that second hand. I imagined that I could reach deep into whatever psychic reserve an angry God had bestowed upon me and use that power to slow that second hand down to a trickle, and then, stop it altogether, stop it cold, and in that instant seize it, seize *It*, seize Time itself in that crystal clear moment where the Will and the World meet, where Moment and Eternity collide, and compel it to surrender itself and give my dog back to me.

But time did not slow; it did not slow a single millisecond. It marched right on and took my dog with it, right before my tear filled eyes.

Of all the eyes I have gazed into, both those living and dead, his are the only ones I can really remember, the only ones that come back to me in those rare moments of joy, or in those all too common moments of sadness and regret; deep, dark brown eyes containing indescribable warmth and love, and a hint of the depth of the spirit within.

The pet store operated out of a narrow storefront in a commercial area, located under the elevated train that cut the borough of Queens neatly in half on its way to and from Manhattan. Only a garish, orange sign taped to the inside window of the establishment promising a "Fish Bonanza!" hinted at what might be found inside. I opened the door and a large bell affixed to the inside frame loudly announced my presence.

A huge red and white goldfish with a genetically swollen body, located in a 25 gallon aquarium facing the entrance, broke the surface of the water as I entered.

A small pen was set up on the floor in front of the fish tank but nothing was in it. A nineteen-year-old girl with a gold stud in her nose and a black *Metallica* T-shirt manned a counter on my left. Two wires led from the front pocket of her jeans into small pods placed in her ears. They screamed something into her brain and she nodded her head in rhythmic agreement.

"Hi," she said, still bobbing with eyes closed.

"Hi."

I waited fruitlessly for her full attention and then pointed to the empty enclosure, knowing full well she could not see me do so.

"What did you have in there?"

"Litter of lab pups. Cute. Only had 'em three days."

Obviously, a remarkably perceptive young woman.

"What happened?"

"Customer bought 'em all up.

"Recently?"

"Day or so ago."

She didn't mind answering questions either.

"Can you tell me who the customer was?"

"Carly was at the register. I was stocking the shelves." She jerked her head sharply to the left and squeezed off a stinging riff on the imaginary guitar that formed in her hands.

"Is Carly here today?"

"Naah. Quit last week."

"Do you think she might have kept any records of the sale?"

"Naah; paid cash, and didn't want the papers on the pups. Just put 'em in a shopping cart with the mice and wheeled them away."

"The mice?"

"Yeah; white ones, with the red eyes, you know? Took all we had of those, about two dozen of 'em. Creepy looking if you ask me."

"The customer?"

"The mice."

"The mice were in the shopping cart?"

"The mice were in a box."

"...and the box...?"

"...in the shopping cart with the puppies. But listen to this... I start walking up to the front, and I hear Carly say 'honey, this is New York, take a walk in the park if you want squirrels.' Squirrels! Can you imagine? Who the hell wants squirrels? I mean that's *whack*; what do you do with pups and red-eyed mice and squirrels anyhow? Put on some kinda Coney Island sideshow?"

I turned and looked again at the empty cages. I wondered whether the prisoners formerly contained there had been pardoned, or otherwise freed by virtue of their summary execution.

"Do you know what he looked like?"

"Blonde, I think; tall, older than me."

I paused to consider the combined wisdom of Bobbie Meyer and Sir Arthur Conan Doyle, as well as my own, oh-so-wise proscription: never overlook the obvious.

"Was the customer a guy or a gal?"

The teenager reached into her pocket and with a black-tipped nail pressed a tab on her I-whatever. She opened her eyes and looked at me for the first time. A blank look accompanied the somewhat dark effect of her *totally*-goth eye shadow, much like any teenage girl would look, I suppose, temporarily removed from her digital universe. She cocked her head in a quizzical fashion.

"That's funny," she said. "I didn't notice."

XXIV

This one doesn't scream.

Much.

No. Not very much at all.

He doesn't like the screaming part.

When *he* works, he doesn't like *any* kind of noise. Whenever he hears noise, he just wants to silence it.

So he usually does.

That part he *does* like.

She's quiet now. Quiet.

Quiet is good. She should probably stay quiet. If she doesn't stay quiet, *she* will probably be silenced.

But she bleeds. She bleeds a lot. A large round pool of the stuff has collected underneath her feet.

The dark circle of red seems so perfect he doesn't even want to touch it.

At first.

OK, so he touches it. Wet. It's wet!

Of course it's wet. And warm, too.

Of course it is. Stupid. It doesn't have fur, but it's still alive.

Stupid.

Even though there's a lot of it, it's hard to get any in this small, plastic water bottle. It takes time. It requires patience.

He has a lot of patience. *Yessiree.* Working with time has *made* him patient. In fact, he's learned that the more patient you are, the more time you seem to have.

Funny.

He has noticed that sometimes, as he gets deeper and deeper into the work, as the seconds begin to drag, as he concentrates, time seems to slow down to a trickle. It's almost as if he can grab it – grab it and play with it in his hands – toss it in the air, spin it around, slow it down then speed it up – and get it to do what he likes.

Yes… Slowing down time.

That's the ticket.

If he *could* slow down time and make it do what he wanted it to do, couldn't he make everything else *in time* do the same? If he concentrated, really concentrated, couldn't he slow down *people* too? Then, once time had stopped and once everything and everyone had stopped along with it; then, if he wanted to, if he *really* wanted to, couldn't he just reach out and *take* someone's *time*?

There. He screwed on the bottle's plastic cap.

He stood up, satisfied. Nothing quite like a souvenir.

He loved souvenirs. Daddy used to get him souvenirs at the county fair.

How he loved the county fair.

How he loved those souvenirs.

He admitted to himself that it would please him greatly to have a whole collection of souvenirs again. But he got in a lot of trouble for that once. He sighed and quickly dismissed the thought from his head.

One must show restraint. Restraint and discipline. In the exercise of this discipline, he has limited himself to the aggregation of liquor in this one vessel. It is, after all, acceptable to reward oneself after a hard day's activities.

How he loved his Daddy.

Poor Daddy.

He made so much noise.

XXV

Bobbie didn't remember how long he had been unconscious. He lay still. The sounds of the city slowly folded in around him, muted only by the brick boundaries of his surroundings. He assumed he could still move.

It was night and a small portion of the moon was visible from his limited vantage – flat on his fucking back in a muddy alleyway – but he could see that it was full. Its wide beams thrust through the evening clouds and splayed its bitter light across the brick of the dormitory wall.

"Fucking with my head. Someone or something is fucking with my head."

"Someone. Or something. Fucking with my..."

The moon; the great timekeeper. Towering, eternal and ever present. A ball of rock revolving around the earth with perfect precision, generating a flawless rhythm with which a man could synchronize his very heartbeat. Or, in his case, measure each and every last pathetic moment of his existence.

Time. A higher power. Perfection-imperfection.

The watchmaker.

His upper body felt as dead as a corpse. His lower half, well, was.

He raised his head with some effort, looking past his prone body and to the dirt and debris of the passage as it declined toward the iron fence bordering the sidewalk. To his right, the windows stood against the dorm's outer shell like sentries.

A brief flicker of light to his left caught his eye. Turning, he saw only the brick of Ricky's house: but then, a low, narrow window, partially submerged under the enduring dirt and debris of the alley.

He hadn't noticed the window.

XXVI

Sometimes he feels sad when he thinks about Daddy.

That's OK.

It's OK to feel sad sometimes. Everyone does. Really.

It's important to be candid and straightforward with yourself, too, and honestly confront your feelings. This is a healthy attribute. It is the key to proper functioning. So many people have told him this is so.

You just can't let feelings get the better of you.

That would be a mistake.

Daddy was oh-so-important in his life. In fact, Daddy made him just what he is today. That's not strange, is it? A son comes from his father, after all, and stays a part of him forever. Just like two people in one body.

Two people in one. Like They are.

He thinks he feels a breeze behind him. He panics momentarily without knowing why and jerks his head around to nothing. All he sees is the narrow doorway behind him.

Through this door is a large open space with a low ceiling. It is divided by a rickety staircase that leads upstairs. The perimeter of this room is lined with old, moldy boxes. A single light bulb hangs from a wire in the center of the ceiling. The light is always off.

A whole lot of work is in here now.

There are other things here, as well. Things that he can't see; things that he can only *feel*. These feelings might be due to his over active imagination.

But he doesn't think so. Because he *hears* them, too. They murmur to him in voices that he can hear, but that are not quite loud enough to fully understand. *Oh-so-many* voices.

These are *not* the voices he *used* to hear. *Those* voices weren't real. No. *He* put those voices into his brain.

Whatever things are behind *these* voices, he is certain that no one *put* them there. They *came,* all by themselves. They just don't seem to be able to leave. Someone is *compelling* them to remain within this enclosure. What's more, the person who is accomplishing this feat is unaware that he is doing so.

He doesn't know why this is, or how he knows these things, he just does.

Funny.

Whatever these *things* may be, they don't bother with him. In fact, he gets the distinct impression that they enjoy his presence very much. They also seem to enjoy his work, which is really quite gratifying, even if they don't articulate their approval as clearly as he might like.

He has felt them watching him closely over the past two days. He swears he feels them smiling. *Smiling.*

Which is fine.

He's been smiling, too.

What's also funny is that sometimes he feels that they are his audience: like a crowd at a baseball game. At other times, he feels that he is their beast of burden – a horse, a donkey, something like that – and that they are his pale riders, driving him hard down a predetermined path.

No matter.

In a corner of the outer wall he faces is a narrow window. Looking up and out the window he can see a brick wall painted blood red by the light of the moon rising above it. A slender finger of moonlight pierces through the glass and crosses his path; a narrow slice of it cuts across his blood soaked right hand and the silver and turquoise bracelet he wears there.

The elements comprising this piece of jewelry were ripped from the bosom of the earth for his use. They were molded, cut, shaped and beaten; veritably *compelled* by his hands into their current form. The Will and the World now converge in this talisman, and he glows with the power of both. He has become the point where the earth meets the sky. The very heavens themselves descend to touch him.

And to guide him, too, he thinks.

He rises from his knees and enters the doorway. He watches as the moon glow travels slowly from his wrists, to his arms, to his chest, to his face. He closes his eyes as the light splashes across him. He smiles, mingling his thoughts with the moonbeam. He feels the power of the ancient sphere soaking through his skin, into his body.

He wonders if the moon can feel his power, too.

* * *

For a single moment, she is conscious, and aware; but her captor is not aware that she is. One of her closed eyes opens slightly; but he does not see.

The outline of his form is before her; he appears as shadow, as wraith. His right hand is outstretched, as if he is asking for something. Or receiving something.

Past his silhouette she sees light, a light from outside, penetrating the horror of this place. For a single instant it meets her gaze.

It is here to guide her, she thinks.

And then it is gone, along with everything else.

XXVII

Most of all, their dreams are filled with blood.

Blood pouring from the pale white throats of hysterical victims, their eyes plastered open with horror, their desperate shrieks brutally cut off by the act of their dying amid the excited wailing of their murderers in the act of their passion.

Yes.

They are asleep, but not asleep. Unconscious but aware all at the same time. They have thrust aside, by the force of their will alone, the nearly impenetrable veil that separates this world from the next, the real from that thought of as unreal. Here, in this place, all that man knows, together with all that he may imagine, is rendered unnecessary and useless.

Here, there be demons.

They fly, sometimes. So many. The efforts of tar-black, hard, leathery wings strain noiselessly past their ears. A brief but sharp wind follows each pass, bringing with it the scents of putrescence and death.

Yes, yes.

They mingle with these minions. The creatures pose little threat to them, as they recognize who They are. They brush their own wings against the darkness. Their scent is as distinct as that of these entities; all are aware of their common allegiances.

They exist simultaneously in this place of power with the world They have left behind. Even now, even here, They are aware of the alley and the man in the alley, and the girl in the basement, and the man with the girl, and all the pieces They have set into motion on the chessboard upon which their body resides at this moment.

The very souls of these others float upon the hot breeze of this place, malleable and vulnerable, transparent to them in every way. From here, They can manipulate events over *there*, changing what people think, what they feel, and what they see.

And what they do.

Their enemy can accomplish similar feats. He is dangerous. Unbelievably dangerous. If They were capable of feeling fear, They might fear him.

But he is controlled by what exists here. He floats along like some twig on a putrid and winding current that carries him where it wishes. The power of this place is a predator that tosses his body in the air, crushes his mind and kneads his soul like clay. He fights mightily against this influence, but fruitlessly, thus far.

They wonder if he believes he can prevail.

The enemy does not realize that this reality is inextricably tied to his own perception. He appears unaware of the simple precept that he controls only what he believes he can. He controls nothing because he believes in nothing. He has isolated himself. He is alone, even here, in the vastness of *this* beyond, where no entity is truly capable of being alone.

They laugh together. *They* laugh because *They* will never be alone. Not now, not ever again.

One of the creatures flies close to them. Too close. A powerful claw rips a deep gouge across their right shoulder blade. The blood flows freely from the wound but They do not attempt to staunch the flow.

They are thrilled. *Thrilled*. Such contact is understandable, as these beings are drawn to them like moths to a flame.

Nevertheless, a display of power is necessary.

Thought is action, here.

A huge hand now exists. It extends from their center, powered by an arm: of sorts. It moves of its own volition and python-like seizes a demon and wraps itself around it. The creature is brought closer for an inspection. Only its head is visible, the rest of its monstrous form hidden in a coil of hairless pink flesh.

Its face, such that it is, is oval-shaped. Two tiny flat ears protrude ever so slightly from each side. They believe they see eyes – red-hot holes, really – but realize that everything else They see is moving, in flux, constantly adapting, becoming. It is changing into something else; into *everything* else. It is a liquid surface, but solid at any moment, a black, oozing mass, yearning, hungering, needing; spreading out now, disassembling itself, massive folds of corrupted, dripping tissue rising out of their grasp and above them, getting wider and wider, enfolding them, filling their vision, sucking them in, wanting and needing; overwhelming power, diabolical hunger, promising everything, and giving nothing at all.

It is silent. Not the slightest resonance, not the most trivial whisper issues from it.

It is singular. It is incapable of comprehension irrelevant to its immediate needs.

It is deliberate. It proceeds in a mechanized fashion. Yet no order or reason within the common man's mental or spiritual grasp attends its transformations.

It is self-contained. It acts out its desires in the exquisite isolation of its unambiguous compulsions.

It is perfect.

They see engorged, reddish veins pulse powerfully across the surface of the monster. They thrill at its might, at its magnificence. They throw their head back and close their eyes, allowing themselves to be seduced, consumed, and absorbed. But only for a moment.

And then…

Their coil tightens, folds and collapses with a shudder upon all that rested within it. It opens slowly, and all that remains is a sticky wet pitch, reminding all of what once lay within. The silence that follows is the unsounded respect voiced by those entities about them.

They are the Power. They are the Way. They control this Darkness and what lies within it. They are the Master of Demons, the Vision-Maker of this dominion.

They conduct their work on both planes of existence. In each They work as the watchmaker works, correcting a mechanism that is in most respects perfect, that in *all* respects *would* be perfect but for the failings of the craftsman, and the bits of dust and oil that mar the machine.

They restore order to the mechanism that is an imperfect world.

Of course, they labor on a slightly grander scale. And while They certainly can't do *everything,* They don't try to. They simply try to salvage those small bits of the world that come across their meager workbench each day.

They try not to be overly dramatic. But, after all, for those who reside in the temporal world, this *is* all rather dramatic. But more than that.

It is Armageddon.

XXVIII

Bobbie forced himself to his elbows.

What was he doing here again?

Oh, yeah.

He made sure his wheelchair was still there and then once more began to slide his body carefully down the length of the dirt passage. He hoped he would be made aware of any sharp objects his lower half came into contact with. He was already aware that what goes down must come back up and found no consolation in the fact that the return trip might be more arduous.

As he slowly pushed himself along the muck, the moon began to show itself fully from behind the clouds, illuminating the alley in a pale white light. Strange shadows rose from the dirt, trailing along the dorm's foundation and then mounting the walls confining this space, making them appear as if they were expanding on either side of him. All of the things embedded in the crust of the alley were visible now, all of them painted a watery white, all of them objects that had once touched human hands, and that, in this singular moment had found themselves here, a small universe captured in this place, containing

ghostly memories

carried upon the lips that had touched that cigarette, the eyes that had read that newspaper, the fingers that had held that bottle, rendered bloody by a

jagged piece of metal protruding from the dirt, like a demon trying to force its way from

Bobbie shifted his weight and jerked his head sharply, as if by doing so he might dispel the scattered thoughts buzzing there like so many insects. As he did, a needle-like object pierced his hand deeply. It hurt, of course, but he was so used to pain that he hardly reacted. Until he lifted his hand to see the white remains of a tootsie pop hanging there.

Like the candy, but not like the candy; it was thinner, bone like.

Because it *was* a bone that had pierced right through Dean Spencer's autographed gloves. He could hear him laughing

...fuck me, Bob? No, fuck you!

It was one of hundreds of bones he now saw all around him, hardly confined to that of any one species, but of several, lying in a semi-circular pattern around the particular pair of casement windows they rested beneath. He looked at the windows and then back at his hand, and then at the open graveyard surrounding him.

No. Not like the candy at all. Not with bits of pink flesh hanging from some, fur of multiple colors from others; skulls, too, some the size of his thumbnail, others much larger, but all of small animals rendered asunder, crushed and torn limb from limb.

He was in the heart of a small proving ground of perversion.

He focused on his hand again and held it up to the moonlight as a small drop of blood seeped from his glove and ran slowly down the length of the recent addition to his anatomy. There was a brief flash again in the corner of his vision.

He looked up and saw he was parallel to the low-lying window on the brick wall of Ricky's house. He crawled a few feet in that direction, ignoring the sickening crunching sounds that accompanied, until he came to a small rise, where he stretched and elevated his body as best he could, to get a better view.

As he looked down and through the murky glass he saw light again, only this time in the form of a dull, oval, glow that seemed to pierce the gloom within. He realized that what he was seeing was a face illuminated by the moon; a strange, yet familiar face, its strangeness not altered by its familiarity.

Time appeared to slow.

He realized the face was smiling.

The face could not see him, but Bob couldn't help but return the smile.

XXIX

He closes the door behind him.

He knows that the exterior surface of this exit blends perfectly with the surrounding wall of the outer room. It is positioned in the far corner of the room least touched by the meager luminescence there. There is no door handle or other visible hardware announcing its presence. When he closes the door, he makes himself invisible.

He walks past her and into the rear of his hideaway. It is set up like a dormitory room, really, only without windows of any kind. Cinder blocks rise on every side of him and there is a concrete slab above him. Quite unlike the basement of any other home on this block, this one was configured as a bomb shelter, originally intended for the exclusive use of the school's students, at a time when one kind of war was ending and a completely different kind beginning. In addition to being virtually impregnable, it has the secondary advantage of being soundproof.

There is a small closet, a dressing area, and a bathroom with a sink and shower. None of these have been used for a long, long, time.

Well, until recently.

There is a heavy steel door in the back that is the exterior entrance to this space. There is a huge padlock on the outside of the door. It is old, and worn, and came apart easily with a few well-placed blows of a hammer. Now it can be closed without really locking.

He removes his clothes, drops them on the floor and enters the shower.

He stands there naked but does not turn the water on. He has brought the bottle with him.

He pours a small amount of the red goo contained within into the palm of his right hand and stares at it. It collects there evenly, like a small pond, not unlike the pond underneath the girl, only in miniature. He slowly arches his hand straight into the air and the pond forms into a single, thin line that drips all the way down the furrow in the center of his palm, past his wrist, along his arm and to the inner crease of his elbow. He takes his index finger and traces the line, so that it becomes a red smear a half inch wide. He repeats this task with his other arm.

He then pours a somewhat larger amount into his right hand again, placing the open bottle on the small shelf on the tiled shower wall, usually reserved for shampoo and the like. He gently massages the liquid into both of his palms, being careful not to sacrifice a drop to the shower floor. He repeats this procedure until his hands are covered completely. Then, starting with his breasts, he slowly coats his chest and midsection, then the rest of his arms. He takes the remaining contents of the bottle and pours it over his head and face, methodically massaging it in as he does.

That heavenly smell; like candy apples. But not candy apples.

He looks into a small, oval mirror he has glued onto the tile wall at his eye level. The grime and dust that have accumulated on the tile for decades do not distract him in the least. This tiny glass gives a distorted view of his features but he approves of what he sees.

He opens his arms wide and looks upward, showing Them what he has accomplished. The perfect silence is their sanction, their voice of approval.

He knows that it is not wrong for him to appreciate the fruits his efforts have yielded. This is the essence of self-actualizing labor. But he also knows that it is not wise to stand around and simply admire what one has accomplished. After all, this is not about him or his ego.

He turns on the water. It makes a loud noise at first; ancient pipes rumble with the effort of what they are called upon to do.

Could this sound be audible from upstairs? He becomes

alarmed for some reason: then confused.

What is he doing here? How did he get here?

The water gurgles from deep within the pipes and empties slowly from the pock-marked showerhead, rust red with the blood of time.

Confused.

Yes. But only for a moment. He just needs to concentrate.

He is reminded of a small task he must complete upstairs.

No, I'm not deaf. Yes.

Fine. I will.

The water turns warm as he gazes into the looking glass before him.

Concentrate.

Red liquid seeps into his half-closed eyes, making them look like fiery hot holes in his head. The water continues to flow over him, but as he focuses it slows, he thinks.

Yes: slower. He continues to concentrate, crystallizing the moment, *grabbing* it out of its continuum.

The water is still wet, but it is suspended all about him now, in the form of droplets and paper thin sheets of crystal, frozen in place. In the mirror his skin appears to be moving, oozing, spreading out and contracting, disassembling itself and putting itself back together again; an undulating red mass in flux.

He is adapting, changing.

No. Not just *changing.*

He is Becoming.

He allows the water to flow again, a little faster, now.

The nail of his left pinky has been filed to a shallow but razor sharp point. He did this a long time ago; no one ever seemed to notice.

Funny. Sometimes even watchmakers, who dedicate each of their days to examining and scrutinizing the world through the eyepiece of their microscopes, don't see anything at all.

He takes his pinky and finds a spot on the top of his head,

three inches beyond his hairline. He presses hard and makes a fine, one-inch slash. He quickly looks into the mirror again and pouts, creating a furrow between his eyebrows. He waits for a thin line of red to run down the center of his forehead. He watches as a vertical crimson column fills the gully he has created.

His blood mingles with the blood of the victim. He allows their combined essence to fill his vision. He permits it to permeate his skin and then to enter his mind. And then, to enter everything else.

Yes.

They are together. They will be difficult to separate. The soft whispers that are her futile pleas surround him. But they touch his ears as only echoes. The voice she speaks with is his. Her spirit, once ageless and enduring, can find no refuge within the suffocating confines of his soul. He has taken her.

No.

It is her *time* that he has taken.

He watches as it slips through his fingers, down the length of his body, and into the drain of the shower beneath him.

The *Now* rushes in. The sound of water fills his ears. The looking glass tells him he is clean and fresh. The pinkish pond of water he stands in gradually clears. He steps from the shower and dries himself with the towel he has brought for this purpose.

He does not know why he has to move the girl from this comfortable place. He doesn't know why he must leave her so close by, nor why he must deposit her in plain view. They did not tell him why and he did not think to ask.

Even now, he doesn't ask.

His free will has been an unfortunate casualty of his recent associations. While he regrets that his destiny is no longer entirely in his hands, he imagines that his situation is little different from anyone else's. After all, how much of their lives does anyone really control, anyway?

He also knows that he is compelled to work in the shadows. He cannot show himself; his work cannot be revealed. While difficult, this is not impossible. But this also means he will not be fully appreciated.

He finds this troubling. It is not unreasonable for a man to expect that he will be recognized for his earnest efforts to please others. It is not irrational to hope that he might be singled out for conducting his business in such an immaculate manner. Further, to have pride in your work is a splendid attribute, a sign of a smoothly functioning human machine.

But humility is an admirable quality, too. We can't change the whole world, can we? No, of course not. There are many things we cannot control. In fact, the only things we *can* control are contained in those very tiny pieces of the world that cross our workbenches each day. The sensible thing to do is to simply concentrate on the task that is at hand.

He feels better now. He is proud of the fact that he is a prudent, practical individual. But he is more than that.

He is a realist.

After all, as the great Clint Eastwood once said, a man's got to know his limitations.

XXX

And now, the face was gone, disappeared into the blackness. Its form seemed imprinted on his mind like some kind of after-image, like the spots you might see before your eyes after staring at the sun too long.

He sat up, rubbed his eyes, and felt his forehead as if he were checking for a fever.

The moon vanished behind a cloud. The alley shrank into blackness, illuminated only by the indirect radiance of the nearby street lights, which suddenly extinguished, leaving only the hazy outline of the place in the sky where the moon had shone to light the world.

It became quiet. No breeze stirred the now blackened detritus of Bob's surroundings. Even the sounds that were always there – the dull hum of incessant traffic, the muted clicks of traffic lights changing colors, soft footsteps and the barking of dogs; the clanking of elevated trains moving residents from this outer borough to the heart of the greatest city on earth; the heated arguments between husbands and wives, and with their children, bellowed out in Spanish or Portuguese or Italian or Greek, or in English, flecked with accents too numerous and diverse to comprehend; the low, rapid breathing of lovers in the heat of their passion, contained within a few square yards of the boxes they called their homes, piled one on top of the other, like wire cages stacked on a rumbling flatbed, filled with chickens being led to slaughter; the wild laughter of inebriated patrons exiting local bars, the banging of corrugated aluminum cans against the iron of garbage trucks, the noise of television sets screaming the joy of reality show contestants and of boom boxes, forcing the vibrating protests of hip-hop into the streets: and of radios – old fashioned devices, now – but still employed by a generation frozen in time, spouting the moment by moment blissful heroics (or stunning failures) of the Yankees, or the Mets, or the Rangers, or the Knicks, all together constituting the necessary milieu of a city's life and blood – all of these things seemed to dull and lose their voices, as if this space was contained within a singular dome, silencing the outside world, preventing it from entering.

Or, perhaps, keeping everything inside it trapped within.

He looked up to a darkened firmament that now appeared as a black goo, a liquid surface oozing across a corrupt sky, in flux, *becoming*, alive, hungering and needing, as if it were capable of plucking him from the ground he rested upon and consuming him, sucking him into an unknowable dimension, empty of anything recognizable except…

…except, he thinks, for that object passing across the sky, floating closer to this world than to the heavens. He didn't know if he was seeing this object with his *eyes,* but he knew that it was *there*, in some way. But not *really* there.

Something. Perhaps only a vision impressed upon the landscape of his mind. Or a product of his cancer, or of stress, or a lack of sleep. Or arising from a guilty conscience that refused to be silenced and that wailed its passions against the barrier of his brain like a rubber ball thrown against a brick wall in a schoolyard.

But no explanation accompanied the specter of a long-dead child's head tumbling in the air before his eyes. Nor was there an explanation for his presence in this alleyway, or for the suffocating silence and darkness that surrounded him, or for the glowing visage of a blood covered maniac just a few feet from where he sat, in a place where he just could not be.

And something else. Yes. Still, there was something else. Behind *him*.

Something shuffled its feet. Anxiety rhythmically pawed at his throat like a syncopated melody, a chorus in perfect tune with the song of the leaves shifting nervously in the windless vacuum.

He reached for a rifle that was not there. He steadied a helmet he hadn't worn in three decades.

A higher power. An unseen foe.

There was something else behind that moon-addled countenance, visible only for the briefest of moments through the ancient grime of a darkened glass, an image obtained in a nanosecond of time, reduced to an indistinct shadow of a memory squashed into the attic of his mind… something else.

Someone else.

No.

Narrow paths linger before our every step: the maybes of our future, the what-ifs of our providence.

Bob's hands trembled as he reached for his cell phone, stored in a small black plastic pouch attached to his belt. The instrument told him he had missed six calls: Nae Tong; he hadn't called her.

A dull pain, a product of the spirit, not of the body, rose from the pit of his stomach to the center of his chest. He did not call her now but quickly composed a text message comprised of four letters.

"IM OK."

He sent the message and then dialed 911. The phone rang once, then again.

He abruptly terminated the call. He never thought to ask himself why.

And then:

An unperceivable click of a wheel; a circular revolution begins; a deviation initiates that, when completed, will constitute what *was*.

How is it that we choose any particular path? Is it our free will that makes it so? Or are we the unwitting tools of other forces of which we are only dimly aware?

A curious idea entered his head. That it was an idea not entirely his own did not seem to matter.

"I don' nee' no stinkin' police."

Bobbie smiled and returned the phone to his front pants pocket. He felt for the .38 strapped to his ankle.

"*I am* the fucking police."

For Ricky

Yeah. That's the ticket.

For Ricky.

XXXI

Dinner had sucked and his beer was lukewarm.

Lark Patina, the owner, manager and bartender of the Dory Inn with the movie star name, slowly wiped a completely clean glass with a towel and stared at Richard with a concerned expression.

He looked nothing at all like a matinee idol. A six foot tall, 285 pound former linebacker for the Boston University football team, he had curly, light-brown hair of an unusual hue that he either never combed, or that otherwise grew from his head in a pattern so haphazard as to give the impression that he was mad. It sprouted from his head like the leaves of a carrot top, spilling across his brow and hiding a series of ugly scars that ran high across his forehead, from his left eyebrow to just over his right eye.

His hands were huge and one could not help but think that their only purpose was to strangle someone. He could flash a look so terrifying as to root a person – whether straight or blind drunk – right to the spot like a sequoia. He looked fully prepared to murder you at the slightest provocation and then go on bar keeping as if nothing unusual had occurred.

Originally raised in a small town in the northwest corner of the State of Connecticut, he had a New England accent that made him sound somewhat provincial. His intellect was anything but. By the time he was twenty-four years old, he had acquired two degrees in psychology and a doctorate in philosophy. He had been the senior editor of the school's Daily Free Press for four years running, the captain of his defensive football squad and a straight A student.

He was an avid reader but he rarely studied. His riveting intellect and analytical mind were bolstered by a photographic memory. He remembered everything he read, heard, and saw. He used to say that when he slept, everything he experienced would simply go somewhere to be stored away until it was needed.

Exactly where all of this knowledge eventually wound up to be assimilated, analyzed and made sense of, he could not say and didn't seem to care. But wherever this *somewhere* was, he knew that his conscious mind had touched this place once, in the immediate aftermath of a terrifying accident involving his Harley Electra Glide, a tractor-trailer, and a mother and her four young children traveling in a 1986 Ford station wagon.

He was cruising north on the Taconic at 75 miles per, in the foothills of the Catskill Mountains in upstate New York. He had been riding for an hour but it was still early. The sun was just beginning to rise over the horizon; the air was crisp, and the 1600 cc's of the Electra Glide pulsed beneath him. The Ford appeared in the road before him as if by magic, just as he cleared a sharp turn in the road and ascended a rise on one of the parkway's most treacherous two-lane stretches.

Seeking to avoid a rapid deceleration, he elected to circumvent the double yellow line separating the north and southbound lanes and pass the wagon, which was doing 40 in the 50 mile an hour zone.

"No Passing," a sign had said.

It would only have taken a second or two.

He surged past the vehicle with ease and looked through its rear passenger window as he did. A girl, around nine, with hair as bright as the sun, smiled and waved.

He slowed, waved back and smiled, too.

This section of road had no breakdown lanes and no shoulders. Eighteen inches to the right of the white line demarcating the northbound lane was the stark boundary of a coal-black mountain wall. To the left was the southbound lane and from there an ancient three-foot high wooden guardrail separating the end of the road from the oblivion of a gorgeous valley 500 feet below. Black and white heifers grazed there peacefully in the shadow of a bright red wooden barn, resting on a small hill overlooking this idyllic scene, with the rich foliage of the surrounding mountains in the backdrop. Lark smiled again, the wind in his face, the exalted freedom of the moment overtaking his spirit along with his common sense.

His helmet was conveniently stored in the saddle bag of his bike.

The southbound trailer – a Western Star 4900 Semi, carrying a double load – was banned from the parkway, of course. He heard later, much later, that the inebriated driver was seeking the next exit. He never got there.

When Lark finally looked back to the road, he saw the trailer coming around the bend 100 yards ahead of him, in the lane he now occupied.

Well, the cab was, anyway. The rear bed of the trailer had toppled broadside onto the surface of the road, followed by the first bed an instant later. Together they formed a screeching "V" of 44,000 pounds of steel that filled the northbound lane entirely. There was no escape.

Everything seemed to slow. He seemed to have all the time he needed to observe, analyze and calculate. But the amazing mind he possessed was of little utility. Certain death was the option residing on his left, an impenetrable barrier was to his right, and braking was no option at all.

So he just acted. He sharply rotated the right grip on his bike that accelerated the machine. The engine roared, responding powerfully and predictably, propelling him in a straight line towards the only daylight available to him; a narrow slice of space between the end of the trailer and the mountain wall. It was a miniscule gap he could not possibly fit through.

In that micro-instant of eternity – frozen forever in a mind not capable of forgetting – he cut sharply across the front end of the Ford, clipping its chrome bumper only slightly, but hard enough to cause the bike to wobble, forcing him to decelerate to compensate and maintain control of his ride. The wagon was largely unaffected, but its driver, unfortunately, was not. She panicked and jerked the wheel sharply to her right.

The Ford struck and careened violently off of the mountain barrier, and abruptly changed direction, travelling in a diagonal in front of him, towards the mountaintop guardrail and foreclosing his last avenue of escape. Neither the sounds of steel grating against stone, nor the sickening rumble of the swiftly approaching trailer, nor the blast of the wind in Lark's ears were shrill enough to stifle the screams of the children inside the car.

His only chance now was to separate himself from his Harley.

As the three vehicles simultaneously collided, he found himself separated indeed, estranged from everything; alienated from the road, from the mountain, from the bike, and from the moment itself, located somehow to another place at another time, a frigid January afternoon on a New England football field, a home game against Vanderbilt, as he leaped high into a bright winter sky and snagged the quarterback's bullet out of midair with one hand, clutching it to him, spinning, twisting and contorting his body; flying, as a spirit, an avenging angel, a caricature of himself, epitomizing everything he was at that time, charting a course in the only direction he had ever wanted to travel, towards the only goal that was important to him then, enduring, eternal, and everlasting.

To victory.

And, in a flicker of time, back again.

The final result was a horror beyond description, an event beyond any normal man's ability to assimilate and still retain his sanity. Or live with, perhaps.

Whether the mother was alive or dead when she coursed through the front windshield and over the side of the mountain he never learned. Three of her children died instantly. The last passed later; much later.

He didn't remember much after that, only…

...only that he opened one eye and peered from the confines of a blanket placed across his entire body, from his head to his toes.

Small white feathers floated everywhere, tenderly stirred into the pure summer air by a gentle mountain breeze, filling his vision and covering the road upon which he rested with a blanket of down. The feathers were splashed with crimson.

His skull rested on a black pillow of asphalt in a dark, wet, sickly pool composed of his own blood, surrounded by blue lights and red lights and yellow lights, amid shouting, confusion, and screams, and the shrieking clamor of all the other sounds that comprise the indecipherable din of a world gone insane.

For a single moment he was conscious, and aware. But no one else – neither the state police or the EMTs or the newshounds perceived this.

They didn't pay attention to him. They didn't pay attention to him at all.

They thought he was dead.

Perhaps he was.

Where he *actually* was at that particular moment was neither here nor there, nor anywhere he could remotely understand. He was somewhere in between. He was aware of the ambulances and the blood, and the fire trucks, the stretchers, white blankets and the oxygen tanks; and the Semi, its load of twenty-five hundred live fowl brutally scattered across the road, reduced to odd bits and pieces of dead and dying animals mingled among the wreckage; and the Ford – or what was left of it – and the remnants inside that once constituted the living, breathing bodies of human beings; and of the blinding sun rising steadily into the sky.

He was cognizant of these things; aware of the reality his body resided in and everything in it, all still accessible to his fading consciousness and vanishing vision.

But there was a *somewhere else* as well. There were other *things* there.

Things that flew.

Hard leathery wings, going round and round, whizzing past his head, leaving a vacant, cold space where they passed, whispering thoughts into his brain as they went by.

And during this razor-thin slice of his ebbing life, as he existed along the faint border separating reality from its *subtext,* and as he felt each dimension pulling on him as if in battle for his very soul, for one brief, strange moment, he understood that he could *choose* which place he could reside in.

The last thing he saw on that asphalt, just before he floated away to a merciful unconsciousness, no more than ten feet from where his head lay, was the head of another; a little girl with bloodied golden hair as bright as the sun, decapitated from her small body, her stunned eyes thrust wide open.

Accusing him, he thought. But more than that. Damning him.

Damning him to Hell.

In a dim corner of the bar hung Lark's many awards and citations, his clippings, his football jersey, his memorabilia. He displayed it all here only because his mother asked him to: otherwise, all this would be stored in the attic of her home in Willimantic.

He cared not one iota for these things now: nor for recognition or reward, or for plaudits or trophies. Or for knowledge or understanding, or meaning.

Once upon a time, he had raced across a grass field of dreams with the limitless vigor and stamina of youth, with a clarity of purpose only the truly innocent can possess.

In a time *before,* he had walked with a proud head held high, down the broad and noble corridors of academia, side by side with great thinkers and skilled writers, men and women of knowledge and wisdom. And he thought he *knew.*

And *then,* he sat alone in a body cast for seven gruesome months, thinking of nothing but the five people he had helped to kill, and of a little girl's head on a lonely highway that led to death, and diabolical darkness, and infinite light: and a choice to be made…

So now, Lark just thought about beer and bartending.

And right now, in the *here and now,* he looked like a gigantic puppy dog on steroids. His remarkable biceps bulged from a T-shirt with a picture of Alfred E. Newman. A caption proclaimed, "What, Me Worry?"

Richard could feel both Lark and his shirt staring at him.

"And you're looking at what, exactly?"

"I'm looking at you being depressed."

"I'm not depressed, I'm thinking."

"You look depressed."

Richard looked up angrily, but that feeling quickly passed. First, Lark was his friend. Second, he was truly huge, had limited patience, and possessed a tendency to act out his irritation.

Lark leaned forward, putting his elbows on the bar. "You *look* depressed," he said, slowly revealing a smile as large and broad as that of the Cheshire Cat. "Fortunately, you can always have another beer!" He popped the tab on a Miller and slid it over the bar top with a flourish.

"For you, Ricky-Boy."

This one was ice-cold and Richard sipped it slowly. This would be his fifth, and he knew his small frame was ill-equipped to assimilate such a quantity of alcohol successfully. Furthermore, he needed to be rested and minimally alert for the next day or so. He pushed the brew aside. As he did, he realized that his admirable restraint was three beers too late, and that he would fall somewhat short of the minimum.

"I told you what happened at the school, right?"

"That was Beer Three."

Lark measured time by the number of drinks his patrons consumed.

"...the animals, Lark, the animals… I told you, right?"

"Beer Four."

"What the hell is going on?" Richard winced at how stupid that remark sounded.

"What the hell is going on?" Lark repeated. He looked at his friend with a grimace that must have looked more like a prayer for relief.

"What the hell is *ever* going on?" he asked again.

Lark knew of Richard's strange and sundry skills. The barkeep had witnessed the practical application of these abilities two or three times, in the form of Richard's ability to avoid a barroom altercation by manipulating a potential antagonist into submission, like a piece of Play-Dough, with words and glances alone. Such alcohol-induced squabbles typically ended with a joke, a laugh, a handshake, and a free beer.

Once, however, Richard had been compelled to reduce a rather large, ill-tempered, and politically extreme patron to the status of a whimpering child; he grabbed three of the fingers on the man's right hand, twisted, and broke them all with an audible *crack.*

It had been unnecessary for him to leave his barstool to do so. He continued raising the glass to his mouth with his right hand as he held on to the wailing customer's fingers with his left. He had not minded that he had presented himself as an outspoken ideologue, but on this occasion the gentleman's numerous remarks about African Americans and Jews did offend him.

Lark had noted this event with only mild interest. After all, he did things like this all the time and hardly considered them unusual.

Of course, only Richard was aware that a motorcycle accident had left Lark's right hand permanently injured and that he was unable to form it into a fist. This disability was never a handicap to Lark; whatever bar-room insurgence his rather persuasive demeanor was unable to resolve was quite efficiently delegated to his left hand to work out.

Anyway, after the patron left the establishment – with three less operating digits than he had when he entered – Lark turned and rang a large, brass ship's bell mounted on a wall at the end of the bar. His habit was to ring the bell each time he received a sizeable tip and apparently entertainment was as worthy as cash in Lark's universe.

Richard had left out any description of the events at Coney Island. He was all babbled out anyway, and even for Lark, this was simply too much information. But like any skilled psychiatrist, hairdresser or bartender, Lark had listened until Richard's mouth had run dry. Richard retrieved his discarded brew.

"It's really quite a mystery, isn't it, Lark?"

He considered Richard's words for a moment. "There is *one* explanation," he said finally.

"And that is?" Richard asked.

"Shit happens," Lark replied.

Wednesday

This is the excellent foppery of the world. That when we are sick in fortune, often the surfeit of our own behavior, we make guilty of our disasters the sun, the moon, and the stars: As if we were villains by necessity, fools by heavenly compulsion, and all that we are evil in by a divine thrusting on.

William Shakespeare

XXXII

He was covered in mud, his arms ached, and he was exhausted. But he was having fun.

FUN. Can you imagine?

But he wasn't playing a game and he didn't have much time to play with. Of course, whatever time he did have would be lost to him in short order.

It took him quite a while to crawl up the incline of the alleyway and wheel his way back to the Ford waiting for him in the lot but he paused a moment to give thanks for the battered vehicle.

A man with paraplegia relies on his wheels with a far greater urgency than most men, who take such things for granted. Without a car he would be totally dependent on Nae Tong for everything. Getting a Coke, or a pack of cigarettes or a morning paper, or getting to work and back; all would be impossible without a human facilitator if not for this vehicle.

The car was specially equipped for a physically disabled driver. Two levers on the left side of the steering wheel – similar to those found on a bicycle – controlled the brake and the gas; functioning legs were unnecessary in order to drive.

It had a license plate with the picture of a wheelchair imprinted upon it by some inmate doing hard time at Sing Sing, the infamous correctional facility located just a few dozen miles north. This insignia was supposed to warn other drivers that he might react slowly to road conditions but typical New York drivers routinely overlooked the distinction. Bless their hearts; they doggedly refused to discriminate against disabled people by altering their berserk-o driving patterns even a little. He got just as many bird-flips as any other driver.

Fine with him. He reached down to his ankle, removed his revolver from its holster and placed it on the passenger seat. He looked at it and smiled.

Bullets did not discriminate either.

An over-sized electric clock was in the center of the dashboard. He watched as a minute passed with a tick of the mechanism. He managed another smile. Time follows him, he thought, wherever he goes. It is the great huntsman, tracking us all, always catching what it pursues.

He hoisted himself up on the arms of the wheelchair and then transferred from it to the front seat of his car in a single, well-practiced move. Once seated he lifted two, small, steel levers on each side of the chair, allowing it to fold, much like an accordion. He leaned toward the steering wheel and pulled a lever on the bucket seat to release its backrest. When it flipped forward he lifted the wheelchair with one hand, deftly removed it to the back seat, righted his seat, closed the car door and started the engine.

He waited, tapping the steering wheel nervously with his fingers until he heard a car start somewhere near the front entrance of the school. He edged the Ford slowly out of the lot with the lights off, just in time to see a sedan shoot rapidly up 92nd Avenue and make a right on Woodside Street. Towards the hospital.

He gritted his teeth and followed the car.

He was not aware how long he had been smiling.

XXXIII

Drinking made thinking impossible and walking only slightly more difficult. While he did not know what effect Lark's supper of french fries, pickled eggs, hot dogs and coffee would have on him later, it had aided his sobriety sufficiently to permit him to walk the two whole blocks back to his house in a relatively straight line.

He passed the gated alleyway separating his residence from the dormitory. The light of the moon illuminated the refuse in the alley. He paused, and then slowly climbed the long flight of concrete steps leading to his front entrance door. By the time he reached the top he was exhausted. He picked up the day-old newspaper lying upon the top stair and entered.

He walked down the narrow hallway and placed his hand on the door of his apartment. The front entrance was always secured and keeping this door locked was unnecessary. His hand slipped off the knob momentarily and he giggled to himself like a schoolgirl.

"That was Beer Five," Lark had said.

The paper slipped from his hand and fell onto the floor.

He opened the door just a few inches and froze. He didn't know why, but he knew that something here was *wrong*. He slowly removed his hand and let it drop to his side.

His eyes brushed a page of the newspaper that had revealed itself at his feet. A small article described a curious event at Coney Island, the death of an old time carny, a fortune teller, and a fixture at the amusement park for over forty years.

The cause of her death was drowning. She had been found in her apartment, fully clothed.

He stood there with the door ajar, listening, sweating in the somewhat warm hall, and instantly sober. Silence met him. In a flash of comprehension he understood, but did not understand, all at the same time. His eyes opened wide.

He began to slowly back away from the door, but there was nothing beyond it that he feared. He continued to inch away, backward towards the entranceway, until he was halfway there. He stopped and slowly rotated his head to the left.

He realized that when he had entered the hallway, he had seen something he had seen only once before. He saw it again now, as he had the very first time he crossed the threshold to his home.

The door to the basement was open.

XXXIV

What is horror?

It is not the stark and brutal inevitability of death. It is not the unbearable pain of an incurable disease. It is not the debilitating dread that accompanies an inability to comprehend the nature of the afterlife, or the fear of obtaining an answer to the eternal riddle of whether we wind up basking in the light of a loving savior or burning at the hands of a three-headed demon in some netherworld.

It is not the paralyzing discovery that no world of the spirit exists at all; not the terrifying realization that after the moments allotted to us by a random fate expire, that there are no more, not here, not anywhere.

It is none of these things.

Horror is what unfolds before him now.

A car pulls up to the emergency room and a door opens to the night. A dark figure emerges into gloom. Misdirected lights leave nothing but shadows. A trunk pops open and a figure is dragged out and dumped on the concrete like rubbish. What is left there is a mere silhouette of a human being.

No one inside the hospital observes this moment. For them it does not exist, not yet.

For him, time has been frozen. This event seems reserved for his eyes alone.

But time watches with him. Another minute clicks by, measured by the clock mounted in the dashboard. And in another minute the car is gone with its driver as if it was never really there.

Bob does not watch the car speed away as it is swallowed by the night. Nor does he hear the screech of its wheels, or notice the small bits of asphalt its spinning tires pick up and pitch upon the motionless body.

All he sees is a person lying alone, in a heap, like a pile of rags. His subconscious mind registers a pool of dark crimson, expanding slowly on the concrete as the seconds pass. But this is not what demands his attention; this is not what rivets his eyes.

He is looking for a small movement, a shallow breath, for any sign of life at all. Anything.

The *now* rushes in again, as it is wont to do, in the form of nurses, and orderlies and shouts and confusion; brisk orders are delivered and obeyed, automatic doors swing wide open, blankets and clear plastic tubes fly through the air. The body is whisked from the pavement, onto a stretcher, and into the hospital.

An arm falls limply from the side of the canvas before it disappears inside. The two men carrying this sorry load share a momentary, knowing look.

Time clicks one more revolution on the Ford's timepiece, and all is as it was before.

He reaches for his cell phone again, not knowing who he might call, or what he might say if he did, but this time he sees nothing but a dark screen. He presses the power button.

Nothing.

The lyrics of an old rock song force their way into his mind.

We're white punks on dope.

Mom and Dad moved to Hollywood.

Hang myself if I get enough rope.

Strange.

He cannot recall the make of the car or its color, or whether it made a right turn or a left at the end of the street. He doesn't know when it will arrive at its final destination, but he doesn't have to, because he knows where the driver is going.

He only needs to figure out where *he* is going now, and what he's going to do when he gets there.

But as soon as he thinks this thought, he knows that it isn't true.

XXXV

The door to the basement was open, and something had opened it.

Impossible.

I placed my hand gingerly on the doorknob, as if I expected an electrical charge.

Nothing.

I pushed the door open fully. It was dark beyond, and the hinges creaked ever so gently.

All was quiet.

I flipped the switch on the staircase wall. A 25 watt bulb illuminated the top of the stairway. A weak bulb also came on in the center of the basement downstairs.

come come come

I climbed down the steps, slowly, deliberately, with one hand on the painted wooden banister and another dragging along the wall to my left as I descended. The steps were shallow and uneven.

yes yes yes

I smelled a musty odor, the scent of rotting paper and mildewed clothing.

Can you feel us? Will you love us? Can we suck you dry?

Voices whispered ever so delicately in my ear.

You'll like us. You'll want us. We're just like you.

My hand shredded chips of paint from the wall as I walked down the stairs, coating the steps before me like snowflakes.

We're all fucked up. Just like you.

Words were murmured gently into my soul. Fragments of my protective ego peeled away, layer by layer.

We're smashed to bits. We're all alone. We need you. We belong together. We're just like you. Down the steps down the steps down the steps come come come.

Psychic knives were being taken to my flesh. Goosebumps appeared on my arms like smallpox, as if insects were slithering there, just beneath the surface of my skin. Still, I proceeded down. But to what?

We're dead and dying dead and dying just like you just like you. Emptiness inside nothing left inside trapped here forever you and we and you and we and we are all together.

Pulled like iron powder to a magnet, like a calf to its slaughter, I didn't know why.

But you will

But I will

Yes Yes Yes

Such sadness, such emptiness

All fucked up just like you

No hope no love no trust no sacrifice

Come Come Come

No honor no courage no faith no future

None of these things

Standing on a square yard of space facing infinite darkness and a raging sea forever

The end of all you know

The ripping of flesh, souls torn asunder

Souls with us. Where you were always meant to be.

I reached the bottom of the staircase, and my legs collapsed beneath me. My sweaty right hand found the banister, halting my fall. The railing swayed dangerously under my weight. I looked around and saw the dim bulb at the bottom of the stairs, a halo around its meager light, and little else. I waited for my eyes to focus and get accustomed to the darkness. I was afraid to loosen my hold on the banister.

My hair began to rustle as if a light wind was wafting down the staircase, blowing toward the center of this space. But I knew there couldn't be.

I felt the slightest tugging at my legs and looked down. As I did my right hand began to slide off of the railing. My left reached for support and found nothing but empty air. I started to fall.

Something grabbed my left elbow and kept me on my feet.

"Careful now, Ricky-Boy."

I turned and saw that nothing was there.

This invisible support then loosened its hold, causing my leg to slide and I pulled all the muscles in my left thigh. I bellowed out in pain and completed my fall, landing awkwardly at the foot of the stairs, unhurt, for the most part.

I squinted and directed my gaze towards the light. The single bulb hung from a wire, perhaps four feet long, attached to the ceiling. I watched as it began to swing on its axis in gentle, rhythmic circles, around and around, its revolutions getting wider at each turn.

The voices stopped and my mind slowly cleared. The bulb continued to swirl hypnotically. I looked up.

A dirty rectangular window hung high on a corner wall. Little light reached through the grime and dust that had accumulated there.

The streets were outside that window, as were the sounds of the city; I was in the middle of a metropolis, but not the faintest murmur from outside seemed to penetrate this space. I began to feel as if I were in a vacuum, a place where sound would not travel, where evil inhaled and held its breath and let nothing out.

I looked around. There were boxes everywhere, ancient cardboard containers of various dimensions that in their time had held who knew what? I rose carefully from my awkward position, thankful that I had not lost consciousness or broken a bone.

I walked slowly around the weirdly appointed space. The dim light did not extend to the four corners of the room and I could not accurately determine how large it was. As I paced my feet crunched on

...peanut shells and the wrappers of candy apples and those huge lollipops you would buy from the vendors that seemed to be...

the hard carapaces of cockroaches long since dead. With each step ancient spider webs wrapped around my legs, as if their silken threads might snare a prey so large. Perhaps they might yet.

The bulb still turned, round and round, round and round, and then, simply stopped.

As did I. I held my breath and tried to sense the slightest movement of anything sharing this space with me. After a moment I let my breath out with a *whoosh*, now fully cognizant of the smells in this place.

Wet paper. Dust. Excrement. Other things so pungent they burned my nose and made the back of my throat ache. I continued my tour, very much aware of the blackness in front of me that the deficient beacon of the small central bulb refused to remove.

I paused before one box. It contained what appeared to be maroon basketball uniforms from a bygone age. I remembered the history of the school's wheelchair basketball team. I resisted the temptation to sort through the box, unwilling to discover what other thing made its home here.

A rustle in the darkened recess. The breeze again.

We're just like you

I couldn't see back there.

come come come

Something. Pulling me into the depths.

Can you feel us?

The music. I heard the music. The sweet refrains of an eternal Bach chorale. Beckoning.

Wanting.

Needing. My legs seemed to move reflexively, seeking the darkness.

As was meant to be

I advanced three steps then turned to look over my right shoulder. A dull light forced itself through the solitary window rising on the wall behind me, radiating a muted battleship gray upon the floor. I reasoned that this crypt could not be much more than a thousand feet square.

More insects crunched underfoot as I continued to advance toward the rear of the basement. The room's already meager light diminished further. As my eyes adjusted, the wall marking the end to this place appeared out the blackness. On the wall was a group of ancient posters mounted in a circular pattern. I took a step closer.

Baseball players... posters of baseball players from bygone eras, in the classic poses of yesteryear.

There, Duke Snider, smiling, with a massive bat resting on his shoulder.

There, Whitey Ford as a young man, crouching on a pitching mound with his famous left arm extended.

Yes, and there, The Mick, swinging for the downs, displaying his archetypal batting stance.

A hum rose behind me. The light bulb began to twirl on its wire like a jump rope in the hand of a little girl, round and round, gaining speed, round and round,

the end of all you know

faster and faster, casting a malevolent light upon the wall before me like a strobe, or in the way an old movie projector might.

As I played out the scene staged for me in this Magic Theatre, I imagined an infernal director robed in red, sitting on a tall chair somewhere, barking hoarse instructions past a long dead larynx, and pointing out his meaning with a gnarled fingertip.

My eyes followed to a spot near the bottom of the wall.

There, Luis Aparicio twisting and turning in the air to make a throw to first base. There, Yogi Berra leaping into the arms of Don Larsen after his perfect game.

But there was another print, not hanging on the wall, but one that appeared to have crumpled into a heap several feet above the floor, seemingly suspended.

As I edged closer towards the poster the drone of the bulb altered. It now sounded like something alive, like *things* alive; not a humming any longer, but a *buzzing,* like a swarm of insects.

But it continued to shed its intermittent beam and the subject of the print became visible: three hideous death masks cast on a black background, all floating from an invisible wire, each staring off in a different direction.

I saw a caption inscribed underneath the masks, advertising the 1981 Mardi Gras in New Orleans. I also saw the picture was not hanging in mid-air, but resting upon something underneath it.

As I reached to touch it, it began to vibrate and flutter, as if a stale wind was blowing upon it, or because something *alive* was beneath it, something barely contained by its fragile paper covering.

Come see come see

I had to see

Yes yes

What was beneath the

A soul with us

Without thinking I grabbed the picture and flung it high into the air across my body. Its gliding form briefly filled my vision.

The light in the room blinked out. But just for a moment.

The strobe returned, striking upon the body, making it appear unreal. The oozing liquids I saw underneath the figure rapidly altered this fleeting illusion.

It would have looked like a dummy of some kind, a slumped figure made of cloth or of cardboard, were it not for the malodorous stench that accompanied it, an unmistakable smell of death and decay. This was not a mannequin, but a human recently deceased. But more; I knew this person.

Far less afraid than I should have been, I held my breath, consciously sealed my nostrils, and moved closer to the heap on the floor. A head became visible; a bald head, glistening with a liquid that had formerly been inside it. There were two gaping holes where there had once been eyes.

But there was more. So much more.

The jaws of the carcass had been stretched – impossibly so it seemed – to accommodate the unrecognizable form that issued from it. It was as thick as a lamb roast but larger, longer, trailing almost four feet from what used to be a man's mouth, tapering to a thinner point at its end.

The body was shirtless and I could see a tattoo of a cobra etched on a breastbone. The tail of the cobra trailed down the left arm of the corpse. There was a dagger etched on its right arm and the dagger was splitting an image of the world. The dagger was dripping blood and the drops covered the planet.

The blood, of course, was real.

I looked past the dagger, down to where legs should have been, and found the remains of only one. The other was simply gone, vanished, pants leg and all, removed from the joint of the hip.

The bulb stopped spinning. It stopped spinning but it had to have stopped at an angle, defying gravity and physics, because its light was now narrowly focused on this body, this former student of mine.

Vander. My God.

I looked to the remains of his head, and then his leg, and realized the obvious; that his deformity – his bad leg – had been removed from his trunk and placed elsewhere.

I gasped for breath. Unable to exhale, I became dizzy and lost my balance. My ears filled with that infernal buzzing again, shrill and painful, and as I fell I covered my ears with both hands.

But this white noise did not originate from any physical

realm, thus, it could not be deterred by any physical means. While I had failed to block out the clamor, I had succeeded in making my hands unavailable to break my fall. So into *something* I fell.

My vision was clouded by tears and my breath was coming in halting gasps. I tried to rise with my hands still covering my ears. But I couldn't rise, because something wet and gelatinous was holding me like a suction. I panicked and rolled, flailing my arms, trying to gain release from whatever it was that held me.

As my body became free of whatever gripped it I heard a *pop,* like a Tootsie Roll being jerked from tightly clenched lips. My back and bottom felt oily and slick.

Her body was fully illuminated, for my benefit, I was sure. Her dress – one that I had never seen her wear – was a brilliant white, with beautiful, embroidered fringes on the hem and on each short sleeve. Her placid face held a Mona Lisa smile and her hands had been carefully draped across her body above her stomach.

They could not have been folded elsewhere because this corpse had no stomach. A cavernous, perfectly round hole the size of a human head – which I had plunged into – had been dug out of Rena's midsection. It had been carefully, neatly, *lovingly* excavated. Tiny punctures surrounded the entire circumference of the opening in her body, which did nothing to affect the perfect *roundness* of the crater.

It looked as if…

As if…

Good God... it looked as if she had been *eaten.*

Phantom hands gripped my body from all sides and tried to pull me down, not to the floor, not to the ground, but *through* the ground. Oh, so far, far beneath the ground. I wished at that moment for ignorance so blissful that it might wipe from my mind the terrible sense of what I knew would be waiting for me there.

An undefined pain coursed through my body, and visions without substance of any kind held my mind tightly. There was no bragging now, no whispers or words, and no music, all of these things reduced to unnecessary pretense. This was the end game and the object of whatever resided here. That object was me.

How do you fight what is not there? How can you battle an enemy you cannot perceive?

My senses sharpened to crystal clarity and an answer to these impossible questions presented itself.

...by *acting*, not *thinking*...

I... am getting... the fuck... outta here...!

Hands that were never there disappeared. An unseen force, overpowering just a moment ago, was gone. Stunned – but not into inaction – I leaped into the air and towards the stairs. I climbed, fell, climbed again, fell again, grabbed the banister and pulled myself up; up towards the light of the hallway above; expecting something would pull me back to a place from which I might never return.

I reached the top of the landing – alive – in one piece – astonished by the reality of what still lay below... and the music began again.

No; not music. The phone was ringing in my apartment.

I was shaking; my entire body was sore. The phone continued to ring. I looked over my shoulder as if I expected something to be there. I crossed the threshold of the basement door and slammed it closed as hard as I could. I stared at it, unsure if this barrier was still sufficient to contain the horrors – seen and unseen – just a few steps away.

The phone. I began to inch away towards my apartment, keeping my eye on the basement door.

The caller was persistent. But he would wait.

I finally entered my apartment but kept the door open.

I would be leaving here soon. I would not return.

A dull pain, a product of the spirit, not the body, rose from the pit of my stomach to the center of my chest as I picked up the receiver.

"Mr. Goodman?"

A man. A sharp pain in the pit of *his* stomach.

"Yes?"

"This is Mount Clair Hospital in Woodside…?"

"Yes?"

"I'm sorry to be calling you so late at night, but your business card was in the purse of a patient we have here, Kara…"

"What's happened to Kara?

"…can you tell me if you are related…?"

"What's happened?"

"Can I ask what your relationship to…?"

"What's happened?"

He is a physician assistant, around forty years old. He's fatigued, but only at the beginning of his nightshift. He would have me believe that he is caring, but detached; sincere, but unemotional. But he is nervous, partly because he is about to break protocol, and partly because of the news he is about to convey.

"…seriously injured, Mr. Goodman. She's here in CCU… Mr. Goodman…?

"How serious?"

"They're in critical condition. Someone should be here right now. Do you know if she has any…?"

I hung up the phone, hesitating for only a moment before bursting through the door, onto the street and into the night.

XXXVI

Kara lay unconscious on the bed; the light bed covers accentuating her slightly swollen midsection. Richard pulled the covers back and placed his hands there gently, ever so gently, looking up towards her eyes. Tears stained his face and it was all he could do to prevent bawling outright. He choked back his anguish.

And then he felt the movement, almost imperceptible, like a feather gliding over the water, raising his fingers ever so slightly.

She is alive. He knows she is a girl, and that she is his child, without having to consider how he knows.

I've got a special announcement and I want to be in a fun place, DIG?

He looked at Kara again and tried to capture any stirring with his peripheral vision. Before him lay his future, just trying to survive a little longer now in her warm, dark place.

He had forgotten for a moment that the doctor was here. If she had noticed his blood covered clothing, she hadn't let on. She wasn't very old, this doctor of medicine, her human feelings not yet hardened to cold steel by a thousand unpreventable demises, her eyes not yet blinded to the suffering of the infirm, her ears not yet closed to the cries of the dying and those who love them.

He sensed her spirit. She held suffering at bay by the force of her will. She had acquired skill and used it as her weapon in daily battles with the horrifying aftermath of blind fate, or poor choices, or bad luck. Sometimes, she prevailed.

She had also gained wisdom, enough to know that every victory was fleeting, that she might hold the bastion for only a little while, and that ultimately she was powerless to halt the advance of time, or death; that we are all so fragile; each of us so breakable, so faulty.

Richard felt her fear as well, and it was this; One day,

whatever it was she was truly fighting against would stop. It would stop and turn around, and reveal itself, and she would see It for the first time. And It would take her in payment for the lives she had stolen.

Richard looked up at the physician, afraid of the truth he might see in her eyes. But he never got that far, really. The Wave swept over him as if it had a weight and a mass all its own, robbing the oxygen from the air, choking him, catching the hope in his throat and making it impossible for him to speak. It covered him in a dank blanket of misery and wretchedness, pushing him far past the point where he could articulate the question "why," to a desolate place where that word had no meaning, where the only explanation in reply was "because."

The Wave forced his eyes closed and compelled him to see. He perceived himself as a character in Dostoevsky's novel, standing there on a rock three feet square, looking out over an endless sea with no other land in sight, with lightning crackling in the air and rain pouring down relentlessly, forever and for always, that black storm cresting, that ageless ocean lying before him until the end of time, he and It, he and It and nothing more; loneliness, true loneliness, killing the spirit and the soul but unmercifully leaving the body alive, leaving nothing but the husk of a man containing his skin, his bones, and his internal organs; lungs breathing, heart beating, body wracked by pain and pouring sweat; unwilling to stand but unable to fall, no reason to live but unable to die; not a scavenger in the sky, not the lowliest insect crawling on the ground, not even the dorsal fin of some fearsome beast below the surface of the water, nothing and no one, forever and for always alone alone alone.

Here is fear, here is the end of all things, where all roads terminate, where all horror truly begins, where It lies and lives and rules and lords over nothing and everything; unspeakable dread where time does not exist, beyond reality, beyond the imagination of any reality, the mouth of the demon, the center, the core, not a star in the firmament nor the faintest hope that there ever was, that there ever could be, that there ever will be, not here.

Forever and for always. He was to be alone.

When he opened his eyes, his hands were still on Kara's stomach, fluttering ever so slightly from the life still beneath her belly. Once more, he looked up at the doctor, his body weak and shaking. He was no longer sitting on the chair but had fallen to his knees.

The physician did not seem to notice. She bowed her head, she turned it ever so slightly to the left, then to the right, confirming everything that he already knew: Life was leaving both mother and child, like it leaves us all.

The doctor quietly left the room. Richard rose, grasping at the edge of the bed for support and seated himself once more in the chair.

He reached into the rear pocket of his jeans for the thin paperback folded there, one that he seized impulsively from his bookshelf as he bolted from his house. He purchased it at an airport many years ago, never read it, and never knew why he had bought it in the first place.

He looked down at the gaily illustrated cover and through his tears, he read:

"On the playpen floor is a dollhouse door and a daffodil bloom and a peacock plume and a portrait of a lamb soaring over the moon…"

What is Outside?

She thinks, but not in words, not in any language, but in the most basic of expressions, on waves of pure emotion and feeling.

Dark dark dark. Warm, dark, wet.

She never questions her existence. She never tries to understand anything. She does not know why she is here.

She does not think about "why."

She knows she is in a shell. Her movements are restricted to a few inches in any direction. When she moves, parts of her stretch the shell around her; it moves with her, but only a little bit. She cannot leave where she is.

But she does not want to leave.

Warm and safe and dark.

She is conscious of the Sound, a rhythmic beating all around her that fills her world. She is aware of the Voice, an intermittent vibration of varying dimension and pitch that permeates her space. These things are always with her. These things are Inside with her.

She knows about Inside. It is warm and safe and dark Inside. But there are also things Not Inside. Often, these things make her feel not safe even though she is in the dark and the wet and the warm and the safe place.

She has not been able to understand the Not Inside. Until now.

Outside.

Inside and Outside.

What is Outside?

She is aware now, for the first time, that there is a Something Outside. It is like the Voice, but not like the Voice. She realizes, too, that it has been with her all the time. It is here with her now.

Something.

"There are dolls with white faces from far-away places and little toy soldiers with guns on their shoulders..."

She does not need to understand the Something, because she understands how it makes her feel: warm and safe, even though it is Outside. But more than that.

The Something is for her. The Something makes her want to reach out and pull it to her. The Something makes her feel

Joy.

Joy is new.

It is Joy, this Something Outside.

"In the still of the room I hear kitty's meow, and feel grandmother's hand lightly brushing my brow..."

The Sound beats slower now. Slower. She moves slower to its beat.

The vibrations of the Something Outside wrap around her. It is louder than the Sound now, but she does not notice. She tries to push against her space and show the Something that she knows it is there, but only the slightest movement comes forth. She doesn't understand why.

"Goodbye kitty goodbye room Fare-thee-well I'll see you soon..."

The vibrations become louder and clearer, flooding over her again and again. For the first time she cannot hear the Sound, but she does not consider this. Her emotions are drowned by the Something Outside.

"...goodbye lamb soaring over the moon."

She becomes something Not Warm, and this is new, this is for the first time; she tries again to move towards the Joy of the Something, but cannot. But she reaches out once more, with all of her strength, and believes she can feel the Something against the very walls of her existence. She feels It!

"Goodbye dolls Goodbye meow..."

And now she hears another Sound, but it comes from her. With this Sound comes everything that she is, and everything that she ever will be. All the joy that she feels has come out, but when it does, she finds to her great surprise that there is nothing left inside. But the Something Outside still rings through her.

"...and farewell to the hand lightly brushing my brow."

For the very first time it is quiet Inside. She cannot move at all. All the things around her are slowly fading away. She is going backward, she thinks. Backward, to the beginning of what was. She wonders if the Something Outside will be waiting for her there.

For the first time, quiet Inside.

And backward.

It is dark now, very dark. All around her has disappeared, and all Inside has stopped. But she still feels safe because she is filled by the Something Outside. It engulfs her and caresses her. It fills her being and touches every part of her.

The fluttering stopped, and the book fell out of his hands. As it fell onto the floor, it opened to a drawing of a lamb with wings flying over the moon.

She feels herself rising; she is lighter and lighter; she is no longer confined to the space Inside, but she is not afraid. Even the Something Outside has gone away. But she is not alone. She will never be alone. To wherever she is going she will carry It with her. She wraps the last moment of her existence around It, brings It close to her, and joins with It.

The last thing she feels is the slightest touch…

The slightest movement.

Joy.

Great joy.

Kara gasped.

Walks on the boardwalk. Taking the first step. Mom and Dad. The first ice cream cone. Triumphs and failures at work. Good friends; family members long gone.

Kara seemed to hold her breath for a moment, suspended between life and death, trying to hold on in a netherworld between the two…

Petty fights and laughter. Bowling: baseball games. Sleepover parties. Birthdays. The high school prom. My first car. Planting flowers in a pot by the windowsill. Ruddy, the dog. A golden fish in a bowl.

…floating there, on the edge, and finally falling off, her chest slowly collapsing, gently exhaling, the strain going out of the muscles in her face, becoming placid and smooth.

She's so young; so very young…

…cool, wet grass on naked feet. Snowball fights. Burned by a hot iron. Dance lessons. A fall down a flight of steps. New clothes. Richard. The last day of school.

He waited for what seemed like an eternity, waiting for the slightest movement from mother or child.

The smell of the air after a rainstorm. Running. The first day of spring. New Year's Eve. Feeding the birds. Richard. A good night's sleep; happy, so happy.

But nothing moved and nothing here was ever going to move again.

The End. There were no credits, there was no dashing musical score and no audience to pace slowly out of the theater. There was only silence interrupted by the beat of his broken heart. He wished he could stop it; he stopped breathing; his heart beat faster; he was gasping for breath, but he realized he couldn't die, that he wouldn't die, not now, not yet.

It wasn't time. There was still one more duty to perform.

He stood on wobbly legs that didn't want to stand, his eyes nearly useless, clouded by tears and the fog of desperation.

A soft radiance appeared over the bed. He saw two shapes inside a delicately illuminated translucent globe. They wanted him to see them, to see how beautiful they were, to see that they were one, and together, and complete. He didn't want to see, and he pushed the visions away.

But there was something that they wanted him to hear, as well, something they needed him to understand. Soft, urgent murmurings rose all about him, like flood waters, and slowly penetrated his mind. But he refused to hear, and pushed the voices away, as well. There was nothing left for him to see or to hear, in this world or the next, not ever.

He stumbled towards the door. It didn't have a lock, just an aluminum latch which he clumsily pushed down, falling into the hallway before an unattended nurse's station. He looked to his right then walked rapidly in that direction.

He couldn't wait for an elevator, couldn't find the elevator, couldn't remember if he came to this floor by elevator; but he found an exit, crashed awkwardly through a heavy metal door, and all he knew now was down, down, down. Nine steps before each landing, and at each he careened off the cinder block of a staircase wall. Down until the bottom; another door and through it.

He wandered blindly down an expansive hallway and passed

a bank of elevators. Next to the elevators there was a watchman sitting behind what looked like a child's desk, reading a newspaper he was holding in both hands. For some reason, he didn't look up as Richard passed.

The smell of disinfectant greeted him as he stepped into the large lobby that was the hospital's main entrance. The tile floor was terribly clean. To his left was a refrigerated vending machine, containing sparse flower bouquets protected by glass. It was standing next to a long wooden bench. Before him was an exit sign, above wide double doors, leading out to the night.

A long white counter lay to his right. A woman was sitting behind it.

She was wearing a white dress, like a nurse's dress, but she didn't look like a nurse. Richard shifted his weight involuntarily from one leg to the other.

She was rustling papers, this like-a-nurse-but-not-a-nurse, reading something before her hidden from his view. The woman had her reading glasses on. They were attached to the back of her neck by a gaudy chain covered with diamonds.

He realized, after a moment, that they couldn't be real diamonds.

He began to walk slowly towards the counter, as if not sure his legs were working. He seemed to feel some great weight pushing all around him. He continued to approach until he was just a few feet away.

The woman stopped rustling for a moment and became still. She had a strange look on her face, and it was impossible to tell whether she was amused or angry or something else. Richard held his breath, and waited for her eyes to lift from her charts and meet his. But this didn't happen because she didn't look up.

Located incongruously on the wall behind the woman was a closet with two doors. Above the closet was a large round clock with two thick, black hands and a plain white dial, like those found in public schools. This clock had a second hand, too; not one that swept across its surface, but one that jerked itself into place, one second at a time, counting off the moments with a motion that looked more like a shudder than anything else.

The clock tells him it is 3:00 a.m.

School is out. Two hours, fifty-eight minutes to go.

And then, like a brief commercial message playing on God's cosmic television, came the unspoken words of his beloved departed, replayed in a private broadcast across the blank screen of his mind.

The school.

The son of a bitch was waiting for him at the school.

He closed his eyes.

XXXVII

When he opened his eyes again, both of his hands were on the roof of a car parked outside the hospital entrance. He looked up and saw before him a five-story tenement, bathed in the dull yellow hue the city lights cast upon it, broken only by a smoldering radiance that cast a flickering shadow against the curtains of an open third floor window. The fabric fluttered and fanned under the confines of the glass as if in desperate escape.

It was cold and wet. He looked at his palms as if he was seeing them for the first time.

He looked to his right, at the path that was the empty street ahead. Hard, moist pavement glistened back at him in the dreary glow of the street lights.

He remembered being on the track team in high school, training alone after school, in the basement, where seemingly endless, deserted corridors lay before him. Training became a test of will, him against those hallways, running the length of them, again, and again.

Sometimes it seemed as if he might turn a corner and be swallowed up by something. Something timeless and patient, without human frailty or doubt or weakness. Something that *knew*. Something that knew he had limited strength, limited resolve and limited character. Something whose business it was to stop him.

It was against this unseen something that he trained. After a very long time, after he developed his running into a discipline, after he had tested and stretched the bounds of his physical limitations, he understood that part of what he'd been fighting so hard against was just himself. He had to free his spirit and will his body to follow.

He still had a long way to go. So long ago.

He paused for a moment to glare at the street ahead as if it were an ancient enemy. And he started to run.

He pushed all the air out of his chest. He began to breathe steadily and deeply, breathing in through his nose and exhaling through his mouth. With every step energy was conserved and the maximum benefit from his efforts realized. He looked up and saw a street sign marking the way, neatly severed in half by the shadows created by the artificial light of the city.

He had eighteen blocks to run. In an instant, every moment was choreographed in advance in his mind, every step a small part of the whole, with a beginning, a middle and an end; a clock ticking at every turn, every pebble and angle on the street a potential benefit or detriment, every second suspended in the air an opportunity to breathe and to rest.

As precious seconds passed a pain arose in his chest and deepened. His breath grew short and it became harder to push the pain away.

Running, Running.

He ran for Kara. He ran for an unborn life that was too small and too innocent to know to question why. For all the innocents everywhere who had their hopes and their dreams and their futures and their very bodies ripped asunder. He ran against life itself; the world he lived outside of, one he could never truly understand and didn't want to try to any longer, not now.

I turn a corner and it begins to rain, slowly at first, then harder. By the fourth block the rain becomes a freezing rain. I hear my heart beating in my chest.

It's counting. It's counting off the remaining moments of my life.

The wind and the rain begin to drive in earnest; the wind is whipping with a fresh and eager intensity. I round a corner and slip, lose my balance, and crash into two silver metal garbage cans placed at the curb for the morning's collection. My right hand seeks balance from the concrete sidewalk; the flesh rips off it as easily as a cellophane wrapper from a piece of candy. I tumble, roll and somehow wind up on my feet. There is a rip in my pants at the left knee. There is an ache where the rip is. My shoulder hurts. I choke back tears.

By the seventh block, I am freezing cold and soaked to the bone. My knee is stiff and it hurts every time it moves. I'm winded and begin to slow down. Two blocks later I can't catch my breath. I begin to walk; each step is accompanied by a heave as I attempt to force air into my lungs.

By the eleventh block I start to run again. My entire body is numb and I am shaking and shuddering uncontrollably.

But I get back into a rhythm and clear my mind of everything except my destination. Exactly what will happen when I get to the school I don't know but I don't care, it isn't important. What I will attempt to do is end this travesty. I will end it with my bare hands if I have to, but I will end it.

So I keep running, head down, running, running, breathing as evenly as I can, until only the sound of my own breath fills my ears. My breath, and then the breath of another beside me.

A hole opens up in the ball of my right shoe. The icy cold of the pavement sweeps through that hole with the wet of the street. I look to my left.

There is a young boy running beside me. I know that he is nine years old. He is struggling mightily against the rain and the cold and whatever other forces of God knows what. He knows that I am here. He slips momentarily and looks as if he is going to go down hard. Instinctively I reach out for him and grab him and keep him on his feet. He takes my hand. I am surprised that he is real to the touch, although I know that he is not real. He stares at me intensely, his eyes bright with fear but with a purpose, too.

We are slowing down together, looking at each other. I realize he is just another lost soul, this child. He is just another lost soul trying to find his way, squeezing from the meager clues of this world whatever small meaning he can, striving towards whatever goals he concludes are meaningful, and all the while fighting; fighting for survival, fighting for understanding, fighting for a moment when his belly will be full, fighting for a moment when his father's arms will be around him and he will have his love, and his pride; fighting for a moment in time when he will not be alone, when all things will be made clear.

Perhaps he is fighting for a moment when there will be no more fighting at all.

He is just another lost soul trying to find his way. What else is there to understand about him? What greater mystery is there? He's just another ant thrown onto the top of a hill and told to Live! Live! But he doesn't know how, this young boy who will one day become a man, who will one day become mad, who will one day take his own life, he doesn't know how. He only knows how to fight and how to suffer, but he tries, good God Almighty he tries.

Look at him run! He's scrawny, but he's not weak. No, there's an inner spark that drives him, that powers him, that keeps him going. It's the same spark that keeps us all going.

Oh, but he will suffer, because the world will come at him again and again, an uncaring, merciless world will come at him again and again, this ant on top of a hill, this little bug crawling around and around in a circle trying to find his way. And I know that this one will never find his way, because he will be crushed on the top of that hill; he will be crushed and beaten and smashed and he will become a casualty; a casualty of war, a casualty of life, a casualty of himself. In the end there will be little left of him, little left at all, and yet he will crawl, still, around and around in a circle, around and around on the top of his hill until he can't crawl anymore, because that's all he knows to do.

Because that's his life; because these are the cards he was dealt.

Huge tears are falling down my face. I'm crying for him, because he deserved better, and I'm crying for myself, because I wanted better. I realize that of the two of us, he had it harder. And I'm crying because I'm selfish, and weak and alone, and because I'm just an ant on a hill with two smashed legs crawling around and around and that's all I know how to do. So I'm going to crawl, just like my father did; crawl and crawl until I can't crawl anymore, until the rain washes my lifeless body from the hill where I was thrown. I'll end up as a husk somewhere and no one anywhere will ever know what I was, or that I was, or what

I felt, or what I strived for, or the obstacles I faced. Even if there is a marker to record my passing it will fade and sink into the earth along with my body and what will be left will be nothing over nothing.

He's smiling. He's smiling and holding my hand and running in the rain. He knows I understand him now. I don't judge him anymore, I don't blame him anymore for anything, because judgment is irrelevant, and blame is irrelevant. The truth is simple – it always was – and I see it clearly. I see that he had his hill and I had mine, and that we did the very best we could. We made terrible mistakes; we had our successes, and we tried. We tried to be the very best that we could, but in the end it didn't make any difference, it didn't make any difference at all, because all that we ever were, were two ants on different hills. And all that mattered, all that matters, that will ever matter, is that we hang on, that we hang onto each other for dear life; that we draw each other as close as we possibly can, that we close our eyes and forge ahead and hope for the best and do our best and just hang on together. For as long as we can.

Just hang on. For a few hours longer. Just hang on.

All of a sudden – like magic, it seemed – I was there at the front entrance of the school. A single street light illuminated the building's magnificent white baroque columns and cast a strange pallor upon the three, wide, concrete steps that led to its gigantic, twin, oak doors. I looked down the street.

Over a half century ago, this quiet lane had been the scene of a glorious opening ceremony attended by General Omar Bradley and Fiorello LaGuardia, celebrating a new age of rehabilitation for disabled war veterans. Then, the doors to this building led to new lives for the brave men who had come home from the World War.

Tonight, they led only to death.

A bolt of lightning crackled in the air. The skin on my forearms bristled. The strong scent of ozone permeated the atmosphere. I realized my left hand was still extended, still reaching out, still holding on to the hand of another.

As I slowly turned I saw that he was gently fading away into the night, tiny piece by tiny piece, minute portions of his body gently breaking away and floating off like so much stardust to who knows where. Soon, the only thing that seemed to be left was a soft, grateful smile on what had been a proud little face relaying to me a message from the beyond, the last message I would need to hear from that place.

When I looked at my hand again, it was filled with small glowing particles falling through my fingers like sands in an hourglass. I stared until the very last of them disappeared.

The four stark columns of the school building loomed over me. Lying on the granite rise before the right entrance door was a large, rectangular, rubber pad that activated an electric eye, opening the door automatically, an accommodation to people in wheelchairs.

The doors should have been locked at this time of night, but they were not; they were slightly parted, just ever so, harbingers of greeting's doom urging me to enter. I walked slowly up the steps, my feet leaden, my footsteps measured. I was soaked and every muscle in my body ached. My hair hung from my head like wet strings.

My hand pushed on the door. With the electricity turned off, it moved, but did not open. I pushed again, harder, and it did, and silently. A pleasant rush of heat greeted me.

There were no lights in the circular front vestibule and I paused a minute to allow my eyes to adjust to the gloom. My gaze followed to the top of the fifteen foot high ceiling. There was a cracked and aged mural painted there, illuminated only by the glow of the streetlight outside seeping through the narrow, rectangular window over the front entrance doors. The mural depicted the history of time; sundials and clocks powered by water, and mechanical watches, and images of our ancient ancestors scratching lines in bones to measure the periods between the phases of the moon.

However we measured it – however we attempted to understand or record it – time passed over us nonetheless, eternal, overpowering us all.

To my left was the alcove shared by the school's secretaries. It had no door, only a portico that led to the two desks sitting there in silent, reproachful order. I stepped inside and approached Andrea's desk. A cheerful, floral-printed box of tissues sat there and I grabbed half the box in a handful and wiped the moisture from my hands, face and hair. The tissues made an audible leaden clunk as I threw them into her empty waste basket.

I stepped into the vestibule again and faced the office of the director. I approached the door and tried its handle. I was only somewhat surprised that it yielded with a soft squeak, offering only the slightest resistance.

I held my breath. The wind whistled through the cracks in the front entrance doors. Somewhere a tree branch brushed against a window. I took a step back and pushed the door wide.

It opened to reveal the formal magnificence of the room. Hanging on the wall facing me was a picture of Arde Bulova of the Bulova watch family. Beneath it was the huge desk that Director Robert Stacey employed to accomplish his daily tasks. The desk was neat and ordered, like the mind of the administrator who used it. A high back, brown, leather chair ringed by bronze metal studs was behind the desk. A banker's lamp with a green glass shade, a blotter, a leather encased cylinder filled with various writing instruments and three silver framed portraits of Stacey's two girls and wife adorned the cherry wood of the antique. An ancient brass "anniversary" clock sat there, too, with a four-sided glass enclosure containing its guts. Three pendulums formed its base and once set in motion acted as counterbalances that powered the mechanism. They silently rotated round and round, counting off the seconds of my life.

And yours, as well, I suppose.

To the right of the desk were three large windows that ran

fairly from the top of the ceiling to the lower third of the wall. In between each window, in elaborate wood frames, were technical drawings of various mechanical watches created by noted craftsmen over the years. Antique wooden blinds, never in the closed position, were drawn high up on each window. Stacey liked the sun that streamed in through these windows. Tonight, the street lights cast only ominous shadows.

Oil portraits of past trustees hung from mahogany wood panels on the left side of the office under which, built into the wall, were a row of ten black file cabinets, each with five drawers. Each drawer was clearly marked. These fifty drawers contained the most vital records of the school, but most were records of its past. Only one cabinet was necessary to contain the present business of the institution and this one was closest to the director's desk.

The room contained no closets or other enclaves where a person might take refuge, so it was reasonable to assume that I was its sole occupant.

Closing the door behind me, I approached the file cabinets. Most drawers were marked with faded labels by year, not by subject, except those in the cabinet closest to the rear. Here, each drawer was respectively marked "financial," "education," "facility," "sports," and "student records." This last drawer was ajar by half an inch, unusual only because of the otherwise perfect order of the office. I opened it.

Inside were the records of each current student, arranged alphabetically, last name first. I selected one randomly. Contained within it were grades, medical records, admissions test scores, emergency contact information and attendance records.

Some files were thicker than others. I reached for the folder of Angelito Cortez, feeling slightly guilty that I was improperly viewing the kid's confidential information. It was thick with immigration documents and contained a remarkably well-indexed medical history. I placed this folder back with the others and let my eyes scan the group in the dim light.

Many years ago I had a friend named Mike. He was a car mechanic and a very good one. He used to say that if you looked at an engine long enough, it would tell you what was wrong with it. I never forgot this simple, enduring bit of wisdom. I waited for the paper to tell me what was wrong.

Then I noticed that two files were elevated, just slightly higher from the rest. I lifted the first of these from the drawer and removed it to the desk. I slumped down in the deep, soft leather chair, which made me feel comfortably small and I turned on the desk lamp, adjusting the shade so that its light would fall only on the folder.

As I opened the file, a newspaper clipping slipped onto the desk. It had been cut from a local paper called "The Magnet," and it documented the arrest of a local boy. He had broken into a pet store. He wasn't there to extract a profit of any kind, but to inflict an evening's worth of physical torture upon the store's non-human residents. He was caught only because he stayed in the shop an entire evening, too engrossed in his work to notice the daylight.

The owner opened his shop as he did each morning, only to witness a teenager – unnamed because of his youth – covered in excrement and blood, sitting in the center of the store, surrounded by bloody feathers and fur, and the pitiable remains of dozens of animals that had made the store their temporary home. The boy had used scissors, a hammer, and a screwdriver as his tools. He was arrested without resistance, arraigned, and referred for psychological evaluation.

Good idea.

What happened after that the story did not say.

The newsprint was smeared. I looked at my hands, but they were dry. I held the article to the light then looked at the folder again. Many of the pages were wet at their sides from the finger marks of the last reviewer. I was not the first one who had read these pages tonight.

The medical file was in a separate brown, plastic binder. It contained psychiatric reports of various scope and breadth from private therapists, hospital administrators, court-appointed psychologists, psycho-pharmacologists, social workers and school counselors; in short, from every conceivable practitioner of the mental health sciences.

This student was not disabled in the way most Waterman students were, in that his arms or legs or ears didn't function. His was a malfunction of the mind. The school, by long-standing policy, never accepted such students. An exception had been made in this case. I read further.

"Narcissistic Personality Disorder," concluded one report. "Antisocial Personality Disorder," advised another. "Schizotypal Personality Disorder," a third. The symptoms of these disorders included a lack of remorse, grandiose fantasies of self-importance, exaggerated feelings of envy and persecution and a refusal to conform to social norms of any kind. Also, "Magical Thinking," resulting in perceptual distortions and irrational fantasies involving imagined other-worldly beings.

The practitioners warned that the patient could be predicted to display an emotional indifference to the pain of others, as well as extreme aggressiveness marked by frequent physical confrontations.

One line in a report stood out: "Patient appears habitually deceitful and articulates complex schemes involving the impersonation of others."

This was an individual who believed he could be anything and practiced the art of convincing others that he was. Remorseless and violent, he answered only to a higher power created by his imagination. Convinced of his superiority and immune to the suffering of others, he possessed a witch's brew of terrifying attributes that, when combined, might yield unthinkable results.

Lovely.

Suddenly paranoid, I checked the door; it was still closed. I noticed that my wet sneakers had made imprints on the director's immaculate, royal blue rug. Like ghostly images, they traced my short steps through the office.

I noticed something else. Two straight lines, one on either side of my footsteps, as if I had walked down an invisible path softly imprinted into the carpet. But it wasn't a path at all, and I didn't need a tape measure to know that those two lines were precisely 25 inches apart, the width of a wheelchair, the unintended marks left by the disabled person who had been here before me. I returned to the file.

In the "miscellaneous" section of the file was a copy of a canceled check in the amount of $250,000.00 made payable to the Waterman School Trust Fund. This had been the price of admission for someone who had never belonged here and who, under any other circumstance, would never have been allowed to become a student.

There were also several police reports, all of them filed while the perpetrator was seventeen years of age or less. There were three arrests for aggravated assault and two for breaking and entering. There were three others for animal cruelty and the events described in these reports shocked the conscience.

One report described a satanic ritual performed in a public park. A small group of dogs and cats had not made out well. In a second there was a tale of thirty raccoons hung like Christmas lights from the escapement of a local bridge. A third described how the carcasses of sixty squirrels had been stuffed into the card catalog drawers of a public library.

Good God.

There was a charge for criminal impersonation in the first degree; the felon moved into the home of a well-to-do resident of a nearby town who had gone on vacation, representing himself as his nephew. He ate his food, swam in his pool, drove his car, and even managed access to his bank accounts based upon forged letters and powers of attorney. He made an impression on the local townspeople who described him as an attractive young man, engaging, friendly and likable.

Everyone likes him and there is very little not to like.

The imposter was most disconcerted at the fact of his arrest and reportedly pleaded with his "uncle" to rescind his "frivolous allegations." He described the matter as a "simple family squabble."

The final report contained the grand prize; attempted manslaughter. This charge appeared to be the only one that had yielded him any substantive jail time. However, he was freed a year and a half later and soon disappeared from the small town of Magnet, Nebraska where he was raised.

He comes from somewhere in the Midwest; for some reason nobody ever asks where or seems to care.

According to a second newspaper article, also in the file, he was released into the custody of his father, a wealthy, connected businessman, known locally for his pride in his only son and his dedication to the family watchmaking business.

...the son of a watchmaker who wanted his boy to learn the trade.

The store had been in the town for four generations. There would not be a fifth; a third newspaper clip announced its permanent closing. Its dissolution had been preceded by the sudden disappearance of its proprietor.

I turned to the admissions application; a necessary document contained within every student's permanent record. It contained mostly standard information: height, weight, home address, emergency contacts, allergies, prior education, and the like.

A glossy photograph three inches square was paper-clipped to the top right-hand corner of the application. It portrayed an angelic young man with sandy brown hair that fell lazily across his forehead. Every hair was spaced closely together, like a lush lawn. His neck was long and lean and graceful. He was smiling warmly, his high cheekbones giving him a delicate, almost feminine appearance. Neither flaw nor imperfection marked a face entirely without blemish and absent of even the most negligible crease or furrow.

He wore a beige shirt with the top three buttons unbuttoned, revealing a naked, hairless chest underneath. His arms made an "X" over his chest; the smooth, delicate fingers of each hand spread evenly apart. I stared at these fingers, and the longer I stared, the more I saw them as having a mind of their own, determined and purposeful. What terrible work had they done? What terrible things might they yet do?

I lurched as the wind pulsed through the hallway outside and pushed at the office door, causing the lock to click against its latch. I stiffened and waited for the doorknob to turn. It did not.

The file lay in some disarray on Stacey's desk.

I looked at the photograph again. I smiled for no reason. He was a good-looking kid, unassuming, with a broad smile on his face.

He fooled us all.

There was a tab to the file, hard and sharp, with the student's name written upon it in black magic marker. I closed my eyes for a moment and ran my hands over it as if I was a blind person reading Braille. I simply stroked it while admiring the beautiful blue of Stacey's carpet, and his handsome family portraits, and listened to the soothing revolutions of the clock on the desk counting down the moments.

It was four forty-five. Seventy-three minutes to go.

The wind whistled at the door again but I didn't pay attention to it. I rose and stepped from behind the desk; I saw no reason to take the time to straighten the file or return it to its rightful place. I walked down the wheelchair made path still visible in the rug. I left the banker's light on, illuminating the scattered paper on the desk and leaving the rest of the room in a pale glow.

I looked at my hands. They were empty, and I felt like I should be surprised. Was I truly going into an encounter without outside resource, without a weapon of any kind?

Apparently.

I had once asked a lawyer how he was able to keep up with the tuition payments necessary to keep his five children in private schools. The bills were staggering. He was a good lawyer and a successful one, but not *that* good, and not *that* successful. But he was religious.

"Do the right thing, and God will provide," he said. He put his hand on my shoulder and smiled.

"One more thing," he added. "Have no fear."

He was earning $300K a year but working seventy-five hours a week. He rarely saw his children. Most of them hated the schools they were compelled to attend. He hadn't taken a vacation in four years.

God will provide.

I placed my hand on the oversized oval door handle. It was cold to the touch but it turned easily. The door opened soundlessly this time. I stood for a moment upon the brass saddle at the threshold, separating the plush carpet in the office from the cork tile of the hall. The rest of my life was before me.

Have no fear.

I proceeded slowly to my right, walking in tempo with the soft, squishing sounds produced by my sneakers. The shadows of the main classroom loomed before me through the portico. An emergency light in the rear did little to mitigate the gloom but I could see that the room had been emptied.

It was as empty as my heart, as vacant as my spirit and my soul.

A sound echoed in the distance. I walked towards the classroom, each step slow and measured, expecting something to jump out at me. I felt like closing my eyes, relying only on my senses, like some Kung Fu master. I actually did for a brief moment but a louder disturbance downstairs jerked them open.

Two staircases were on my left; the first, twelve steps down to the level below; and the second, eight steps up to my office. I closed my eyes again. The sound of Marty Rodriguez dragging and lifting his half-body up to my perch reverberated in my ears.

I chose a staircase, grasped a handrail firmly and led myself down.

Another emergency light cast a soft glow upon the smooth, hardwood borders of the pool table. The conference room to my left was black. I hesitated for a moment and listened.

Nothing.

Domingo's station was closed; the aluminum curtain sealed the opening to the kitchen. I looked at the round tables placed around the room. I approached one and ran my hand in a circular motion around and around its smooth surface. Round and round; it was soothing, like meditating (wax on, wax off). I chuckled to myself. Then, a whisper behind me…

"Hi, Derrick."

I jerked my head in the direction of my voice so hard that I pulled a muscle in my neck. Then, from the kitchen…

"Secund helpings waiten por jou Mr. Cookie Man."

Startled, I crouched behind a table and peered over its edge: at nothing. Then, from my right…

"Very funny, Marty. No, I have not seen the Devil Dog."

There was no one there, but in fact they were all there, only inside my head: Marty and Derrick and Dorio and all the others.

"Chips Ahoy, have you seen him?"

I grabbed my skull with both hands and tried to shake the demons from their current residence.

"Yeah, Death is free, too…"

I scrambled to my feet, stumbled in place like a cartoon character running on an oil slick, and finally bolted blindly past the kitchen and down the passage leading to the pool and the dormitory.

Twenty feet down the hall I stopped – exhausted and breathing hard – and leaned against the corrugated aluminum paneling that made up the walls of the corridor.

The aluminum began to vibrate, resonating as if affected by some giant machine. Of course that couldn't be, because there wasn't any machine, but the walls were shuddering anyway, so much so that my fingers began to hurt. I pulled them away as if they were over a hot stove. I turned and saw the wall was pulsing like a tuning fork, as if it were midway between two dimensions, neither here nor there.

Disparate noises came from somewhere down the hallway: nondescript yet terrible sounds, and like some dull-witted fool I mindlessly turned and walked towards them.

There was laughter in the kitchen behind me, I think, but it didn't matter. I smiled stupidly and quickened my step. I was marching down a division between what was real and what was not. I no longer had the ability to discern the difference between the two.

Oh, joy.

Something barked.

Have no fear.

The pungent smell of chlorine filled the air, and it became quiet for a moment. I halted as I approached the swinging doors leading to the pool. The round portholes near the top of each door were clouded over, like retail shop windows whitewashed to disguise the goings-on inside before a grand opening. I took a step closer and saw that the windows were obscured by steam, like you might see on a shower door, usually, when someone is in the shower.

I looked down the hallway and considered running past the doors.

Nah.

The aluminum walls of the corridor had melted away; on this side of the building the walls were tiled a bright, baby-blue and were spotlessly clean. I placed my back against the wall parallel to the doors with my palms outstretched as if feeling my way and edged towards the pool entrance.

My feet glided silently on the floor. There was no sound, not here.

I realized I was staring at a large, round clock hanging on the wall opposite the doors to the pool, one with black hands and a plain white dial. It had a second hand, one that clicked into place one small second at a time, counting the moments.

I was ready to look through the windows but before I did I noticed a dim glow forcing itself through the bottom of the doors, broken intermittently by dancing shadows that indicated someone, or something, was inside.

I slowly reached up with my left hand and placed it against a porthole. It was warm to the touch and wet with dew. I became bolder and exposed myself fully before the doors, wiping the left window clean of moisture with my shirtsleeve to reveal… nothing. Moisture from inside the room was still obscuring the view.

There was a vertical crack between the two doors and a soft, warm, wet draft whistled through it. As I stood there, something slowly wiped a three inch diameter circle upon the inside of the window.

I didn't see the hand as it crashed through the small window and grabbed me by the throat, quickly cutting off my air supply. With me in hand, so to speak, it retreated backwards, taking my head and the rest of my body with it. I crashed against the door, my face sliced neatly by broken glass remaining in the window.

The doors were thrust violently outward, the hand released me, and the force propelled me a full six feet backward. I landed hard against the tiled wall under the clock and slid to the floor.

I was half conscious and bleeding profusely but still aware enough to see the mist pouring from beneath the doors of the pool house. I sat there for a moment, exposed and vulnerable, until sheer fear compelled me to scramble to my feet. When I stood up I heard the second hand of the clock above my head lock into place. Then another sound took hold.

Coming from inside was a piercing whine; not made by a human, and not originating from any one creature I could identify. It warped into a mad cacophony, a chattering that seemed almost artificial, as if produced by a machine that had an unlimited power source, and that was going to go on and on forever.

The doors beckoned, but the gracious invitation was truly extended by a universe gone mad.

I accepted. I stepped across the threshold of the doors as the mist parted for my benefit. The pool was drained. It smelled of mold and human excrement and a reddish crust circled the inside of its perimeter. Debris littered its beautifully tiled deck.

I listened. I heard a scurrying sound around my feet and something flashed by, too quickly for me to catch a clear view of it. I moved forward slowly, shifting my feet along rather than taking steps, and kept my back to the entrance of the pool. I looked to my right, and to my left, wary of another attack. The vaporous fog closed around me.

Moving to my right, my hand found the cedar wood of the saunas. Each of the pair had a small window. For reasons of safety, neither door had a lock, but both had a temperature gauge. I wiped the first clean and saw that the temperature inside was off the scale, past the red zone of the device at nearly 275 degrees. Nothing human, nothing alive, could be inside.

I heard a sound at my feet again and then felt a sharp pain in my left ankle. I cried out. A shape whizzed by and ripped at my right calf. I crouched down and felt my legs. Blood flowed freely through the tops of both of my socks. I looked up.

A squirrel stood on its hind legs not more than three feet in front of me, staring directly into my eyes. Its small chest rose and fell rapidly and fog steamed from its small mouth. Its eyes were a golden red, as if they were caught in the beam of a flashlight. But I didn't have a flashlight. Tiny needles protruded from its mouth and I could see they were dripping with blood; undoubtedly my own. It held my gaze like a bull facing a matador.

Another flash whizzed by a foot away, and then another. Still this animal stared at me.

Teeth tore into my left hand, and then ripped at my knee. I looked around wildly and saw dots of red in the mist, appearing and disappearing into the vapor.

The dead have always appeared to me in human form. They have never made physical contact.

A thin red watch band hung round the squirrel's neck. The watch on the band hung from its throat like a medallion. It leaped, and as it did – *I* did – swinging out wildly with my hands. My flesh contacted its form, hot to the touch. I stepped backward, trying to retreat to the sauna, but before I reached it an anvil in the form of a human fist appeared out of the vapor, drove into the left side of my face and knocked me to the ground. I tried to get to my feet but halfway up I was struck on my right side and went down again.

That strident, maddening, penetrating clamor rose again. With it rose the mist, obscuring all, and effectively blinding me. I smelled the odor of decomposition and rotted flesh, from man or beast, or both. I held both hands to my ears and screamed as if I could ward off this madness with the sound of my voice.

The racket ceased as quickly as it had arisen and the mist cleared as rapidly as it had formed, cleaving the pool lengthwise like an infernal blade and retreating to the far walls of the space.

A figure appeared at the end of the pool, a vision of a young man I had known and liked, who I thought was alive and well and still of this earth, but who I now knew could not possibly be.

Marty Rodriguez had a pipe stuck through his chest and from that pipe his precious fluids flowed. He was in his wheelchair, an appliance he had resided in for much of his brief lifetime. I wasn't sure where the rest of him resided at the moment.

A slick puddle formed underneath the wheels of his chair. The puddle emptied itself into the pool. Around the edge of the pool was an array of small animals, each with two red dots that now substituted for the eyes they had enjoyed in their previous lives. They were positioned side by side, lined up one after the other around the perimeter, all of them motionless, all of them facing me.

Marty twirled himself in small circles in the puddle he had created and the wheels of his chair made a sickening sucking sound as he did. He stopped abruptly with his back towards me. After a long pause he turned around, so quickly that my breath caught in my throat.

His head was bowed as he glared at me; only the whites of his eyes were visible. Terrible black circles waited underneath each orb. Sickening, bluish-gray veins stood out on his face. They throbbed down his neck to his arms and finally to his hands, which held the circular rails on the wheels of his chair. The veins exited there, piercing the flesh on the back of his wrists and wrapping themselves in a gluey, undulating mass around the spokes of both wheels.

One corner of Marty's mouth rose in a dreadful attempt at a smile. He spoke, making a gurgling sound as he did. Blood flowed from his lips and down his neck.

"What I wouldn't do for a Domingo burger."

He laughed, coughing up more blood and small bits of flesh. He released one hand from his chair. The veins detached themselves from the wheel and slowly retreated back into his flesh until they popped fully into place. Marty wiped his mouth and kept his focus on me.

"It wasn't fun getting here, Ricky. No fun at all. It's not fun being here."

Something picked me up and threw me half the length of the

pool. I slid across the wet tile on my stomach, finally stopping prostrate before my former student.

Marty wheeled towards me, rapidly closing the short gap between us. Just as quickly he leaned back and seized the wheels of his chair, skidding to a stop within a few inches of my face. Tracks of blood trailed behind him. He leaned down, placed his hand under his chin, and smiled.

"No laughs, Ricky. No laughs here at all. Do you understand?"

I was picked up from behind, from my belt and from around my neck, and carried like a missile toward the sauna doors. I thought that my head was going to careen into those doors, but just before it did something lifted me upwards, so that only my face smashed against them. I managed to twist my head at the last moment, saving my nose from being broken. I was turned around to face my antagonist. Two muscled arms held me in place, my feet off of the ground.

A head appeared from the mist and pierced my clouded vision and tear-filled eyes.

"No laughs, white boy, you dig?"

Derrick's eyes met my own. They were no longer eyes at all, really, but black auroras containing centers that glowed a deep red, as if embers were within each. He released his grip and I crumpled before him. He leaned down.

"So eager to get here, are you whitey?" he snarled with a smile. He hit my head with the heel of his hand. "Listening to some bitch with a crystal ball. As if *she* knew. As if *anyone* knows."

He leaned closer still, his lips touching my ear. His breath was hot.

"Are you really ready for what happens next?"

He grabbed me by the hair and turned my head. Marty was at the far end of the pool with his back towards me, ready to resume his circle-making. He peered over his right shoulder.

"Are you really ready for what happens next, Ricky?" he said.

Instantly I was face to face with Rodriguez, close enough to see every distorted and damaged line and furrow on his blood-spattered skin.

"Are you ready, *Ricky-Boy?* Are you *really*?"

I passed out.

XXXVIII

I found myself outside in the hallway, face down on the cool tile floor. I tried to lift my head. It was heavy and wet with my blood. Sputum dribbled down my swollen lower lip onto the floor, making a thin red line.

The doors of the pool building were closed. Red beads of light coated with mist flashed beyond the vertical crack at the center of the doors. I rose slowly and continued down the hallway, sliding my right hand against the tiled walls for support. I left a trail of blood behind. A squeaking sound accompanied the slide.

I came to the junction between the dormitory rooms and the outside. Without hesitating, I turned left.

All was quiet. Two of the three banks of overhead light fixtures, each containing four fluorescent bulbs, were dysfunctional. Three bulbs in the fixture furthest down the hall were in the same condition. The fourth flickered on and off, putting forth a soft pink glow one moment and a lightning strike of brightness the next.

Dayne Dorio's room was opposite the last fixture at the end of the hall, invisible but for the intermittent brightness provided by that one bulb. My hand sought the corridor's left wall for support, and I tried to catch my breath.

I passed the door to Derrick Vander's room. It was open a few inches, but it seemed to be undulating, widening its breach an inch or so, then retreating to its original position. I reasoned the movement was caused by an open window inside the room.

Marty Rodriguez's room was next, and that door was ajar as well. As I approached I felt a soft wind blow and on that wind were voices, communicating not in words but in thoughts, pulling at my mind, trying to bend what little cogency remained there.

I felt a gooey substance underneath my left hand. I turned and watched as my appendage slipped and sank into the wall as if it were putty. I felt a hot sensation and looked on with fascination as my wrist, then my forearm, disappeared beneath a surface that boiled and bubbled in a variety of colors.

I had booked an LSD trip, customized just for me. I had been invited to a private dance in a ballroom located on an avenue with no name, where the neighbors never drew a breath, and where no atmosphere survived to carry your screams.

I pulled back with what strength I had but the wall held fast.

Down the hallway, the doors seemed to transform into that same viscous substance; each spilled out from their frames into the hallway, filling the floor with a gelatinous liquid which began to loll and roll, like some fantastic sea, against the borders of the corridor.

But the doors to the rooms belonging to Vander and Rodriguez remained intact and their faces were fixed on the entrances of their former residences. They looked directly at me, accusing me, as if I had murdered them, or as if my inaction had caused their deaths. They moved their lips and began to speak but I couldn't hear them above the noise of the supernatural waves lapping at my feet.

Blood poured down my face, from my nose, and my ears, and filled my mouth with the salty, metallic taste of my essence. I leaned forward as far as the wall would allow, so I could listen to the voices of the dead.

I watched their mouths move. It was a question that they asked, the same question, and I looked from one to the other, numb and exhausted, and leaned forward and listened…

There was a popping sound; the wall released me and I fell to the ground with a thud. With the floor as my pillow, I looked down the hall. Everything was as it should have been, except for the darkness, and that single bulb flickering on and off. Marty and Derrick's rooms were sealed shut.

I closed my eyes and imagined that I could just float away, far away from all of this, somewhere where nothing that had happened over the past three terrible days would matter. For a moment I felt myself become lighter, a weight lifted from me as my head rose ever so slightly from the floor. I tried to look down to the watch on my right wrist but it was as far away as the heavens from the earth.

But the floating stopped, and the feeling of weightlessness stopped, and I slipped back down to earth. The cause was a thunderous discharge that propelled me back to awareness; a blast that exploded midway through Dayne Dorio's door, putting a hole the size of my fist in the wall just a few inches above my head. Chips of tile fell over me like hard snow, covering my hair and stinging my eyes.

I managed to roll to the parallel wall. As I did, two more blasts resounded, obliterating the rest of the entrance and adding additional holes to the corridor walls. The door's locking mechanism fashioned itself into a missile and hurtled towards me. As it flew by it slashed my right arm, one of the few places from which blood was not already flowing.

Human beings, or things that once were, screamed in agony from beyond the shattered remains of the door. I pressed my face against the floor, trying to wish away the maelstrom. Around me everywhere were chunks of brass, pieces of tile and wooden shards of varying sizes and shapes.

When silence returned to the hall I pushed myself to my feet. My entire body ached and every movement caused me pain. I moved toward the room at the end of the hall.

A thin slice of Dorio's door hung precariously from its frame; nothing more than silence and shadows emerged from within. I slipped carefully through the opening, past jagged spikes of wood.

Each dormitory room was fairly identical. A handicapped-accessible toilet and sink were on the left. A bed rested against the wall on the right.

My eyes dropped to the chrome plated .38 caliber revolver at my feet. I took a few tentative steps forward. A thin filament of smoke rose from the barrel.

An eager radiance entered the room from the street lights outside. It forced its way through a crack between the drawn curtains that covered the windows opposite the entrance to the room. One window was open and the curtains rustled gently, altering the substance of the shadows. I crouched down and touched the gun, quickly withdrawing my hand. I looked up.

In the far corner of the darkened room was a mound that appeared to be a huge pile of clothing thrown haphazardly onto a chair. I approached cautiously, step by step. I was aware of a slow drip from the faucet in the sink behind me.

The smell of burning flesh filled my nostrils. The broad shoulders of a man became visible, a man lying face down on the heap on the chair. There was a gaping black hole in the center of his back. His left arm hung limply, but his right arm was invisible, buried beneath him.

Breathing through my mouth, I stepped closer, still unable to identify the corpse. Trembling, I grabbed the body by its right shoulder and tried to turn it over, but it would not yield. I tried again with both hands; the body turned but didn't fall; it remained on its back, the eyes of the dead man staring at the ceiling, his head hanging loosely on his neck.

There was a terrible pit the size of a man's fist where Dayne Dorio's chest had once been. His beautiful, almost feminine face was clean and untouched. He almost looked as if he were sleeping.

Then I saw that his body was being supported by the arm of a wheelchair. In that chair, underneath Dorio, there was another. But it was the knife I saw first; a huge, unnatural looking thing, six inches wide at the hilt, protruding through the stomach of its victim.

He had been just fifty-five years old. Only a few strands of thin white hair remained on his head, growing from the center of his scalp and flowing wistfully across his right eye. The cancer had all but ravaged his body. His legs had turned to twigs long ago, but now they were only vaguely reminiscent of human appendage, empty props to give him the form of what he once was. A vacant holster hung loosely from what remained of his left ankle.

Judging from the look on his face, his death had been agonizing.

For one last time, Bobbie Meyer had played the role of the killer. The man who had the courage to save six men by terminating a woman and her child – and who had willingly traded his soul for their lives – had ultimately sacrificed his life to save for me something I had little use for: My own.

I dropped to my knees and stared at the face of my friend. What stared back was the face of death, the face of the future, of all of our futures.

And Death spoke to me.

"You and me, Ricky-Boy."

When I turned to face the voice, he was still in a wheelchair; why I could not guess. He was staring at Dorio's body.

"I couldn't let him kill you, Ricky. You know that. You know I couldn't let anything happen to you."

Bobbie Meyer continued to stare at the body, but now sneered with disdain. "He had it coming, the prick." He looked at me for the first time.

"Don't we all?" I asked, not expecting a reply.

He flashed a curious little smile.

I rose and walked a bit closer to Bob's body. I reached slowly, carefully, into the front pocket of his shirt. His car keys were where they always were. I looked over to Bob's specter and, without speaking, asked him if he minded.

He didn't respond. But he did mind.

The apparition looked down and lifted his left pants leg; he realized his ankle holster was there but that there was nothing in it. He laughed weakly and shrugged his shoulders. Death sometimes works in strange ways, and sometimes those ways are strange even to the dead.

"Funny how the world is made," he said, eyes still downcast. "So many possible roads to travel, so many possible outcomes."

He moved his wheelchair like a rocking chair, forward a few inches, then back, then forward again.

"There's so much that cannot be controlled," I said.

"Yes," Bobbie agreed. "But that's not the end of the story, Ricky-Boy." He grabbed my wrist hard with his left hand. "You can't really end the story at all."

A cool white fire seemed to burn from behind his eyes. He leaned forward in his chair and kept his grip on my wrist.

The volume and intensity of his voice increased. I realized where these sounds were coming from and how far they really had to travel to get here.

"You're not writing a book at all, kid. You dig? Just a small chapter. But it's an important one. It determines the next one and the next. In whole, in part, a little, a lot… you just don't know for sure. But that's the deal, and those are the cards.

Bobby sat with his back towards the doorway. I smiled and turned towards the open window as Bobby loosened his grip on me.

I heard him slump back into his chair. I wanted to go, but I didn't. Not yet.

"You gotta play the cards, Ricky," he said. "You gotta play the cards you're dealt."

As I turned from the open window I felt a slight breeze rustle my hair. I heard the curtains flutter gently. Somehow, this made the sound of the gun all the more surreal.

A lean arrow of smoke pierced the back of Bobby's head and exited from the center of his forehead. He peered up, eyes crossed inward.

"Oops," he said, dumbfounded.

A bullet passed neatly through my left arm with a notable "squirting" sound and my body twisted from the force of the impact. I was still on my feet, which I thought was strange. I grunted in pain, acting in perfect character with my human form. Getting shot, after all, was still a new experience for me.

Bobby was just staring.

"Doesn't look so bad there, Ricky-Boy," he said.

I looked down. A thin but steady stream of blood flowed out of the fresh wound. I looked back at Bob. He shrugged his shoulders.

"Of course, I could be wrong."

I am, now and again, struck by the fact that the deceased typically exhibit little sympathy for any living person facing his demise. It's not that this makes them bad people. It's just that their perceptions have been altered, and that they exist on a dramatically different plane where death is – well – just not as big a deal as it once was.

I have also come to believe that our afterlives are mere extensions of our lives in this world. Put another way, the reality each of us ultimately sojourns to is not dramatically different from the one we created for ourselves during our lifetime.

In any event, regardless of the specific locale they may eventually come to inhabit – by virtue of their righteousness or wickedness on Earth, if you will – few among the dead seem to wish to return to their former dimensions. Although this may seem strange, it is a truism that few of them truly pity you any prospective escape from yours.

I looked from Bob, to my wound, then to Bob again. A second shot rang out. I jerked my head to the left, and the bullet whizzed just past my face, making it seem as if my momentary shift had somehow been responsible for the failure of the projectile to hit its intended target. For some reason, I laughed.

Bob misguidedly took this as a cue for him to chuckle and

shrug again in exaggerated fashion, thinking no doubt that I appreciated his cosmic canard.

My eyes followed the dissipating dart of fog to its point of origin.

"Did you think…?"

The words rolled slowly along the pinpoint of mist. There was a slightly rounded pronunciation to each word. This was understandable, as deaf people cannot hear themselves speak and thus possess a limited ability to detect and correct the fine errors of their elocution.

Celia stood there – all six feet and one hundred seventy-five pounds of her – with both of her hands on Bob's .38. There was a Mona Lisa smile on her face. A soft, delicate curlicue wafted from the end of the gun's barrel. I staggered. She looked at me, still smiling, and cocked her head.

I looked at her without comprehension.

"Did you really think…?"

"Did I?" It was the only thing I could think of to say, and it seemed an appropriate response.

She took care to enunciate her words so that those of compromised mind and body would have less trouble understanding.

"…that I would allow you…"

"You…"

"…to take away…"

"Because of Rena?"

"…the very best part of me…"

"It was you all the time."

"…leaving only everything broken and rotten…"

Demons.

"…without taking away…"

"Kara…"

"…everything… "

"Everything."

"…that was important to you?"

"I am thoroughly confused," Bob said. His words seemed to register with Celia. Which, of course, was impossible.

It was then that Celia's words returned to me, a line borrowed from Shakespeare's King John:

"Be stirring as the time; be fire with fire; threaten the threatener and outface the brow of bragging horror."

The famous phrase is rarely quoted in its original form. The modern day translation is this: Fight fire with fire.

Celia straightened her back for a moment and surveyed the death scene. Her head tilted back and her chin rose and pointed skyward. She closed her eyes and like some beast began to sniff the air, searching for that most ancient of scents, carried on moonbeams and windless nights, the perfume of mortal conflict, and victory, and of the end of all things.

She pointed her left index finger at me, then slid it across an invisible line in the air and aimed it at Dorio's body, then in Bob's direction, then back to Dorio.

"One against the other, so simple to exploit your weaknesses and fears. Like chess pieces on a board, so easy to play."

In the corner of the room, to my right, a dark shadow began to form, appearing out of nothingness. It coalesced into the rough shape of a human being, or what once was, and its former identity slowly became recognizable. A tinge of crimson, like molten metal, formed the outline of the figure. Hot red holes substituted for eyes. This afterimage was all that was left of the sandy-haired boy with the perfect face from a small Midwestern town.

"Dorio?"

"Just your run of the mill psychotic. Nothing to fear from him, unless you're a small animal. But so easy to instruct and guide. It was so simple to turn him round and point him just so: toward a reality only slightly dissimilar from the one brewing in that tempest in his mind."

"The main classroom?"

"Well, that *was* his idea, can't take any credit for that. Inspirational work, if it was a bit messy. The foreseeable product of a diseased, destructive and irrational mind. Purposeless violence from a psyche out of control. Despite his considerable potential he was always going nowhere. He headed down a path he created for himself, which ultimately led him to the exact place he resides right now."

She seemed to peer directly into Dorio's shadowy mass.

"Where he'll always be. Forever and for always."

Dayne Dorio as wraith continued to grow, his scarlet margin expanding. I began to sweat profusely as the temperature in the room seemed to increase precipitously. Whether this was because of my wound, my emotional state or something else I could not tell. In all of my considerable experience with those things departed, *this* I had never seen. I began to get the distinct impression that this apparition was the greater threat, despite the alarming peril Celia presented.

Bob, displaying no concern whatever, rolled his eyes and shook his cheeks until they jiggled.

"Everybody's got to get into the act."

His Jimmy Durante impression was actually quite good. This bit of theater, however, did little to improve my situation. I took a step backward, shifting my eyes back and forth between Celia and Dorio's phantom. Celia continued.

"Now Bobbie, here; Bobby was a little challenging. Facing terrible pain and the prospect of death most every day, well, there wasn't very much to work with. There weren't many things that could be used to motivate him or move him to action. There wasn't much left for him to be afraid of except the unbearable weight of his guilty conscience. She smiled. But there was one thing..."

"Me."

"You. His love for you, *Ricky-Boy.*"

"Hey, only *I* get to call him that."

Bob was clearly failing to appreciate the gravity of my position.

Brilliant lines of fire, like solar flares, erupted from Dorio's form and spread to the far corners of the room. Its mass seemed to double, filling the room with a brightness that burned, generating a heat that scorched through the body and the mind. And through space and through time.

"He's gonna blow!" Bob shouted.

Celia spread her arms wide, thrusting her considerable chest outward in Dorio's direction. She tilted her neck forward unnaturally and opened her mouth impossibly wide. A horrifying double row of razor sharp teeth appeared from nowhere. I blinked in disbelief as they grew, becoming sharper, protruding more and more as they struggled to fit within her maw. Sickening dark gray goo quickly formed, rapidly plastering her lips and her chin. The stench that accompanied this transformation was unforgettable.

Her entire face flattened as if she had just entered a wind tunnel. Her eyes burned red. From every inch of her body there began to radiate a force that I could not see but that I knew was there. Her body seemed to bend and curve, dilating into an invisible vacuum as if she were being sucked through a straw.

Dorio's incorporeal form withdrew, collapsed within itself and disappeared. A voice boomed within my subconscious, from nowhere, and from everywhere, all at the same time.

We are the Power and the Way. We control the darkness. We are the Master of all Demons. We are the Dream Maker.

By the time I looked back at Celia she had regained her normal appearance. I swooned momentarily. She noted my condition.

"Egotistic fool. Did you really believe that you were the *only* one?

In the eddies of our lives run currents of irony so swift they would carry our very breath away if we recognized for one instant that they were there.

"But how…?"

"How? How did we get this way?" She threw her head back and laughed.

"You idiot; who cares how or why? We *are*. You're full of questions, and every one the wrong one." She paused, and her voice grew low and deep.

"I will tell you this, my poor little Ricky-Boy lost; it starts with whatever stardust is placed within us by an angry God. It proceeds with an iconoclastic event that sets everything in motion. And it ends with us becoming such stuff as our dreams are made on.

"And then?"

"And then? Well… then you control *It*, or *It* controls you." She smiled.

"I'm just like you, Ricky," she said, cocking her head and smiling gaily.

"But not like you."

"After a lifetime of believing in my own singularity…'

"…your own ego..."

"My uniqueness…"

"…your confused words and thoughts…"

"A casualty of life…"

"No! A casualty of yourself! Gads!" she exclaimed with an exaggerated flutter of her eyelashes. "Your thoughts are yours, but their ends, none of your own. Don't you see? The demons control *you,* Richard. They drag you into *their* world to play each night. You follow along every time, don't you? Didn't you ever learn you had a choice? Didn't it ever occur to you that you weren't just put here to *succumb*? You reduced yourself to the status of a victim. A victim of the spirits. A victim of the dead. The victim of a hag on a boardwalk shouting prophesies into your all-too-willing ears.

"But, most of all – poor, poor, little, Ricky-Boy lost – you are a victim of yourself. Conceived from chaos, with chaos self-imposed by your own bad thoughts, all you see is bedlam. If you weren't simply running away from it all, you were isolating yourself, like a two-year-old locking himself in a closet, and numbing yourself senseless with drugs and alcohol."

She knew everything about me, and so much more than I knew about myself.

"*You* were so *easy*, Ricky."

My head slipped downward, my eyes drifting to the gold Bulova on Bob's wrist. It said that it was 5:00 a.m. It was keeping real time.

I dropped to one knee in a small puddle composed of my blood. Celia crouched down and looked me in the eyes. She lowered her weapon.

"It was you all the time, Ricky. You followed the path that you laid down. You tortured a reality from your own visions." She rose slowly, keeping her eyes bonded to mine.

"Visions through a glass, darkly."

"Now I get it," Bob said. You're a loon!"

Celia swept her arms theatrically across the room.

"All of you, like broken toys in the attic, chaotic and dysfunctional. Devoid of faith, consumed by fear, unable to control your environments and unwilling to control anything else brewing inside you."

Her voice became cold as ice.

"Decidedly imperfect."

I recovered momentarily. "And you have used *your* talents for what? To murder?"

"How unworthy a thing you make of me. You would play upon me; you would pluck out the heart of my mystery! No, Ricky, not for the sake of killing… for revenge."

The lady doth protest too much, methinks.

"You opened all the wrong doors, Ricky. Now you have to live with what's come through."

She smiled grimly. "Or not." She raised the gun again. Her

voice lowered to a whisper. *"To die, to sleep…"*

I breathed pitiful murmurs in response.

"…to sleep, perchance to dream…"

"…but here's the rub; for in that sleep of death…"

"…what horrors will come…"

"And in the excruciating silence of those horrors, Richard, you will find…"

"I will find…"

"What We have found…"

"And that is…?"

"…and that is…" She clicked the hammer of the pistol back for the final time.

"…perfection."

And then she was gone.

Celia crumpled at my feet like a house of cards, revealing another behind her.

Angelito Cortez – immigrant, watchmaker, hero – held the aluminum arm of his wheelchair in his right hand, which he had presciently detached and used to strike the back of Celia's head. He had employed his left arm to elevate himself to a height sufficient to accomplish his task, and he remained paralyzed in that position.

The arm that gripped the metal rod was still extended across his chest. He seemed frozen in place, like a batter the moment after he has hit a home run. The muscles in his forearm were massive, taut and still straining; soft beads of perspiration dotted his head. His facial expression was a mix of horror and surprise.

"Did you hear?"

Angelito nodded his head quickly without taking his eyes off Celia's fallen body.

"Get the police, Angel."

He remained where he was.

"Angelito!"

Cortez dropped his makeshift bludgeon, hesitated for a

moment longer, then turned and wheeled down the hall, leaving me and the reflection of Bob Meyer alone in the room once more. I struggled to my feet, holding my injured arm with my hand. My hands were soaked in my own blood.

"See you in the next world," I said.

"See you in the next world," Bob replied.

I smiled gently at the voice from that other world. He didn't need to add the next line of the Jimi Hendrix song.

I wouldn't be late. I wouldn't be late at all.

I would be right on time.

"Bobbie…"

I thrust out my right hand. He grabbed it, and like a small child I hugged him and cried.

We were both dead men, indulging ourselves for a moment.

I think we were entitled to that.

Epilogue

I am driving on the Taconic State Parkway. I am forty-five minutes north of the school's parking lot where I commandeered Bob Meyer's old Ford.

It is equipped to be driven by a paraplegic. Bobbie, of course, has no further use for such accommodation.

I look around and realize fall is coming, arguably the most beautiful time of the year anywhere in the world.

The trees are beginning to change colors. There are so many of them, passing by so quickly, too quickly to be able to reflect upon any one by itself.

As soon as I think this thought, I wonder if it is true.

I am approaching the Croton Bridge in central Westchester County. It has always been one of my favorite places. It passes over the New Croton Reservoir, a vital source of fresh water for New York City. Traffic signs warn others to reduce their speed to 25 miles per hour.

This old car still has an electric clock as a centerpiece on the dashboard. I manage a smile. Time follows me wherever I go. I suppose it follows us all.

I look in the rearview mirror and then at my hands. I am confused for a moment. But only for a moment.

The bridge has two separate spans, one going north and another going south. The southern overpass traverses an expansive section of the reservoir. It is a modern affair of steel and concrete construction.

The northern-bound overpass is less than a half city block in length. It is an ancient but beautiful wooden structure, despite its pitiable state of repair. Its low guard rails are the original ones left from the bridge's construction in the mid-nineteenth century. The trees from which they were constructed were alive when John Quincy Adams was president.

To my knowledge, there has never been a serious accident here.

The old Ford's wheels rumble loudly as they hit the approach to the bridge. I look to my right, past the old baseball card placed on the front passenger seat, and through the window to the world beyond the confines of this vehicle. The length of the narrow reservoir seems to pulse eastward for as great a distance as the mind can imagine. I have seen this sight many times before. But today, I can see the end, I think.

It is utterly beautiful. I do not doubt for a moment that if there is a God, that he lives right here, in this faultless splendor, in the simple purity of this one moment, in the stunning silence of the perfection before me.

I grip the wheel tightly. The graceful, curved archway of the bridge casts a shimmering, glistening reflection on the still water below.

The last minute passes on the Ford's old timepiece with an audible tick of the mechanism. I stare at the clock. It is an attempt, I suppose, to keep a special moment of one's life still and fresh for a second longer in the mind's eye.

I cross to the dead center of the small span…

The world may be capable of dissection such that the concepts of good and evil can be identified and grasped. Random forces neither good nor evil intervene.

Our perceptions may be painfully real or mere products of our own visceral imaginations. There may be truths so brilliant that they become as absolute as the stars themselves; others that cast their pale light only so far as the reflections our colored glasses allow.

Our lives may be our own, or not. It may be, as the Great Scribe tells, that our faults lie not in the stars, but in ourselves, that it is the nature of our own imperfections that inexorably compels us to blame the heavenly bodies themselves for the self-imposed catastrophes that befall us.

Maybe all of our destinies are in the gentle hands of a loving God. Or, perhaps we are only sparks in the bonfire that is the cosmos, grains of sand in an infinite universe that somehow think we are more, and who proceed through our fleeting existences blithely unaware that it is a timeless ocean that carries us where it wills.

Maybe an answer is to be found in the cacophony of our muddled thoughts. Maybe it waits to be discovered in the silent whisper of a spirit, or the paralyzing hush of an unborn child's final breath.

I do not know.

But I do know this:

My name is Richard Goodman. I am an illusion. My life has been a mortgage, my time on this earth borrowed from an anxious loan shark, shuffling his feet and checking his watch under a lamppost on a corner at the edge of forever.

The sun, that most ancient of timekeepers, is rising now over the reservoir. The moon, its distant cousin, is still visible above the horizon.

Goodbye moon.

Goodbye lamb soaring over the moon.

THE END

Acknowledgements

The author wishes to acknowledge the following writers who provided the fertile soil that nourished this novel:

Clive Barker, Louis-Hector Berlioz, Jorge Luis Borges, Carlos Castaneda, Fyodor Dostoyevsky, M. John Harrison, Herman Hesse, Harlan Ellison, James Herbert, Stephen King, Dean Koontz, Edmund Rostand, William Shakespeare and Kurt Vonnegut

Additional thanks to the faithful readers who critiqued my initial drafts:

Andrea Aboulafia, Matthew Aboulafia, Rita Aboulafia, Erica Heymann, Phyllis Heymann, Michael Mascia and Dana Thomas

...and special thanks to...

Mike Evans and The Tubes – rock on, my brothers – and the good people of *Magnet, Nebraska*

Other Books by David I. Aboulafia

Snapshots from my Uneventful Life

Library Tales Publishing, Inc. (Summer, 2015)

ISBN-13: 978-0692331491

ISBN-10: 0692331492

COSMIC
EGG
BOOKS